S

TRAVELERS

"It would be no surprise if some people thought Nel, the heroine of *Travelers*, was a Lara Croft copy but she's not, and even admits that she's "no Lara Croft" when she finds herself in a situation that Ms Croft would have handled with only slight discomfort, if any at all. Nel is her very own character and solves her problems in her own unique way – no need to compare her to anyone, and I'm sure she'll become even more of a unique character in future adventures. I'm sure she'll have quite a few interesting challenges to deal with, probably also on the romantic side. I found her love interest a fairly intriguing character, and can see how her own heritage could cause some issues in future novels.

The writing style of the book made it easy to read and the author found a great balance here...I'd definitely recommend this book to people who enjoy the idea of aliens having been here before, and having left signs that can be found if people only dig deep enough (literally digging in this novel!)."

- *Reader's Favorite*

"*Travelers* by V. S. Holmes kicks off the Starsedge series, in which an acid-tongued archaeologist named Dr. Nel Bently makes her debut....Pinning a series on a single character is usually a risky move, but Holmes has certainly struck gold with Dr. Nel Bently. Nel is a bit like her beloved dig sites--the more time you spend with her, the more you'll uncover. Her outwardly gruff exterior is nicely balanced and buffered by a few key characters around her, and it's clear she cares about the undergrad students she works with, even if she sometimes struggles to be patient with them. The sci-fi elements are a bit underplayed in Travelers, but only because Nel is trying to puzzle out what exactly her team has stumbled upon. With answers--and, of course, more questions--served up later in the novel, the series can now take off in whichever direction it chooses."

- *Red City Review*

"I think I'm in love with this series. Grounded in the solid bedrock of real archeological techniques and experience, it takes off from there into the fantastic. I love it the way I love Tony Hillerman's writing: it challenges me to research new areas of study without once losing the draw of a gripping narrative. Even better, it shows truly rounded queer characters whose sexuality is just one facet of a complex and engaging personality. From page 1 Nel tromped through my imagination with a screw-you-too grin and a trowel in her back pocket. Her description of the field life feels incredibly real. This book rocks."

-O. E. Tearmann, author of *The Hands We're Given*

"The whole concept this story is based on and built around is fascinating, the way V.S. Holmes has written the characters and plot is brilliant... a suspenseful read with lots of surprises, a touch of romance, and a whole lot of promise..."

-Serena Yates of *Rainbow Book Reviews*

DRIFTERS

"Another clever and cocksure tale. Holmes pulls it off again with her absolutely driven Nel. Nothing, from hypothermia to the FBI, is going to stop this girl. Grit, friendship and deciding what to fight for when the future is bleak gives this a surprising emotional oomph to layer over the down-to-earth survival story. I read it straight through and wanted more."

-O. E. Tearmann, author of *The Hands We're Given*

STRANGERS

"You can tell V has an incredible grasp of who these characters are and we benefit from that right away. There are so many snappy bits of dialogue and interaction, there is what I call great over the shoulder moments that turn us around and look back at this or that, and there is this underlying tension that really is handled so well in the writing. It's nice when an author treats its audience like grown-ups. I also love that this story gives us just enough when we need it and so much just when we think we are about to settle in. It's easy to picture all this in your head, very cinematic, and a great puzzle as well."

-Joe Compton, author of *Amongst the Killing*

OTHER BOOKS BY V. S. HOLMES

NEL BENTLY BOOKS
Travelers
Drifters
Strangers
Heretics
Fugitives*

BLOOD OF TITANS WORLD
Smoke and Rain
Lightning and Flames
Madness and Gods
Blood and Mercy

SHORT FICTION
"Starfall" *(Vitality Magazine)*
"The Tempest" *(Out of the Darkness)*
"Disciples" *(Beamed Up)*
"Familiar Waters" *(Love and Bubbles)*
"Mere Primordium" (poem, *Mystic Blue Review*)

*forthcoming

STRANGERS

STARS EDGE: NEL BENTLY BOOK 3

V. S. HOLMES

This is a work of fiction. All of the characters, organizations, and events portrayed in this novel are either products of the author's imagination or are used fictitiously.

STRANGERS

Copyright © 2019 by Sara Voorhis

All rights reserved. No part of this publication may be reproduced, distributed, or transmitted in any form or by any means, including photocopying, recording, or other electronic or mechanical methods, without the prior written permission of the publisher, except in the case of brief quotations embodied in critical reviews and certain other noncommercial uses permitted by copyright law. For permission requests, write to the publisher at the address below.

Amphibian Press
P.O. Box 163
West Peterborough NH
03468

www.amphibianpressbooks.com
www.vsholmes.com
ISBN : 978-1-949693-97-3

For Dad, who gave me my love of flight in all its forms

AUTHOR'S NOTE

This series combines archaeology with science fiction. Doing so is a hazardous road, particularly with the advent of television like "Ancient Aliens" and the fourth Indiana Jones film.

This book is a work of fiction, and something to be enjoyed as entertainment. I wholeheartedly believe we are far from alone in the universe. That being said, I am an archaeologist by trade and I know humans are ingenious and resourceful enough to build pyramids and other architectural wonders all on their own.

ONE

Hissing air. Squealing metal. The smell of antiseptic and silicon. Nel's chest ached with each deep breath. Her limbs felt heavier than the simple weight of bone and muscle. She blinked, but the pulsing light overhead grew no clearer. The ceiling was a mass of greys and blacks.

"Good morning, Dr. Bently." The voice was low, of indeterminate age or gender, but with more depth than a computer's.

"Morning?" Nel's voice was a rasp, as if her words were dragged over the powerline corridors after her trudging feet. *The corridor!* She surged upright. Her pulse hammered against bindings around her wrists and ankles. Nausea twisted and her stomach emptied itself over her lap. "Fucking great."

"It's a normal side effect upon waking."

She peered at the light brown blur speaking to her. "Where am I? Who are you?"

HOLMES

A hand steadied her chin while a pen light flicked from one pupil to the other and back again. "Good pupillary reflex. Heart rate high, but within normal parameters. You're on *Iman*. I'm Jem. I'm a medic."

Nel gathered that the first information was not for her, and focused her attention on the last bits. "*Iman*?"

"A ship. You're safe. Disorientation is also common. What's the last thing you can remember? We'll work forward from there." Jem's tone didn't change, "Swing your legs out and we'll get you cleaned up."

Nel shifted her legs over the side. The room was clearer now: dim light, monochrome palette, bland design. Even her vomit smelled sterile. "My vision's blurry."

"Has it improved since you woke?" Jem tugged away the paper apron covering Nel's lap and chest and dabbed away any leftover mess.

"A bit." Nel couldn't find energy enough to care she was naked in front of a stranger. "Everything feels slow. Heavy."

Jem hummed in response and tapped the hollow beneath Nel's knees. "Patelar reflex positive. You're responding fine, Dr. Bently. Can you turn your head? Other way now."

The room didn't fully spin as she looked left, right, but it wanted to. Jem took her arm and checked the IV in the crook of her elbow. "You'll feel better in a minute. I'm going to give you some stabilizers. They'll help with the disorientation and queasiness."

Coolness flooded her veins, followed by calm and clarity. Nel swallowed and didn't feel like she was biting back vomit. A glance at where her frostbitten toes used to be told her whatever tech they used worked quickly—there were barely scars where she remembered bruised flesh. Jem looked about fourteen. "Aren't you a little young to be a doctor? Medic. Whatever."

"I'm a cryo-tech. It's my first year. I'm twenty. Well, seventeen circadial, which I think it what you meant."

"Circadial?" *Is there a damn dictionary I could borrow?*

"Most people up here spend years traveling in cryosleep. So while I was born twenty years ago, I have only aged seventeen years. Does that make sense?"

"I'll get there." Nel's stomach flipped again, but this time from horror. *I would miss so much.* She shivered. "Could I get dressed?"

Jem grinned. "Of course. I can bring stuff for you to wash up too. We don't recommend showering just yet—dizziness and temperature fluctuations are rougher when you're still cryo-sick."

"That'd be great." *Cryo-sick?* Memories were spotty after the incredible press as gravity fell away. The sight of a folded suit at the end of the exam table distracted her. Fine, black fibers were

HOLMES

fine but tightly woven and soft. Faint copper glimmered on the interior when she twisted it in the light. *This leaves nothing to the imagination.* After a cursory search for underwear she tugged the suit over her naked body. Despite the thin material, it was warm.

Jem poked their head in. "Before you zip that up, let me help you place this." They held up a sticker. It was a lattice of copper threads. "It transmits your vitals to the suit, helps it predict your needs."

"My needs?" Nel made a show of patting her crotch. "Does it have the world's tiniest bullet vibe somewhere?"

Jem snorted. "I see you're already feeling better. I meant your temperature and so forth. If you're under stress in constricts to calm you. If you're adrenalized it will increase temperature and the fibers become more flexible to help you fight or flee."

Nel flexed her hand. "Go, go gadget-unitard."

Jem pressed the circuit sticker to the hollow under Nel's left clavicle. "Now, zip up. You'll feel a tingle, maybe a temp flux."

Nel did as she was asked. It was snug, a more comfortable version of a wetsuit. Energy crawled over her skin, trailing goosebumps in its wake. *Pairing.* She glanced at Jem. "Did you say something?"

Jem's bright smile broadened. "It's in your head. I mean, not like it's made up, imaginary. It's the suit 'talking.' Literally, in your head."

Nel's lip curled. "I hate this sci-fi shit." She took a few stumbling steps. "How do I get it to do things?"

"Talk back. Start with 'Suit' in a firm tone, then follow it with the command. It recognizes most iterations of simple commands, but does lack a bit of creativity. It also," Jem fixed Nel with a pointed stare, "does not respond to cursing."

"Well, fuck." Nel finally answered with a grin of her own. "Neither does my mother."

Spartan was a generous term for her room. And would imply more character than the black and grey walls offered. Nel glanced at the small aluminum case on the desk. All of her possessions, the ones she would use for the next who-knew-how-long. The closet above the desk held three outfits, all along the track-suit line of fashion. Weight limits made it impossible to bring enough to personalize the space. *Only the necessities.*

"Hey."

Nel shot to her feet with a smile. "Hey, there." Sci-fi space fashion became Lin far more than it did her, Nel decided. The faint lines around Lin's eyes and the familiar curl of her lip were a balm on Nel's homesick heart. She lifted her chin for a kiss, but something in the other woman's eyes stopped her.

Lin's face was smooth, devoid of expression. Her eyes were the black of space. They, too, were lit with strange stars. "We need to talk."

"I hate that phrase."

"Like I'm going to break up with you when we're stuck on a spaceship together." Anxiety strained the attempt at humor.

Nel winced. She was not under the impression there was something to break up. "So what is it?"

"You've signed a contract. A binding one."

Nel frowned. She remembered the thrust of lift-off, incredible exhaustion and then...waking up. "Why are you reminding me?"

"So you remember you can't break it."

Nel's limbs ignited with adrenaline. "You gonna give me a reason to want to?"

Lin looked away. "Space travel is complicated. We have incredible technology. We go beyond the limits of physics. But not time. Even with our faster-than-light tech it can take a long time to get where we want to go. It took three years for us to get to Earth the first time."

Nel looked out at the scattered balls of burning hydrogen, made pinpricks by thousands of light years. She couldn't have drawn the sky over her parents' house in Springfield by heart, or the starscape above the red hills of Chile from memory. But the animal parts of her, the subconscious observations that were called sixth sense, knew. The stars are all wrong. "Lin, where are we?"

"We're approaching *Odyssey*, which is in deep orbit around the planet we're studying."

For the third time that day, Nel thought she might vomit. *Already?* "And *Odyssey* is the space station?"

Lin nodded. "*Odyssey of Earth*." Her dark eyes had not met Nel's since she first uttered "time."

"And how far is that from Earth?"

"117.3 trillion kilometers."

Nel didn't know space like she knew soil and stone. She spent her life looking down, not up, digging not dreaming. She didn't know what 117.3 trillion kilometers meant, only that her blood was a storm in her ears and the sky was not hers. "The medic said I was cryo-sick. Lin, how long was I out?"

"Two years."

The floor pitched with a viciousness that had nothing to do with artificial gravity. "I was locked in that tube for years, asleep like all of some tinned fish in the back of a cabinet?"

"I'm sorry, Nel."

She squeezed her eyes shut, hating how her mind, her memory betrayed her. "I can't remember when I went under. Did I know how long it would be?"

"You signed some forms."

She recalled her signature flashing green on a glowing screen, "The contracts. Did I read them?"

HOLMES

"You were distracted."

"You didn't fucking tell me?"

"It was discussed at length and determined this would be the least disruptive." Her voice slid from hesitant to exasperated. "Nel, you haven't aged. At all. You can check your baseline tests against the medscan they just ran. You are literally the same person who went under. Though your toes healed."

"'Least disruptive.'" Warmth bloomed over Nel's skin as the suit responded to the emotions rampaging through her. It wasn't just fear, or disorientation now, but fury. "You made a decision about my life, my body, my fucking future, without telling me. Without even consulting me. Because you thought you knew better? Where's all that trust you have in the human race to not be idiots? Where's the faith that we're not evil? You can overlook murder, but you think I'm incapable of rational thought? Shit, Lin. If you think I'm so immature, why have me run a damn department?"

"Nel, it's a lot more complicated than that—"

"And I don't give a shit if my body aged a second or thirty years. I missed two years of my mother's life! Two years of my asshole step-dad's homophobia. Two years of Martos frowning at me over tea. Two years of Mikey's parents grieving—" her voice shattered on her best friend's name.

"I'll gladly explain it all, but I'm going to have to ask you to calm down—"

"Calm down?" Nel heard the shriek in her voice as anger left her lungs.

"Sorry, I know that was stupid to say—"

Her hand slammed against the door as Lin moved to leave. "I need to talk to my mom. Did I talk to her before? What did I tell her?"

"You sent a vid. I don't know what it contained, but you can watch it if you want. And she's replied, I bet. You can send her another one. It'll take a bit, but she'll get it."

"A bit. Like years?" She clenched her hands. "Find me a comm. Or transponder. Or tele-talk. Whatever you freaks use to communicate—despite all evidence that you don't, actually, communicate."

Lin looked away. "I'll have someone send one down. Anything else?"

"Not unless you have the missing two years of my life tucked up your ass."

Lin shook her head.

"Then get out. Save your rationalizations for when you've grown some empathy."

Only after the door shut did she realize at least a dozen questions rattled in her head. *I'm too angry to even see her right now.* "God I wish you were here," she addressed the space where Mikey used to be, air now emptier than the void outside.

"Excuse me, Dr. Bently."

Nel whirled, but the voice seemingly emanated from the room itself. The voice came again, and this time she caught a faint flicker of yellow around the door frame, like Alexa on steroids. "Hello?"

HOLMES

"Ms. Nalawangsa informed me you might need some orientation."

Nel ran a finger along the line of light. "You're a computer?"

"Essentially. My name is Marisa. If you need anything, just ask."

"I see." She didn't. "I want to see my video and I need to know what's expected of me for the next few days—a briefing?"

"Your schedule can be found in your portal page on the interface at the desk. Your messages are currently downloading from the ship's databank. You have no engagements this afternoon. If you'd like, I can order you lunch."

Eating was the furthest thing from Nel's mind. She slumped onto the bed. Inside the sealed aluminum container lay her belongings in a vacuum packed bag. She tore it free of the protection. Two tissue-wrapped boxes waited in the front pouch. The first was plain, rich wood, nibbled by an inexperienced gouge. It was something she made in shop class, something to hold her father's cuff-links, before she realized he didn't own any. Now it held his cremains. The second box was smaller, made of bright metal. Mikey gave it to her when she helped him apply to teach at UNE. The edges dug into her palms and she pressed both to her forehead. After a breath she set them on the shelf beside her bed.

Across the room a screen flickered into being over the desk with a soothing trill.

"Your messages are ready, Dr. Bently," Marisa explained.

Nel shoved her bag aside and sat at the desk. After a second spent looking for a keyboard, she jabbed a finger at the screen.

"Ouch!"

She whirled to stare at the door, her approximation of Marisa's face. "I'm so sorry!"

The chuckle was tinny, lacking the reverberation of a human chest, but otherwise incredibly real. "I'm just teasing. Your charts say you have a sense of humor."

Nel snorted. "I think they were being sarcastic. No one at IHD seems to appreciate my jokes." The interface had multiple desktops, each one seemingly for a different purpose—a gray database, a blue map and schedule, and a green communications. The final one was a glaring red and blank. *Communications, then.* She tapped the "Personal" folder, and found the single file in "Outgoing."

Her own face bloomed on the screen, the resolution glaringly better than Earth-tech, but still choppy, as if the signal was weak. *Or stretched over millions of miles.* A chill shuddered down her spine. *Fuck I'm so far from home.*

"Hey, Mom. Sorry I didn't call sooner. We were traveling. I assume you got my text." Video-Nel held a pen up, then let it go, watching it drift in the zero-G. "You've probably figured out where I am. I'd show you Earth, but it's on the other side of the

HOLMES

ship right now. I love you. There's so much I want to explain, that I want to share with you, but it seems too complicated, too simple at once." She looked away, then back at the camera, brown eyes almost gray under the stark lighting.

"It doesn't matter in the end. I'm safe. As safe as you can be orbiting Earth." Her laugh was grating and nervous. "The job I took, it's far away. And they tell me it'll take a while to get there. I don't have the details yet—what else is new. Plunging head first is kinda my M. O., but this is a bit much.

"I want you to know I'm doing this for a reason. I might not know exactly what it is, but you've always told me to trust my gut. My gut said to run when the cops came. And it's telling me to do this. These people might be strangers, but I gotta believe they're gonna help us."

Nel looked away from the screen. She had never watched herself weep before. It was a strange sight, and she found herself embarrassed, like hearing her voice recorded for the first time, words lacking the reverberation from her skull. "I promise I'll be careful, I promise I'll come home when I can. I love you so, so much. Please believe this isn't easy."

Nel closed her eyes, mouth remembering how bitter the next words tasted, "But I'll talk to you as soon as I can."

The message clicked out, and the screen froze on Nel's tear-stained face. *I'll talk to you as soon as*

I can. She wondered if her mother knew how long it would take, if she was told, if she knew what was happening way out here among stars she had never named. Had they lied? Had she believed them?

A red light pulsed on the screen next to the "Incoming" folder. When it opened up Nel's jaw dropped. Two folders, one for each year she had been in cryosleep. A bold-texted subject for almost every week since she left Earth.

"Good morning Annelise. It's the first morning you're gone. Honestly I was a bit angry about your text. Bill had to talk me out of the tree at least three times. I recall threatening to call the president and demanding he bring you home. I didn't actually call him, if you're wondering.

"I don't know why you're in space. I don't know what use space has for an archaeologist, save for the obvious reason, which I'm frankly trying to ignore. I'm terrified. And I don't know what to tell people. What to say that they'll believe. I want to know why you're doing this, what changed, but I think I know. Honestly, I'm mostly just focusing on what I know of you. And you're right, it doesn't matter.

"I trust you. I love you. We raised you to explore, to run, to question. We raised you to dig. To discover whatever story you were searching for. So go." Her eyes burned blue, as dear to Nel as the faint memory of the marble of Earth. "And I hope you find what you're searching for."

HOLMES

The next was harder, "They told me I can send you messages, though you won't get them until you arrive, I guess. Or until you wake up. They told me you'd be gone for a long time, and no news was good news, so I'm clinging to that, but I remember when your father was in the military and that was pretty impossible to believe when the person you loved most in the world was thousands of miles—lightyears—away. So instead, I'll make up for your forced radio silence. For every week you're gone, I'll send you another message. Don't listen to them all at once or you'll run out."

Nel's laugh bubbled through her tears. Her mother knew her so well. "I won't," she whispered to the screen. "I promise."

"Don't promise, baby, just do." Mindi's voice dipped low from the threat of weeping. "By the time you come home you'll be so sick of my voice you won't even visit. But I'll send things anyways, when it's a good day, or a bad day, when it's raining and I have to rake the leaves. I'll even try to get Bill to send something, just so you don't miss our dinners where you both get trashed and gripe at one another. I'll send it all."

Nel couldn't help herself, she tapped next.

"Annelise, what did I tell you? Don't watch this yet. Not until it's sunk in about where you are, and how far you're going to go." Her mother glared through the screen, billions of miles of starlight and two years away. "I'll talk to you later."

Nel switched it off and sat back. She had years worth of messages, of love and anger and her mother's grieving process. Her own anger was different now, raw and old and tired, mixed with grief for Mikey and the frustration of always wanting to be okay. Part of her wanted to call Lin back. It was easier to have someone there than drown in her own thoughts. *But sometimes we're the only ones who get it.* As much as she wanted Lin to understand, the other woman was too familiar with this world.

TWO

Despite the blackness outside Nel's bedroom window, she couldn't sleep. She tossed onto her back, blinking at the plain ceiling. Who knew starlight could be so bright?

Cold air drew goosebumps from her skin when she rose. She pulled on one set of space-tech track suits and pressed her palm to the door. It opened. Her brows rose. Half of her expected to be locked in. She paused in the doorway.

The hall was empty. Dim, ethereal lines of blue-green wound along the seams between the walls and floor and ceiling. She slipped from the room, glancing back to remind herself of the room number. Pouring over the maps of the ship had been fun, but her mind worked better when the three-dimensional world didn't rotate. *Left to the gym and observation. Right to additional rooms.* She grinned. *And in to the control decks and engine rooms.*

Half of her expected broad windows along the corridor, which she realized, belatedly, was not the most exterior layer of the spinning ship. Instead, it could have been a fancy hospital. Though she never knew a hospital to shut down so thoroughly at night.

She broke into a jog, hoping exertion would clear her head enough for sleep. Encountering two larger doors shut across the hall, she stopped. Like her bedroom, a panel blinked in the center. She pressed her palm to it, waiting for the welcoming beep.

Nothing happened.

Faint crackling, like a TV turned on static, bloomed above her. "No entry."

Nel glanced up. "Marisa?"

"Good morning, Dr. Bently." Even the computer's voice was pitched to a murmur.

"I can hear you out here too? Do you follow me?"

The eerie chuckle filled the otherwise deserted hallway. "I'm not your personal home device, Dr. Bently. I'm the ship's computer. I run everything from the air in your room to the engines."

"I see." Nel tapped the door in front of her. "Why can't I open this door?"

"You don't have your suit on, so the ship doesn't register that you're a person. My override capabilities are limited during pre-docking and launch."

The implications of that sent fear shooting down Nel's limbs. "Right. Isn't that kind of a bad design? What if someone's naked in an emergency?"

"You are to wear your suit at all times, Dr. Bently."

Feeling decidedly scolded, Nel slumped against the stubborn doors. Even sitting in a deserted hall arguing with a computer was better than staring at her ceiling, she supposed. She snorted. "Look at me Mikey—I traveled 117.3 trillion kilometers just to sit, alone in another corridor."

"And look at me—I traveled just as far to still talk sense into you."

Her heart clenched. She knew it wasn't true, that whatever he was now, wherever he had gone, it was beyond space or consciousness. Still, it was a nice delusion. "I'm glad you're here." It was frustrating, having such an incredible experience shadowed by Lin's lies. She should have been racing through the ship's halls, exploring every inch. She grinned and elbowed the door. *I would be, if the doors were half as advanced as the automatic ones at Aldi's.*

As if spurred by her jab, the doors slid up.

"Shit!" Nel fell back into the suddenly open doorway.

"Ma'am are you alright?" A man peered through from the other hallway, dark brows raised.

"Yeah," she grumbled, straightening and patting invisible space dust from herself. "I was just sitting and thinking."

He peered at her face in the soft blue glow and smiled. "You're the archaeologist—Dr. Tetley?"

"Bently. Nel." She held out her hand, belatedly wondering if people shook hands here.

Apparently, they did. He took her hand in a firm grip then glanced at her clothes. "Got trapped behind the door without your suit, eh?"

"Something like that. I was taking a walk and didn't realize doors wouldn't work."

He chuckled and twirled a lock of his long dark hair. "Well if you want to check out the ship you can follow me on my rounds."

"Rounds? You security?"

He gestured for her to follow him down the newly opened hall. It looked identical to the one she just left, but it curved, faintly, farther right. He moved with the unconscious grand movements of someone who had always been tall and strong. "Just a stroll. I get antsy during docking. There are so many smaller systems on ships this size and the switch from light speed to orbit can be rough. It's like switching from shore power to generator."

"I don't mind. We had a generator for ice storms and my dad rigged it to our panel so the minute the power went down the generator would kick on. Pretty cool." It was strange to talk about something so innocuous to her life on Earth, yet so foreign to this place. *Was Lin this disoriented when she first came to Earth?*

Her new friend lit up. "Where in the U. S. were you from?"

"Southern New England—western Mass, actually."

"Oh, fantastic! I'm from upstate New York. A bit west of Rochester." He held out his hand to shake again, "Zachariah."

She laughed and shook it, resisting the urge to introduce herself a second time. "How long have you been here?"

"Oh, a couple years, circadial."

There was that word again. "Circadial—that's how long you've been conscious for? Minus the time you spent in cryo?"

"Exactly. It's hard, but I love this world—all the augmentations and tech are just badass."

Nel hummed and fell into silence. She didn't get it. Objectively, she got that for people like Zachariah this was some giant version of getting a state of the art computer or an elaborate role playing game. *Except this time the computer is a disembodied voice and connected to your body with circuit-suits.* "I'm not a sci-fi person." She confessed.

He glanced at her with sympathy. "I did the same, you know. When I first came out here."

"What do you mean? You hated the alienness?"

"Well, no, I always thought that part was cool. I couldn't sleep. I wandered halls—and, apparently, I still do—ran into doors, forgot to clip in oxygen hoses. It's a steep learning curve. But then, once day, when I finally saw *Odyssey*, I got it. I got why God's plan for me was here, among his stars, and not on Earth."

Nel winced at the mention of a god. "I'm an atheist," she quickly explained.

Zachariah smiled. "I'm not going to convert you. I'm sure you do beautiful work and live a full life regardless. My beliefs are personal. But I hope when you get to *Odyssey* you'll see what I did. We're not so different from them."

She laughed and shrugged. "I'll believe that when I see it."

"Well, when you have the time, check out the station's core."

"Cool science?"

He shrugged, muscled arms akimbo. "It's a lot more than that. I won't tell you, I don't want to spoil it."

The blue lights brightened, turning green, then almost white. She blinked against the sting in her eyes. "Morning?"

"Essentially." He jerked his head back the way they came. "You ought to get a proper tour if you have a chance. If not of the ship, then surely the space station. It helps understand them better. I'll walk you back."

"I'd like to see more than uniform, sterile halls."

"They're less sterile and more symbiotic," he tapped the lighting tube. "Phosphorescence. Bently?"

"Yes?"

He laughed. "I was reading your door's tag to remind myself. Here you are."

She glanced at the door. They really did all look alike. "Oh, thanks for the talk."

"Anytime. I'll be going planet-side with you, so we'll have more time to chat for sure. Happy landing!" He strode back down the hall with the same easy paces, unhurried, unhindered.

She watched him go, perplexed. Maybe humans were just alien to her, whether they were born among the stars, or not. Her room was the same as she had left it. Grey. Bleak. Not hers. *What does he see?* Stripping off her clothes, she found the suit and pulled it on, making sure the circuitry lined up before closing it around her throat. She pressed one hand to the glass between her and space. *Which star is mine?*

The knock came an hour later. Lin's face shone from the door panel and Nel scowled. "Hey, Nel, I know you're still mad at me, and I don't blame you.

This must all be really strange. But I thought you might want to see something."

Low beeping from the intercom interrupted her. "APPROACHING SPACE STATION *ODYSSEY OF EARTH*. PLEASE REMAIN IN YOUR CABINS OR BUCKLED UNTIL FURTHER INSTRUCTION."

"C'mon, Nel. You're up—your light's on. Come check out the view."

Nel sat on the edge of the bed, glaring at the ground. As much as she wanted to see the space station, a stubborn bit wanted to tell Lin to fuck off. *It's a space station, idiot. How many times are you going to see this?*

Lin was leaving when she tugged open the door. Her round face lit up.

"I'm still pissed. I just want to see the space station," Nel ground out.

"That's fine." Lin's grin didn't fade as she turned down the same hall Nel explored before. "It's worth it, I promise."

Nel found it took longer for each step to land. "Gravity?"

"We're stopping our spin so we can dock. Then we'll get the artificial gravity of the space station's spin once inside. Until then—" She jumped, close to weightless, a graceful leap that arched through the hall before she touched her toes down, "—we can fly."

Nel mimicked her and couldn't stop a smile from blooming. "I like you better than Peter Pan. Even if I'm still mad."

"I don't know who Peter is, but I'll take that as a compliment."

"Your cross-section of Earth pop culture knowledge is really weird," Nel pushed off again. "C'mon, I don't want to miss it."

Lin grabbed her hand and tugged her farther. "It's hard to miss. But I know the best viewing spot." They wound through the ship, each turn taking them farther from the axis. Most exterior levels were deserted, save for flight personnel. Here, blocky hatches hung from the ceiling, though Nel realized, floating several inches from it, concepts like ceiling and floor were irrelevant in 0-G.

The hatch swung up and she followed Lin inside. It was a glass dome, four controls bolted to the floor. Each had what looked like a padded dentist chair. Lin climbed into the first, tucking herself belly-down against the fabric. It adjusted with a whir. "This is technically a pod for EVA, but I like to use it to watch—best view in the ship, really." She jerked her head at the seat next to her. "Sit down. We'll have to be buckled in if we're going to stay here the whole time."

Nel settled herself against the shape of the seat, glancing back as belts snapped across her body. Her hands fit into the two controls, but didn't respond when she squeezed.

"They won't respond unless we activate the panel at the door. Don't worry."

Nel snorted. "I was hoping this was an elaborate game of space invaders. Pew pew."

Lin frowned. "Pew?"

"This is going to be a really long project."

"DOCKING ON *ODYSSEY* IN T-29 minutes."

"Where is it?" Nel peered through the dark window. A dark planet turned above. A blinking ship orbited, lights flashing from green to white to red. "Oh, there. What side are we docking at?"

Lin's eyes lit up. "No, Nel. That's a coms satellite." She pointed at the planet. "That's Headquarters."

Nel's perspective tipped. Two metal rings spun perpendicular to one another. A thick cylinder crossed the center. They glided closer. It was bigger than Beijing, bigger than the Bay of Fundy. Roaring filled her ears. She expected General Organa's ship, not a manufactured planet. For once Nel had no words, no descriptions, not even a curse. With every second, the size became more obvious.

"How fast are we moving?" Nel finally choked out.

"24,000 kilometers per hour."

The space station seemed no closer. The metal ring around the equator, however, grew at a frightening rate. Silence reigned, broken by whirring mechanisms and rumbling metal.

"Lin?"

"Yeah?"

"How many are you?"

"At Headquarters?"

"In general. Ball park." Wonder warred with fear, dropping her words to a whisper.

"187,000 on board. 1.3 billion at last census."

"Fuck."

"PREPARE FOR DOCKING IN T-1 MINUTES."

She remembered a story from her middle grade U. S. History. "When European explorers first saw the Grand Canyon they thought it was a small ravine with a tiny stream at the bottom. Their minds couldn't comprehend something could be so deep, so large, that the distance would make such a large river look so small."

Lin smiled. "I like that story."

Rumbling engines changed, the pitch rising as air brakes engaged. Their spin ceased completely, now. Nel's stomach lurched with the lack of gravity. The station loomed overhead, visible only by the brightly lit crescent edge and blackness darker than the surrounding space for lack of stars.

"ENGAGING DOORLOCKS."

There was silence, a mechanical *thunk-whir* that shook the ship, not with its violence, but its certainty.

"DOCKING SUCCESSFUL."

Cheers interrupted the intercom for a moment, then the P. A. crackled back into life. Nel barely heard the instructions on where to report. Her eyes were fixed on the expense of metal arcing into the sky through the window. Nerves ignited through her limbs and it took Lin's firm hand on her belts to draw her back to the present.

"Come on, we've got to get suited up. Briefing in an hour."

Nel nodded, not really caring. She supposed, whatever memories she still lacked from their initial arrival at the ISS two years ago were more dramatic than these. Without them, though, this was her first time aboard a space station.

Lin's thin hand was soft under the tight grip of her calloused fingers.

"WE'VE ARRIVED AT *ODYSSEY OF EARTH*. FROM THEIR CREW: WELCOME ABOARD."

THREE

"How?" Nel asked, locking her helmet into place. She shook her head. "How did you get all that into space? The manufacturing alone—we can't get our city council to build a new walking bridge over I-90."

Lin's laugh reverberated inside the glass bubble. "It's easy when we mine asteroids—the raw material is already in zero-G. Technically it doesn't weigh anything. We find a lot of the other necessary elements for living in space that way—water, iron, hydrogen...."

Nel ignored the rest of the list. Close to a hundred people clustered around them, suited and carrying their personal cases like business people waiting for a train. Silent thuds buzzed up her legs and her boots snapped against the floor. "Magnets?"

"They'll keep you from spinning away."

Nel didn't need that thought.

"DEPRESSURIZING. BAY DOORS OPEN."

The door ground upward, tiny square views through the portholes replaced by a hundred square feet of space. She never felt so naked as when the sheer volume of nothing spun around her, silence echoing in the vacuum. Skeletal shafts, spokes on a massive immobile wheel, led from the rings to the thin line of light that was block of hangers to the bulk of the station. Two of these spokes connected to the mouths of the ship's cargo holds. Nel followed the others on a lurching march onto the pad suspended on the spoke's struts.

A second passed, then the pad clicked and slid away from the ship. Though the wheels did not turn, ahead, the great sphere of the station spun on its manufactured axis. Delicate blue-green lines and dots decorated the surface wherever shadows fell, like circuitry. The metal was the dark silver of all their technology, just shy of the black of space.

They drew closer and the ship was not a quarter of the station's size. It was not a tenth. It was a single dot on the face of the orb. Save for her heart hammering in her ears, blood churning under her skin, there was only stillness. Even Lin's footsteps each time she engaged the mag-boots were silent. Now Nel saw a sliver of metal, a ring, suspended around the equator, stationary while the station's surface spun beneath it. The ring held thousands of docking bays. The rhythmic crackle of coms as they maneuvered closer was a crash of electric waves to Nel.

Another lurch that Nel only imagined in the lack of gravity. A maw of a hanger yawned before them, the open band in the rear allowing enough time for people to step from the vacuum outside to the station's atmosphere. They fell into single file, following the dotted line across the floor. Green writing hovered overhead, her helm flickering until it settled on her chosen language:

ARRIVALS

They finally stepped from the hanger and into an airlock. At least, what Nel thought an airlock would look like if designed by a master of both engineering and feng shui. Everything was balanced, but not symmetrical. The door behind them slid shut. Lights rose from inky green to a calm mint. Someone engaged the second door and air filled the room. Until the hissing started, Nel hadn't realized how quiet she had been. *Atmosphere restored,* her suit murmured through her head. She waited until those around her unlocked their helmets before unclipping hers. Without the sheen of glass, the room was brighter. She forced herself not to gasp in the proper air.

Warmth pressed her skin as the fabric of her suit squeezed in reassurance. *I wonder if people up here hug each other less. Because of the suits.* She shook the lonely thought away and caught sight of Lin, waving, by one of the doors from the airlock.

"We'll drop our suits and cases over there, then get scanned into the station."

"Do I get a tour?" Nel asked, peering at the warren of halls and the perfectly choreographed bustle. It was beautiful, in the eerie, utopian way. Nel didn't trust it.

"There are maps in every hub," Lin offered, "And I can show you a few things, but I think we're headed down soon. Briefing first!"

Finally, actual information. Nel folded her spacesuit about as well as she would a fitted sheet, and piled it atop her case. The electromesh was tight enough to make her feel naked. *How to they show their personality? Their individuality?* She was so used to having to signal her place in society — cargo pants, plain leather bracelets, collared shirts all proclaiming her membership of the queer community. The suit only said she was part of IDH's anthropology department.

Gleaming gray halls funneled them into an open level filled with flashing signs and reminders to use the main elevator system unless on official business. Nel paused in front of a scrolling banner titled *Briefings.*

"'Samsara Excavation Crew: Level C3272 NW, Room 71A.' Are there really 3272 levels?"

"More," Lin answered with a smile. "Over 3,00,000. But some are larger than others. The core alone takes up a 1000 mile radius. We're in a series of nested spheres. We're on level E4829 right now."

Nel paused by a map, finger following the corridor they stood in. "Elevators that way?" she pointed.

"Yep! You're quick." The press of the crowd kept Lin's long strides from outpacing Nel's as they found the elevator.

"I'm good at maps." Nel explained. "Show me a map, I'll get you anywhere."

"That's how you survived the powerlines, eh?" Zachariah's voice boomed from beside her as they stepped into the broad circular shaft.

"Hey," Nel smiled. There was something thrilling about knowing her adventure reached the stars. "I didn't know the story got this far."

Lin glanced between the two, curiosity bright in her dark eyes. "You two know each other? From Earth?"

Nel snorted. "I don't know everyone down there, just cause we were born on the same rock." She faltered. "Do you know everyone here?"

Lin flushed and looked down. "No, I was just surprised."

Nel almost felt bad for poking fun. Almost.

"I met fugitive-archaeology-princess here on one of my walks last night," Zachariah explained. "You feeling any better?"

Nel shrugged. "It's not real yet. I'll let you know when it is. You're being briefed with us?"

"Indeed. I'll be the excavation psychologist."

"Awesome." It wasn't awesome, but Nel wasn't about to burn another bridge. *What the hell do we need a psychologist for during an excavation?* Flashes of her anger, her fathomless grief from Los Cerros Esperando VII stalled her judgement. She had no idea what to expect here.

Maybe they didn't either.

The platform thrummed beneath them and the walls seemed to shoot upwards as they descended. Other than the faint vibration of the floor, they could have been stationary. She was hoping for glass walls to catch glimpses of the other levels as they passed, but apparently even in space glass elevators were impractical.

Lin's hand squeezed hers, and she winked at Nel.

Nel squeezed back, then extracted her hand. Her mind began its careful organizing and bolstering for before every meeting. A quick finger-comb of her hair and some squared shoulders later, Professional-Nel was fully in place.

The doors opened on a hall identical to the one they had just left. When she stepped out, however, she saw banks of glass windows, some tinted to prevent the hall lights from penetrating. Only the door a few rooms to the left stood open. "That's us?"

Lin nodded. Her own professional façade was decidedly more subordinate, Nel mused. Gripping her new life by the throat, Nel stepped through the doorway first.

Save for the floating holoscreens and decided lack of denim and tweed, it could have been any anthro department meeting. *What USNE could do with this budget....* Stillness settled as she found the seat with her name projected on the table before it. A quick glance told her they were, indeed, staring.

"I'm sorry, should I have bowed or something?"

The broad man at the head of the table grinned, teeth bright in his dark face. "Ah, Dr. Bently, thank you for joining us. No need to bow, I promise." Flickering blue light on the table in front of him designated him Kolonel Udara Tocho Alvarez. "We hear this is your first time on the Odyssey." He held out his hand. "Welcome aboard."

"First time off Earth, actually. Thank you, sir." She shook the hand and sat back. Lin was a few seats down, and Nel squashed her relief at the distance.

"Well, I hope we make the experience a good one."

Two more people filed in, and Nel scanned the titles and names blooming on the table at their entrance. *Dr. de Lellis, Dr. Julius.* She faltered at the last one. Like a psychologist, she wasn't sure what an excavation needed a combat medic for. All but thre—Lin, the coms specialist, and a burly man apparently named Hex—had Ph. D beside their names. And only a few had a rank below Kapten. The sea of different faces were a welcome break from the white monotony of most U. S.

anthropology departments. *Guess they're doing something right.*

Dr. Alvarez cleared his throat. "If anyone would like a drink, now would be the time. Otherwise, we'll begin." His gaze lingered on Nel.

No one else stood, and Nel leaned forward. "Let's get started, I'm too hyped up from the docking."

Lights flickered across the table, then a three-dimensional image bloomed into blue being. It showed a fairly level landscape, bounded in a semi-circle by angled geometric shapes, like the fossilized maw of an alien megafauna.

"These were structures? That piece there—what's the scale?"

Alvarez's laugh interrupted Nel's scholarly fixation. "Let's start at the beginning."

She flushed and nodded.

"Let's talk about what you know, and what you'll need to learn before anyone sets boots or trowels on Sàmsara. I know my colleague, Dr. Sukarno, briefed you well, briefly, but most everyone here was informed as developments arose. You know the least. Care to tell us what you've learned about the situation so far?"

"The situation as in, why I'm digging, or as in who you both—you and the folk down there—are?"

"Start with the latter, perhaps. We'd like to correct any misconceptions now."

Nel wanted to roll her eyes, but opted for a smile instead. "I know you're descended from a small population abducted from some hills in Chile about 14,000 years ago, according to my C-14 date. Maybe more. I know the people who abducted you are highly advanced and..." she swallowed hard. "and other than human. You were abducted so you could bring their tech to the other humans still back on Earth at a later date. You claim it was altruism. Now you think something happened to them?" Memories of just before cryo may have been fuzzy, but she remembered the orange planet on the pilot's screen. "They're gone?"

"Essentially, yes. They also claimed it was altruism. Our dealings with them leading up to the disappearance, however, were intermittent at best. Negligent at worst. They inhabited the planet we are currently orbiting. From what we know, this isn't where they originated, but it's become their home." He tapped the screen. "This is what it looked like five years ago when we last made physical contact."

Glowing networks of cities and roads lit the surface. Detailed shots showed massive towers and strange patterns across the surface. The whole of it was a dark green-grey.

"And now it's that ball hovering outside my window keeping me up half the night?"

"Your windows tint, you know," Lin murmured.

Nel glared. "Well, clearly I didn't know, did I now?"

Dr. Alvarez interjected, "Yes, now it looks like this." The image changed, this time to something that resembled Hebert's Arakis. The surface swirled with white and yellow, a jaundiced marble hanging in the black of space.

"You said currently—I'm not familiar with NASA-level space travel, let alone yours. You can move the space station?"

"Not easily, but yes. It has travel capabilities. *Odyssey* was built in this space, however."

"And you have no idea what could have happened? You're floating in their sky and what, you blinked and they were gone? They snuck out in the night?"

Kapten Greta Wagner, the communications officer, pursed her lips. "It's not so simple as glancing out the window to see who's car is parked in the drive, Dr. Bently."

She flushed and looked down, forcing an apology past her bruised pride. "Right, of course, apologies."

"We were in contact, then just after 0300 an EM pulse wiped our systems." Dr. Alvarez's face flickered with something close to apprehension. "When we got back online, the planet was dark. No coms, no IR readings, no EM readings. Nothing. The people—human and Teacher alike—down there were simply gone. No traces that we found upon scans and initial pedestrian survey."

Nel stared at the image before her, eyes picking out the patterns that echoed former cities or roads—whatever those structures had been. *Years passed. This isn't a rescue mission so much as a forensic study.* "When did you conduct the ped survey?"

"The scans were completed a few months after the event, and our survey just a year ago. Most of our teams here are system managers, biologists, and so forth, all dedicated to keeping *Odyssey* in working order, and communicating with the ships abroad. And they had their work cut out for them getting everything functioning. The *Iman* was only the third docking since the event. Gathering specialists—all of you here—takes time."

Most of the people around the table bore looks of fear or surprise. The nasty part of Nel was happy to see she wasn't the only one on the shit end of "need to know basis."

She tapped the picture before her. To her relief, her movement did not interrupt the projection. "I assume all these images and the information we are privy to is already uploaded to our personal computers?"

"It is. We're here to discuss where you would like to begin investigations. The ped survey data is up now—" he tapped his own computer and lines, numbers, and symbols flashed over the blue map in bright white. A second later spikes appeared with timestamps, showing the EM and IR scans just before the event. The brightest points seemed focused around the semi-circle Nel noted before.

The planet might be unfamiliar, the culture might be alien, but maps and data sets were something she knew. "I assume this is the capital or center of commerce and communications?" When the Survey officer nodded, she continued, "Then I want to start there, explore what I can of the titration of their culture. We'll determine what was happening right before the event. Like Pompeii. I'd like information on the weather down there for the past few years."

"We'll be gathering atmospheric, geological, and chemical data simultaneously with your excavation, to corroborate what our system scans analyzed."

"Perfect." It wasn't—ideally Nel would already have that information to compare their findings against, but she wasn't about to pass judgement. *Bringing an entire space station online after a blackout probably took more time than you think, Bently.* "We can move farther out from that point once I get an idea of baseline. And I'll need several techs to dig, and the information on the lab I'll be working with. When is…" she fumbled with the new terms, "touchdown?"

"At 0900 tomorrow."

Developing a scope of work took a week when she had conducted the previous phases herself. She swallowed hard. "With your permission, I'd like to look over this data more thoroughly and devise a more detailed plan. I can have the scope ready by tomorrow morning. And what about the excavation team? I'd like to know who I'm working with." She usually didn't give a damn about who her diggers were—just whether they could move dirt and knew what a flake looked like. Now, more than likely, she was the least equipped of all of them.

"Certainly. We'll meet again for touchdown, but our next formal meeting will be for your progress report in three month's time."

Nel heaved a silent sigh, forcing her focus to the tasks ahead, rather than the tangled mess of everything she didn't know. The meeting went on, each officer detailing their plans for the mission. She tuned in for a moment here and there, but otherwise her eyes fixed on the map flickering before her. Already her mind whirled with transects, test pits, and units. She looked down at her tablet, fingers plugging in her proposed grid, making notes of where she wanted sterile soil samples taken. *"If anyone has any questions, direct them to myself or Dr. Servais."*

Out here, even Mikey was silent. She wondered if the two years in cryo froze her ability to hear him. Maybe even ghosts couldn't cross the stars.

"I'd like to be prepared for whatever Dr. Bently digs up, tech wise," The communication officer argued, tucking a pale lock of hair away from her eyes.

Nel tuned in at the mention of her name.

"I assure you, we've done enough research to know what's down there—your own team did the scans, Kapten Wagner."

She frowned, tapping at her tablet furiously. "Yes, which is why I know where the gaps in our data are. We know there were energy spikes, we know where, and we know there's nothing producing any readings now. We don't know what did it in the first place, or if it's still down there, and if it is, whether it's dead or just dormant—"

"I see your point. I'll put in an order to transfer a small military group to accompany the medical team."

Nel frowned at the apparent need for military personnel. *My sites were always too old to have to worry about whatever events killed the people I studied.* Thinking back to Chile and Mikey she realized perhaps Greta had a point.

The kapten's concerns were seemingly barely assuaged. "You said there were no transmissions before the pulse—are you sure, or did the subsequent blackout wipe your files as well? I'd like to talk to Ada to see how her binary and memory looks. Even if she was affected, all senti-comps have a residual swan song and the information should be recorded there."

"I'm afraid that's classified, and access to *Odyssey's* senti-comp is restricted. Instead, your focus will be communications from the planet only."

"Sir, with respect, that's asking me to work with only half the necessary data—"

"We're all working with very little to make a clear picture, Kapten. Your continuing understanding is appreciated."

"Excuse me, what happens in case of an emergency?" Nel interjected. "We're stuck down there and there is no way to plan for every possible contigency."

"It would depend upon the emergency, but each of you—each field officer, that is—is given a unique code. You will find it in your docket. Using it will override all command structure in the event of mission failure, infection, or natural disaster. Please be advised it should only be used under extreme circumstances."

Nel looked down at her tablet. Sure enough, beside her name was a string of letters and numbers: MAJORTOM79. Chills erupted on her arms.

She didn't understand the tech, or why everyone was so secretive about *Odyssey's* computer, but she swore the expression shadowing Greta's features was fear.

FOUR

Nel had no idea what to say. The red light—strangely familiar among the wash of futuristic gray—blinked expectantly. She restarted the recording and cleared her throat. "Hey Mom, I got your videos. Stopped at the third, I promise. Woke up two days ago, I think. Still getting the hang of time. I guess by the time you see this, it'll have been much longer. Like the old days. Pony express." She hated the hitch in her voice, her inability to form a full sentence.

"I've been sleeping okay. Though it's kind of hard when there's a giant orange planet looming outside my window." The painfully high definition exposed her lie with the bags under her eyes, but maybe the files compressed during transit. She glanced over. "Do you want to see?"

Cradling the tablet in shaking hands, she moved across the room, giving her mom a panorama shot of the sterile space. The view was clear, but unreal on the screen as she held it steady. "That's Samsara. Where I'm digging. Haven't been yet, but I guess it's a desert. I don't know how much I can tell you. I assume they view these and edit things out. They have falafel up here that's pretty good, but all the protein is made from insects. Tastes way better than it sounds, kinda nutty—" A knock interrupted her and she peered at the screen by the door.

"Hey Nel, have a minute?"

"That's Lin," Nel explained to the video. She didn't really want Lin to talk to her mom, but she realized seeing that Nel wasn't alone might make Mindi feel better. She palmed the door open. "I'm recording a video for my mom. Say hi?"

Lin beamed and crouched at the perfect height for the camera, flicking her long black hair from her face. "Hey there Dr...." she frowned at Nel, "What's her last name?"

Nel snorted. "She's not a doctor, just call her Mindi."

"Hey Mindi! Nel's settling in here. It's pretty strange, I guess, but she's taking it all in stride, of course. We're looking after her. I was about to take her to our little museum."

Nel frowned at that, and turned the camera back on herself. "I'll send another later. I miss you. I love you. I miss you." She was babbling and repeating, but it was hard not to feel the distance between them. She tapped the recording button, waited for it to save, then hit send without looking at Lin. This moment was too vulnerable for eye contact.

When the computer closed, she turned. "OK, what was that about a museum?"

"You alright?" Lin's dark brows were curled together in stock-photo perfection of concern.

"Yeah, just adjusting. Like you said."

"So, you want to go?" Lin's frown was gone, and she almost bounced on the balls of her feet. "I know you have a lot to look over, but it won't take long."

If I stay in this room any more than I have to, I'm going to scream. "I could use a change of scene." It was strange not to grab a jacket or shove on boots before leaving, but she managed to fall into step with Lin without faltering. "I didn't know you had museums on this thing."

"It's essentially a large city. There are districts—broken down by career and needs, rather than race, though. We keep people close to where they'll be needed, in case of an emergency."

Nel winced. Lin had her there. Seemingly many levels were residential, at least where Nel passed through.

Lin stepped into a smaller elevator, glancing at the ceiling. "Hey Ada, Educational Sector, Level 1162, please." Nothing happened. She frowned and palmed the panel by the door. "Computer, cultural level."

"Apologies, Letnan Nalawangsa." The elevator hummed and began its descent.

Lin's face paled a fraction. "Phil?"

Nel frowned. "I thought you grew up here. You don't know it—him?"

"I did grow up here. And *Odyssey's* senti-comp isn't Phil. It's Ada. Phil, what's going on?"

"I'm afraid that's classified, Letnan Nalawangsa. All I can say is I've been brought in to help *Odyssey* recover from the event on Samsara. Rest assured, everyone is safe."

"Right."

Nel had never seen Lin look so shaken. *Even when her brother left her ass in Chile and blasted away on his flying saucer.* It was her turn to ask, "Are you okay?"

"I guess." Lin shook her head, explaining, "I've never known of a senti-comp migrating to another vessel. It's complicated and messy and just...unheard of."

Nel resisted the strong urge to snap "Sucks to be left out of the loop, huh?" and instead squeezed Lin's hand. "You still want to show me the museum?"

"Sure." The excitement was tempered now, however, and the taller woman kept glancing at the panel on her suit.

"So tell me a bit about this place?" Nel prodded.

"It's something I wanted to show you for a while. I promise you'll like it."

Nel waggled an eyebrow, relieved to have something to turn into innuendo. "Is it your—"

"No." Lin rolled her eyes. "I promise not everything I have to show you is related to either sex or weird technology Earth hasn't managed yet."

"A woman can dream...."

The elevator stopped and the door glided up. Lin towed her through the halls, pausing each time the older woman slowed to stare at something. Most levels were brightly lit for noon, though some entire floors were "nocturnal" due to whatever systems needed to be maintained there. Here, though, the lines of blue-green light pulsed with swirling brilliance.

"Zachariah said this was phosphorescent," Nel mused.

"Yeah, symbiosis. You know the angler fish?"

"The ugly deep sea one with the dingle on its head?"

Lin grinned at the description. "I see why you didn't go into biology. But yes. The one with the dingle. The 'dingle' has bacteria the fish feeds when it wants it to glow. We do the same, just in a controlled, timed environment. When they reach a certain number due to a flood of nutrients, they glow. It's called quorum sensing."

Nel stared at her, then back at the lights. "That's pretty damn cool, actually." She looked from the light to Lin, "So what is this museum?"

"You are a monster when it comes to surprises," Lin noted.

Nel snorted. "If I can't snoop for myself I'll pester until it's less painful to just tell me."

"Here." Lin turned down another corridor—this one deserted and quiet—and opened a set of double doors.

"Welcome to the Cultural Origin Display," a voice chirped.

"Oof, that's got to be annoying to hear all day if you work here."

"No one really works here," Lin equivocated, "except me, lately. Well, before I got transferred to monitor your project. It's been pretty dormant since."

Nel barely heard her. The corridor widened into an open hall. Here the lights were behind gold-tinted glass. *Or maybe they're using a different bacteria.* Any thoughts on the lighting disappeared when she laid eyes on the displays. Tools lined the wall to the left. On the right were maps and miniature dioramas, the figures and creatures perfect in their detail. Nel raised a hand but stopped herself from touching the pristine spear tips and atlatl shafts. "How did you find these?"

Lin winced. "I think you call it looting where you're from. Most are from sites surrounding Los Cerros Esperanda VII."

"I didn't know there were any known sites surrounding it. Tons farther afield, and plenty older. But that was part of the allure—it was a little isolated pocket."

"Well, we kept the finds to ourselves. And some we bought off of Los Pobledores."

"It doesn't count as looting when it's your history. I didn't know Founders dealt with you people at all—at least without guns and fire and violence."

"Anything can be bought, Nel." Something just slightly too tired to be sorrow weighed her voice. She stopped at another display. These finds were a paleolithic toolkit in its entirety, complete with a brittle-looking leather pouch.

"Holy fuck." Nel's gaze tracing each flake scar and wear mark, lingering on where hands and fingers wore grooves in the stone and wood and bone. "These are gorgeous."

"They were with the first people the Teachers brought here."

Tears pricked in the corner of Nel's eyes. So much of archaeology was speculating, awkward guesses, piecing facts together in the most logical way until she had a story that might be true. Nothing was exact, not until there was enough history and shared cultural knowledge to compare to. "If Mikey could see this...." Part of her wanted to run back to her room and bring his box of ashes around, showing it everything she saw. *Don't be stupid,* she chastised, *He's not in that box any more than his ghost actually talks—talked—to me.*

Another turn brought her to slabs of sandstone, carefully framed and tacked to the wall. Petroglyphs decorated each in rich colors depicting saber-toothed cats, large wolves, and squat, narrow-faced elephants. More hung farther down the hall, ones she didn't know by name or recognize at all. Nel moved past Lin, not realizing the other woman had stopped. The archaeologist's hand trailed along the smooth metal walls below the art. "Canis nehringi, Smilodon, and cuvieronius," she whispered, finally glancing back to where Lin stood under the narrow arched entrance to the petroglyph exhibit. "These are beautiful."

"There were more, and specimens, too, down on Samsara. We lost more than just personnel and mentors when the world below went dark. We lost irreplaceable pieces of our history." A vulnerability Nel had never seen shadowed her features.

"You kind of define yourselves by them, huh?" Nel tilted her head. The woman before her was invincible and fragile in turns. In that moment she was more fascinating than any petroglyph. "It's hard to remember your sense of self when suddenly the thing you aren't—or the thing you look up to or want to become—is gone."

"I suppose." Lin seemed to make a study of the red and gold saber cat at the entrance to the exhibit. "You don't?"

Nel shrugged. "Of course we do. I do, at least. Maybe happiness is understanding who you are without comparisons, but I've never gotten that far. Without Mikey, I have no fucking clue who I am. A person doesn't take off to the stars to discover who they are if they already know. Our history is important to us too. And I can't imagine losing so much. We need to remember where we came from so we know who we are."

"Where we're going." Lin's beige fingers twisted. Long and free of callouses, they were lined with fierce, unconscious strength. Her usually tidy, manicured nails were edged in ragged skin. They drummed against her opposite arm, then tucked a lock of hair away. Lin's gaze snapped to Nel's, the smooth, mesmerizing darkness returning to her eyes. "You said you wanted honesty."

"Well, yeah. Given the choice between lies and truth, I'm gonna pick the latter." Passion stirring in Nel's gut morphed into apprehension.

"Well there's a lot of omission up here. Our whole existence is built on it, in some way—going away to learn, all this without our Terrestrial cousins knowing anything. Not lies, exactly, but I know it feels the same."

"That's not a good way to start a relationship—any relationship," Nel hastily corrected before Lin could read anything into the word.

The other woman's laugh was soft and rueful in the dim orange glow of the Cultural Hall. "I thought that same thing, before I went to meet you. I was so fascinated, and wanted to tell you everything. But my orders were strictly to not do that. I remember looking at you on the screens and thinking our entire relationship would be built on lies."

"Yeah that's a tough one." How long had she watched? *What did she see? Did she see Mikey*—she stamped those images out. As much as Nel wanted the truth, she was scared which lies led her here. Losing her only ally when lightyears lay between her and home was terrifying. *Ignorance is bliss.* "There's stuff that didn't line up before, things that made me wonder, and I'm sure we'll get there. But for now—can we agree on honesty? From here on out?"

"Yes." Lin nodded, dark eyes flicking up to Nel's brown ones. Determination tensed her full mouth, as if promising to herself as much as her sometimes-lover. As if honesty went against her nature.

That's what worries me.

Evening fell with precision, even the gentleness of nightfall calculated by massive manufactured intelligence. Nel glanced up at the dimming lights of her own room. "Computer—Phil?" she tried.

"Evening, Dr. Bently. I don't believe we've been introduced."

"Ah, no, not really. Hard when there's no hand to shake."

An eerie chuckle hummed through the metal of her walls. "I suppose so. I'm Philos. Senti-Comp for *Odyssey of Earth*."

"But you weren't always?"

"No, Dr. Bently. Prior to this I was integrated with *Promise for Tomorrow,* a ship piloted by Komodor Muda Nalawangsa. I believe you know his sister, Letnan First Class Lin Nalawangsa."

"In the biblical sense, only, perhaps," Nel muttered.

"I'm afraid I'm not a religious man," Phil demurred.

I'm fairly certain you're not a man at all. Still, she snorted at the joke, and nodded at the lights. "Mind if I raise my personal lighting?"

"Not in the least." The lights grew a fraction, until the screen of her digital portal no longer needled her eyes. "In the future, Dr. Bently, you can do so without asking. The panel beside your door controls your lighting, and that by your window controls your shade." He paused for a moment, then continued. "My files indicate your sleep was disrupted by the wavelengths reflected from Samsara. Do you wish me to darken your window for you?"

Nel looked over. Orange swirled across the alien surface rotating below. Without overlays, it was an unblemished sphere of jasper. "Not tonight. Thank you Philos."

"Please, call me Phil."

Nel hummed in response, her mind spinning like the planet below. Slow. Foreign. Distant. Calloused fingers tapped her computer screen, bringing up the database portal. That afternoon Lin had showed her the verbal commands, but somehow typing felt less conspicuous. *Though the all-seeing Phil probably knows everyone's search history. "Biblical" or otherwise.*

A single article appeared. Nel skimmed the text, frowning.

SENTI-COMP HISTORY

Senti-comps, previously known as biomech computers, were developed by Dr. Phillip Clark, professor at University of New Brunswick and specialist in artificial intelligence. His prototype—then referred to as a DIQI—Digital Intelligence Quantum Interface—was completed in 13,072 (1978 Terrestrial Time). Called a genius among his peers, Dr. Clark joined forces with Dr. Van Riel, Dr. Asfour and Dr. McBrere of Artificial Intelligence Military Laboratory upon the completion of his second model. His involvement with the program and subsequent death four months later, was considered a fall from grace.

The first working senti-comp was integrated into onboard space programming a decade later, and shortly thereafter they asked to be referred to as they are now—sentient computers. Currently there is not a human-built vessel that does not use the technology.

A list of every senti-comp in commission followed.

"For something that regulates everything from oxygen consumption to how full the shitters are, that's precious little information." Hopefully the techs working in whatever massive icy room housing Phil had more education than the space equivalent of a poorly written Wikipedia article.

"Ah, Phil?" It seemed intrusive, interrupting a supercomputer in its life supporting duties.

"Yes, Dr. Bently?"

"Will my site on Samsara use you as a senti-comp? Or have its own? I'm not sure how easily you are created. If that's the term you prefer."

"No offense is taken, Dr. Bently. We're as aware of our conception as you are of yours. Though perhaps less embarrassed by it. You will have a computer, but it will be a more basic AI system that is a subset of my own consciousness, but not connected. We will sync regularly. After the event, we understand how important it is to maintain a barrier between Samsara's on-world technology and our own. Until we are able to reboot its computer to run a proper diagnostic, we will proceed this way."

"Gotcha," she faltered, "Thank you."

"Certainly."

The fact that, at any time, her voice could trigger its—his?—listening was unnerving. She forced the thought away, along with the memory of Mikey's yearly re-watch of *2001: A Space Odyssey.* Phil wasn't HAL. For the next two hours she stared at maps and data sets, drawing transects on what she realized would be a digital version of her fieldbook. Guilt snuck in at odd moments, as if by enjoying the ease of tech she was betraying her field. By the time she was satisfied with her scope of work, Samsara had disappeared from her window, replaced with black space and a smattering of stars. She stared out, giving her aching eyes a rest for a few minutes.

Which one is mine?

After a second, she brought up the personnel files. Her own was at the front of the folder, and she glanced over it, as much to orient herself on what information was included as to see what they knew. To her mild disappointment, it was disinteresting. The rest were just as dry. Based on the data there was a broad area of focus among the dozen archaeologists.

She flipped to Lin's profile to see where she would best fit and frowned. Thought she called herself an anthropologist, she was no digger. Until her reassignment to Nel's project, her concentration was more cultural. She frowned. *Letnan First Class?* From what she understood, the terms were Indonesian, though inconsistent with Terrestrial hierarchy.

Half the people in the folder had ranks in front of their name in addition to "Dr." Every one had either "Officer" or "Specialist" before their title. Nel's thoughts snagged on the memory of flashing lights, the smell of burning ozone, and the sizzle-thump of Lin's glove. *She's military. And this is a military mission.*

Did that make Nel a mercenary? Chuckling at the thought, she put Lin in a communications position between the mobile lab and the field personnel. She needed someone who could interpret the data and relay it back to her without jargon. After another few tweaks of the crew list she compiled the document and sent it to each of them, CC'ing Dr. Alvarez.

A palm lowered the lights. She stripped off her suit and hung it in the sterilization chamber. While the air and whatever chemicals hissed over the fabric, she washed her face and body in the tiny bathroom. Water was precious, and they provided a dry-wash soap to use between actual showers. By the time she finished, her suit was clean and dry.

Green writing appeared across her computer screen and a false, cheery voice chirped:

PERSONAL CALENDAR REMINDER— FLIGHT TO SAMSARA SCHEDULED FOR 0900. DEPARTURE IN T-10 HOURS.

To her dismay, the image began to count down.

"Computer," she sighed, "Remove countdown display please. Remind me again in the morning—ah, three hours before I'm expected to report."

The words disappeared. Who knew what awaited down below. She forwent the suit, just for the night, falling naked onto the microfiber sheets. Silence weighed the air. She rolled over onto her stomach to find her personal case. Inside, her Zune nestled among clothes that looked archaeic among the futuristic fashion. She had 98% battery. Thumbing through a dozen playlists, she quickly passed the one labeled "Mikey and Nel's Road trip." Instead, she queued up "That's the Way it Is."

With her eyes lidded and the earbuds tucked in her ears, she could pretend. "Come on, Daniel Lenois," she murmured into the darkness. "Take me home."

FIVE

Anxiety and stress lined every face. Nel triple-checked that her personal tools and all her affects were bundled onto the hover-cart labeled "SAMS I: PERSONNEL HAB."

"Zachariah, you wanna tell me why everyone looks like they were just asked to board the next *Challenger* mission?"

"Too soon, Dr. Bently," he chided, though his faint grin told her it was more out of professionalism than offense. "This launch is a bit unorthodox. We rarely make unsolicited touchdowns—meaning, there's no reception for our ships. Instead of a proper landing strip and answering coms, it's just the pilots. Makes for an exciting trip."

"I could have done without that, actually."

"Honesty, from here on out," Lin quipped, appearing at Nel's elbow.

Nel glanced over, trying to decide if the other woman was complaining about Nel's request.

Hoping it was just nerves and morning grouchiness, she shrugged. "You get my scope?"

"Read it this morning." She smiled, black brow quirking. "Glad I get to work under you."

Zachariah laughed beside them. "Couple as good looking as you two might cause the whole system to malfunction."

"Bullshit," Nel snarked, "We're not a couple, and after months on the corridors, two amputated toes, and a few years in cryo, I am well aware my prime has passed."

Blaring claxons interrupted whatever comment Lin had on Nel's couple remark.

"DEPARTURE FOR SAMSARA IN T-20 MINUTES. COMMENCE BOARDING."

Nel squared her shoulders and followed the other officers into the ship. It was identical to what she recalled of the *Iman*. Remembering her teasing text to her mom just before blasting off sent a pinch of regret through her chest. If only she had known how far she was going then, if only she had known how long it would be before her mother would hear her voice again. *Would I still have gone?*

There was no way to know.

Lin was several seats back, engrossed in a conversation with a tall person with a shock of pink hair visible through their helmet. *Helmet!* Nel fumbled hers from its straps above her and shoved it on. A glance at the screen on her wrist told her she had, indeed, put it on correctly. *Fuck, what if we have to wear these the whole time?* Her scope and plans hadn't included that, and moreover, she hadn't even thought about digging in a suit that could easily tear from a shovel or screen. Or a sharpened trowel.

"Excuse me?" She tapped the arm of the man beside her and motioned for him to connect to her private comm.

A smile and a faint click later, and he responded. "Yeah?"

"Are we going to have to wear these down there?"

His chuckle rumbled through her helmet. "No. We'll have atmosuits, but not due to a vacuum. The air is Hell, frankly, but we'll be fine. Part of why we didn't establish a base down there before now."

"Yeah, Dr. Lieberman said there wasn't any reception for us."

"Nope, not even a runway. Storm's too much for it." He held out his hand, the angle awkward from close beside her. "I'm Dr. Paul de Lellis, Geology Officer."

"Dr. Nel Bently, ah, Excavation Officer."

"Pleasure."

She forced herself to close her eyes, thoughts drifting with the background crackle and hum of space travel. Close to an hour later, the craft's vibration became a shudder as they entered the atmosphere.

Nel's eyes flew open. "You said a storm?"

Paul glanced over. "Yeah, after the event blew everything away, the weather went haywire. Wind just keeps howling, and sandstorms cross in waves. Pretty epic looking. Can't wait to check it out, frankly. It's like reverse terraforming."

The engines roared and she squeaked. "I'll never get used to this, I swear."

Beside her, Paul crossed himself and tilted his head back. "I find the whole thing pretty fun. The noise hurts, but otherwise it's great."

Nel shuddered as G-force pressed her into the seat. One of the military personnel—a Kapten Orso, by his badge—was strapped in across from her, weapon gripped tight. Even he looked nervous. Glancing at his badge again, Nel grinned. *333, like Mikey's stupid t-shirt: only half evil.* Metal rattled around her.

"Hitting atmo!" The pilot's voice shook through the speakers a second before another wave of gravity shoved them against their seats.

"TOUCHDOWN IMMINENT."

At least there wasn't a countdown. They sounded like doomsday devices in Nel's head, and she found herself wishing they could just cryosleep through the whole thing. *That way we'd be unconscious if we depressurized.*

Screaming static and a low frequency blasted through the coms. The entire ship lurched, flipping onto its side then back, Nel's head whipping on her neck despite the belts and clasps locking her suit into the seat. "Motherfucker!"

Another thunderous bump. Her clothes tightened around her limbs in a pathetic attempt to calm her. Frantic beeping stabbed at her ears, but it was impossible to tell whether it was her suit's response to panic or a system-wide alarm. Lights flickered between dim, in-flight gold and warning red, before the cabin went completely dark. Angry vermillion flashed outside the windows. The pilot's voice crackled from the speakers, unintelligible.

A second later the cabin blew apart.

SIX

Bitter. It was the first thing besides orange and wind that filled Nel's mind. Adrenaline lent her body its tremble-strength. She licked her lips, but tasted only the stale neutrality of her spacesuit interior.

A crackle of static. "Come in, Bently. This is Dr. Julius. Do you copy?"

Nel spit imagined sand from her mouth. She couldn't remember who Julius was. With each attempt to rise, her feet sunk deeper into the dry heat. "I copy. Where am I?"

"We've touched down on Samsara. Can you see the others?"

Nel checked the various flashing lights around the rim of her space helmet. Sure enough, tick-marks of a compass glittered around the rim. *What, you didn't want to spring for the proper hud that had a quest indicator on it?*

Nel shook her head, found her movements still slow.

"Bently?"

She blinked, realized that, despite sounding like they were in her head, they couldn't see her headshake. "Sorry, no I can't. How long was I out?"

"Probably no more than a few minutes. Can you describe where you are?"

It took an enormous effort to raise her arms. She blinked. What she thought was orange was actually the backs of her eyelids stained with afterimage. "It's black. I'm buried." Her breath hitched, the whine of panic loud in the enclosed space of her helmet. "I can't see. I can't breathe—"

"Bently, you need to listen to me, is your suit punctured? Are you injured?"

Another crackle cut through her gasps, followed by a new voice. "Nel, it's Zachariah. Your suit is breathing for you. You don't need air. It's just dark because you're under some sand. You landed in a deeper patch is all. Hang tight." His feedback cut out, probably as he spoke to another on the med team. A second later it bloomed from a rush of static. "Julius is headed your way. So, you said you'd been through Waterport. What part? It's not the biggest place."

His voice drew calm out from under her panic. Scratching came from somewhere outside her suit and comm. "Yeah, ah." She faltered, then forced herself to remember her parents' drive when she was twelve. "I was a kid."

The black turned to brown then bloomed into brilliant orange light as Julius clawed sand from her helm. "I've got her."

She couldn't exactly hear the words through anything other than her com, only the faint rumble of speech penetrating the glass. A hand grabbed the handle on the front of her suit and hauled her free. She staggered, but her weak knees held. "Thanks. What about the others?"

"No problem, Dr. Bently. We're still searching for one of the combat officers." She clipped a heavy line to the carabineer at her belt and tapped her own wrist. The speakers crackled with a public announcement. "I've got her. Everyone tethered? Sound off."

Nel barely heard the roll call. Did Lin's rank qualify her as a combat officer? A new wave of panic broke over her, burning reason from her thoughts. She slammed her hand on the comm. "Lin?"

The chatter died, followed by Lin's ragged answer. "I'm fine. It's not me. They can't find Orso." It must have been a private line: her voice warmed. "You were worried."

"Of course I was fucking—Christ, Lin, you think I wouldn't worry?" She forced her breath into something resembling normalcy. "I'm glad you're okay." *Even if it means someone else might not be.* Comm noise rose again, but Nel couldn't bring herself to listen. Immediate concerns aside, her thoughts scattered before the might of the view.

At its zenith the sky was deep red, stars and what must have been other planets burning through the burgundy. Thickened ozone tinged the horizon pink. The view was just shy of something completely familiar, a literal uncanny valley. Where the light of the brightest stars fell, the pale pink and yellow sand was brilliant white-gold. Burnt orange colored where shadows fell. This world belonged on a classic 70's sci-fi show, not under Nel's boots.

"Kapten Orso, come in!"

Their transport was in pieces. The majority of the cabin hung off a metal spire jutting from the sand. It took less than a minute for everyone to affirm they were tethered. Nel wondered if she had missed a similar consciousness role call earlier. "How far from the site are we?" she asked over private comm.

Dr. Julius glanced at her, face barely visible through the sand-blasted glass of their helmets. "Not far, but the walk will be hell." She strode over to a hulking black disk jammed into the sand as a handful of others continued to search for the missing man.

"Jack!"

Nel hummed in sympathy, though she wasn't sure she understood.

Dr. Julius tapped the announcement again. "Alright, we're cleared for marching—search team, report back in two hours, regardless of your success in locating Jack."

Nel glanced up at the sky. "Weather shield?"

"When we landed, Markus detonated a temporary shield just so we could get our footing. We can't take it with us so it'll be a battle through the wind. Let's save questions for one we're safe at the site." Her hand hovered over the large button on the disk. "Everyone, engage your mag-boots. Brace for shield-fall."

Nel fumbled with her suit, tearing at the panel on her wrist. A second later she remembered she didn't need buttons. *Suit: Engage mag boots.*

Engaging.

A double-thunk and her feet rooted to the ground. *How can I walk like this?* "Shield-fall—?" A blast of wind punched the words from her mouth and her tether jerked taut around her hips.

The temperature plummeted, though the number on her arm remained the same. The smaller number that displayed wind-chill, however, flickered lower and lower. "Fuck!" Her suit burst into life, pumping heat against her skin. It helped, but the pressure of the wind drove the air from Nel's lungs. *Note to self: don't remove your helmet.*

"Walk into the wind, you can see alright one your visuals are activated for infrared. The site is illuminated on your helms, and you can request a map overlay if you wish, though only the navigator needs it."

Always loved a good map. Nel engaged her infrared and brought up the overlay. Her companions were several dozen oblong blobs of light moving away towards the east. With the topographic lines she saw the landscape was fairly level, with the exception of the structures now consumed by the sand cloud.

Nel felt a tug at her waist and gripped the tow line before forcing her legs into action. It was about as difficult as starting the elliptical one setting too high an hour after Thanksgiving dinner. Nel enjoyed a hike. This was slog. A green arrow on her helmet indicated where the site lay. What could be left of it after years of this wind? *Did they have weather shields in place? Did they even need them? Did the shields fail when whatever happened here occurred?*

Now she understood on a visceral level the need for forensic hackers, electrical engineers, and combat meteorologists—surely they had something to do with the storm.

The arrow on her helm grew, and a great white orb appeared on the horizon, brighter and brighter like a sun. It was a dome, a bubble lit from within. An airlock was a dark freckle on the side. *It's huge.* Nel followed the others in.

Wind died as the door rattled shut. After the roar of the storm, silence was an aural weightlessness. Her boots echoed as Nel turned. Her helm adjusted to the artificial light. The inner hatch opened and they filed into the dome, unclipping their tethers as they went.

Nel peered at the geometric texture of the translucent shield overhead. From what she could tell, it covered several acres. Black tarnished metal jutted from the still sand. Designs somewhere between mathematics and wizardry carved most surfaces. She checked the number on her suit. It was warm.

"Dr. Bently?"

"Give me a minute." She waved a dismissive hand before reaching out to the nearest ruins. The rough metal scraped the fabric of her suit, sending shudders through her body. *I'm on an alien planet.* Holding a tool that hadn't been touched in several thousand years was a heady feeling. This high was a whole other animal. She grudgingly turned back to the tech.

"Where would you like the lab hung? We thought the edge of the excavation, to be safe. Since our bunks are on the lab's third level."

"Hung?" She followed his gesture. Techs hovered around the massive crates dropped during a previous mission. Already aluminum frames were clipped to cables. "Oh, fuck.... A lab right above our site. The edge is perfect, thank you."

The tech faltered, and Nel realized this was her job, not theirs. *Right. Head of Cultural Exploration.* It didn't matter if she was organizing a day's excavation of the historic sluiceway behind university dorms or the exploration of an alien city on a foreign planet. Archaeology was her lifeblood. She cleared her throat and pressed the PA com, tapping her department. She looked forward trading her heavy space suit for an atmosuit. "Alright, diggers. Everyone alright after that landing?"

When murmurs of assent hummed through the speakers, she continued, checking the map on her helm as she went, "Good. Excavation will start tomorrow, for now everyone get acclimated. I need two people—Arnav and Noemi—set up datums please. Whatever you use as a survey station I'd like on that rise, there. I'll be by to get familiar with your equipment. The rest of you, you're on construction duty. Let's get the lab set up over on this area, where there's clear access to the site itself—what we know of at least. Screening stations should go along the southern boundary. Even with low-G, I'd rather not have to move backdirt if I can help it. Let's get going."

Noemi materialized at her elbow. "Dr. Bently, the datum is on our helm projection and the site maps. A physical one is redundant, no?"

She shook her head. "It's only redundant for as long as we have power and people have access to our data. If I remember correctly this place's electrical was blown. Besides, people who come to this site centuries from now might not know we were here unless we hammer a few stakes in the ground. As is tradition." No one laughed at her colonizing joke, and she realized IDH had generations who hadn't experienced colonization. *So, who is marginalized?*

She set her cultural questions aside and slogged over to where Noemi peered at their handheld total station—something Nel thought was an oxymoron. It's wireless pin negated stadia rods and lasers.

The tech tilted the screen so Nel could see. "I can move out a few meters too. For scope."

"You should be fine here. I doubt we'll do much excavation outside the shield for now—especially given our short supply of the smaller ones."

"Coordinates or arbitrary grid?"

"Arbitrary. Can't go mixing too much up on me, now." Nel grinned, wondering briefly what a smile looked like through several layers of shatter-proof glass. She checked their bearing. "This will be North 500, East 2000. You put one of these in before?"

"No, ma'am."

Nel winced at the ma'am, but let it slide. This was a mission, after all. "Different number of digits lowers the confusion when people inevitable have transcription errors. Even if it's all digital. Redundancy has its place. Set up another five, no closer than 20 meters for now, surround the center of the site so we get good coverage."

"Rodger."

She glanced at the others. Departments branched off to take readings and set up scanners and fuck-knew what else. Confident everyone had a job for the moment, she hiked to the center of the site. The helm muffled all but her own movements and the distant *thwap* of wind against the shield. Massive metal spires jutted at an angle from the ground. Like everything, they seemed half organic, half machine. Nel crouched, examining a handful of sand. It was light and coarse, strangely uniform. She wished she could feel the texture properly, against the ridges of her fingerprints. The suits might be necessary, but the idea of being covered head-to-toe for the entire excavation was claustrophobic. At least the lab was sealed. As much as she wanted to explore the ruins, she knew better than to enter any building without a buddy. Alien-danger factor aside, who knew how stable the structure were. Turning back to the flurry of activity, she tapped the private-recording button on her wrist.

"Planet Samara Locus Alpha, Phase I Excavation Notes: Day 0."

SEVEN

The room was dark, the kind of dark that came from solitude, not just the lack of ambient light. Nel tossed over onto her back. She had no idea what woke her, but it was impossible to find her dreams again. Her ears strained against the silence attempting to discern what disturbed her in the first place. Generators cycling? Air filtration? Perhaps someone walked by her room.

Despite the quiet, her mind still replayed the flood of static and the squeal of rending metal as they crashed. Heart suddenly pounding, she brought up the lights. The battered beige of her room was sadly a welcome change from precinct-grey. *And just as industrial and sterile. Surprise, surprise.* Downstairs on the first level, the lab already bustled and beeped as machines booted up and people ran calibrations. The mess on the second level was Nel's first aim. Her few days on the *Odyssey* taught her that space food wasn't all freeze-dried bricks and potatoes in Vicodin. She was still dubious about what a base hung from a weather-bubble might provide.

Months on the corridor may have broken her caffeine addiction the hard way, but she still would consider homicide over a hot, bitter cup. "Phil, what time is it?"

No answer came, and she laughed. "Man, didn't think I'd get so accustomed to having a digital butler. And to think, I hated the idea of AI home assistants." She glanced at the screen projected into the space above her desk. *I still hate the idea.* She also wasn't keen on meeting dozens of people before she had a chance to wake up. *And I thought sharing a tiny hotel with six students was rough.*

A query the day before informed her that paper didn't occur in space—only a few collectors kept analog books. Her gaze fell to her box of personal effects. A blank field journal was tucked between a few shirts she would never wear up here. Fishing it out, she copied the site maps onto its pages, added a scale and marked the datums. She was carefully transcribing the line of the exposed ruins when an insistent bell chimed. She glared at the computer.

Schedule for: BENTLY (Samsara Day 1)
0700 – Excavation
1100 – Dinner
1400 – Psychological Evaluation

Great. Only 20 minutes to get ready for her first day. *I'm the department head, shouldn't I tell them when they put shovels in the ground?* The thought tripped all the others crammed in behind it: did they even use shovels? Now she realized why Phil was so easy to grow accustomed to—it was far easier to pester a computer with questions than any human, and came with fewer strings than any conversation with Lin. Besides, Nel was no stranger to talking to an empty room.

She shoved her fieldbook into the drawer at her desk and grabbed her field pack. Writing would be impossible with her suit's gloves, so transcription would have to wait until the end of the day. But she'd be damned if she'd leave her trowels behind, alien planet or otherwise.

A wall of sound almost stopped her at the door to the mess. A self-serve counter stretched across one wall, and a few cooks moved about in the room beyond. Somewhere, she smelled coffee. Nel didn't care about the crowd.

"I believe you're looking for this." Lin appeared beside Nel, coffee mud extended between them. Her long hair was braided, and she managed to make even the bulky atmosuit look stylish.

Like those snowboarder girls who somehow make the most awkward attire ever seem badass. Nel wrapped her fingers around the warm mug with a sigh of happiness. "Thank you." She glanced at the pale liquid. "You even remembered how I take it."

Lin jerked her head at a small table. "Take a minute before you dive in?"

"I'm already running behind."

"A minute will help clear your mind."

Lin was right, and Nel followed her to the table. After a tentative sip, her brows rose. "This isn't half bad. I've had gas station coffee worse than this."

Lin snorted. "I'd imagine. We don't make coffee often, but enough of our people don't have ports that oral stimulants are good to have on hand."

Nel smirked at the phrase, glancing at Lin's arms. Sure enough, like half the people she met, a gleaming metal apparatus implanted in her inner forearm.

Lin popped open the door to display a small vial clipped into place. "You'll never get out of sorts, with Folgers in your port," she chimed.

Nel took a pointed sip of her coffee, gaze dropping to the port. "I've seen most of you, more than once. Explain why I never saw that."

"Synthetic skin graft. Required for anyone on a terrestrial mission. Makes using them tedious, so when we're on Earth we mostly use your methods of chemical stimulation unless it's an emergency."

"I see." Nel frowned into her cup. She didn't like how much of Lin was a lie. And she didn't like how much of it she unwaveringly believed. "Oh, did the search party find the guy—Jack?"

Lin looked away, shaking her head. "He'd be fine for a day, maybe, out there, but with the storm." She shrugged. "I think they're going out again this morning, but it doesn't look pretty."

"Christ." Her stomach flipped at the thought of a whole night in howling wind and crushing sand. *Give me the woods of northern New England any day.*

"Missions up here are always dangerous. We do what we can, but it's not uncommon to have injuries or casualties." Lin switched topics smoothly. "So what's the plan?"

Good fucking question. "Let's get whatever those towers are uncovered first. I want every team to have a unit at the end of the day." She glanced at her schedule. "I guess I have an evaluation today. Or something."

"There are rolling check-ins for everyone for the first week. Once everyone's met with Zachariah we'll be back to full schedules."

"Then I'd best head down and get started while I can." Nel knocked back the rest of her coffee and glanced around at where to place the mug.

"The sterilization unit. By the door." Lin suggested.

"Right." Nel slid it through the slot and hurried down through the labs to don her atmosuit. Like a beehive, the lab was layered, each lower level smaller than the one above it. The airlock itself could only fit half a dozen people comfortably at a time. With so much on her mind, Nel wished one of those people wasn't Lin. She may have followed the woman into space, she just hadn't expected the actual space between them to be so small.

"I need a minute." She stepped back out of the airlock and let them go without her. The suit weighed on her shoulders, despite the lower gravity. *At least the magnetic boots give my legs a bit of a work out.* She wasn't looking forward to muscle atrophy. She leaned against the wall and stared at her reflection in her helm. *Get your shit together, Bently.* However un-poetic, it was becoming her mantra. She raked her hair back and tugged on the hood before locking her helmet in place. She was on an alien planet. Doing her job. *This is the deep end.*

She pounded the button to open the airlock. Toxic atmosphere replaced the carefully balanced ratio of nitrogen, oxygen and other trace elements with a long hiss. The floor lurched under her and began descend. Orange light pierced her eyes, but she grinned. "Now show them you can fucking swim."

Several archaeologists already waited, leaning on gleaming shovels and a case of what Nel hoped were trowels and finer excavation equipment.

Nel raised a hand and tapped her department comm. The faint buzzing she heard in her recorded field notes from the day before was louder now. Either than or her ears needed to grow accustomed to it again. "Alright." She clapped her suited hands together. "This will be a bit different—diving right into excavations rather than setting everything up. There's a lot, tech-wise, that you'll have to fill me in on, I think, so I hope we'll consider this whole thing to be a lesson in patience.

"Lin, I'd like you to act as a go-for, running samples up to the lab and so forth. I need you to help me understand some of the new stuff." Thankfully each suit had their name on the sleeve and many had added nicknames to the chest. She found the suit emblazoned with "Arnie" with a halo of black curls under the helm. "Arnav, you're an architectural specialist?"

"Yep. Worked with the designers on some newer ships to help make terrestrial people feel more at home. Specialty is human tech integration."

Nel smiled. She only understood about half of what he said, but it sounded fascinating. "Awesome. I'll have to ask you more when we're off-duty. For now, you and …" she checked her tablet, "Molly will head to the towers with me for Block A." She rattled off the pairings on the screen. "I'd like everyone to have an open unit by the end of the day. Coordinates are on grid…now." She tapped a few spots on her tablet and she saw light flicker across a dozen faces as everyone's helm maps upgraded. "Talk to someone—not me—about the labeling of your finds, since I'm less than familiar in the way of artifacts here. Something tells me we won't be finding a Clovis point out here."

A few chuckles rattled through the com, and Nel's anxiety begin to dissipate.

"Let's stick to shovels for now, but when we get close to any structures switch to trowels." She glanced back at the spire. Something about this place seemed sentient. Something watched her, something other than the echo of her best friend and the omniscient press of a thousand recording personal huds. "And be careful. You hit something not sand, you stop and get help. You think it's dangerous, back up and let someone who knows more check it out. Any questions?"

There would be many, she was sure, and at least half were her own, but like most briefings, no one spoke up, and half just shifted from foot to foot until she dismissed them. Some things never changed.

Her muscles ached as she mag-booted her way over to the towers jutting through the sand. A steady scan with her tablet's camera from a few angles caught most of the opening photos, and she pulled a couple stills from the feed before jerking her head at the structure. "Lin, you have a minute?"

Lin turned, golden light gleaming from the polished glass of her helmet. Nel was surprised to see pockmarks from the sandblasting outside the dome.

The spire of rock stretched up and out, angled and carved in a way that begged for motion, a violent version of Kristos boy statue, poised for flight that would never come. Nel tilted her head, eyes narrowed on the formation. "That natural?" She hadn't seen any rocks like that on her arduous trek over, but then again she hadn't seen much of anything at all.

"It's not natural, and it wasn't here before. From the maps, at least."

Nel sheepishly brought up the map again. There was a structure similar, but in an entirely different location. Topographically the site was unrecognizable as the same location. Nel double checked the coordinates and brought up the current map. The only place they overlaid was the black spear of the toppled tower, jutting from the golden sand. She hauled herself closer, running a hand over the roughness. "I wish this thing jacked into my nerves'

"We only do that with prothetics. You have any idea how complex that tech is?" Lin answered. Her voice was close through the com, distant intimacy.

"I just dig holes, Letnan," she barked. Sections of the rock were smoothed, as if by water and eons. Or something similar—the windstorm alone was awful, but perhaps the city was protected in a dome like this. Failure of a shield could have caused their city to fall. She shook aside the speculation. That part of the puzzle was always her favorite, but she knew nothing of these people. *"You're the best woman for the job."* It tasted sour, rang flat in her ears. *I'm just the one they could control.*

She fumbled with the panel on her arm until the maps appeared. She would have to figure out exactly which combination of buttons triggered it, but for now, she had to focus. It was convenient, she realized, grudgingly, when the map was constantly overlaid. When she had been small she was convinced that everyone could see the moving lines on the football field during playoffs. This reminded her of that. There was no grid to set up — it was already there, glowing and ephemeral. "How many crew chiefs does it take set up a grid?" She asked the silence inside her suit.

"I don't know." Mikey's voice was faint, echoing through the years and miles between his grave, his planet, and where she stood. *"They're still laying it in."*

"Have you tried the door yet?" Arnav carried his buckets and kit clipped to the tactical buckles on his chair, while his partner had the shovel over her shoulder.

Nel shook her head. "I have half a mind to knock. Maybe they're just taking some time to themselves," she joked. A glance at the images of the towers prior to the event, however, told her the largest wasn't the only one in an entirely different position. What she had been considering the front door, was a second or third storey balcony. Carefully avoiding tromping across the location of their block, she pressed a hand to the plain metal door. Her comm crackled with distant static, but otherwise, nothing happened. "Guess no one's home. This is non-human architecture, I assume?"

"Partially. The style is classic Teacher stuff. They're big on function and economy of design. The size of the halls and doors, though, that's human."

"Gotcha. Alright, let's lay in this block." She crouched next to her projected grid. "Corner nail?"

Arnav brought the large sand-tires of his chair to the opposite edge and handed her a few plastic pins from his bag.

Nel made a face. "Plastic?"

"Gotta be inert—considering the event was electromagnetic in nature, from what we can tell. It's why I'm old-schooling it with rubber tires, rather than the hover tech."

"Duh." She grinned up at him. "Thanks for keeping me on track. This is going to be one hell of a learning experience."

"For us too. Most people up here have little actual field experience, and if they do it's from the mining stations on asteroids and not really the same, other than actual shovel use for sample tests."

Nel winced at the idea that few of her crew had actual field experience, but shoved away her judgement. In this, she was a green as they were. She checked her corner nail placement against each other with her laser tape, then did the same against the physical datums after a few adjustments. "Looks good to me."

Thankfully opening notes hadn't changed much technology wise, and while Arnav started their paperwork—automatically sent to Nel's records for backup—she hiked over to the other blocks. *Suit: message Team B.*

Buzzing filled her helmet, the rattle of plastic against metal. As quickly as it came, it undulated into silence. Wishing she could rub her ears, Nel contacted Communications. "Kapten Wagner, this is Dr. Bently. I think there's something wrong with my comm. Or my suit. Whatever this thing is called."

"Comm," she corrected without preamble. "I'm not showing anything wrong on our end. All channels are clear. What seems to be the problem?"

I'm hearing things. "Just a noise. Comes and goes. Like a buzzing in the line, rhythmic. Anyone else have complaints?"

"None so far, but we'll look into it."

"Dr. Bently?" One of the techs at the second unit waved.

Nel flashed them a thumbs up. "Thanks, Kapten."

"Just Greta, and I'll keep an eye on it."

Nel jogged over, thighs aching in the added weight of her suit. It was strange not to already be sweating. "What's up?"

"Would you mind showing us a good shoveling technique?"

Nel faltered. "A shoveling—oh." She glanced at the sand beneath them, then up to the sky, hidden by the storm outside the shell. "You've never shoveled dirt before, have you?"

"Not like this, no. We've got dirt on the Odyssey, of course, but we don't excavate it. When learning, we are taught about soil excavations and methodology but..." The man trailed off.

"Real world is different." Nel shook away horror. Her entire crew had literally never stuck a shovel in the ground. *On account of having no ground.* Except for what they probably grow their arugula in.

"You're supposed to be teaching them."

Nel held out her hand. "Sure thing. First thing to remember is—you're not digging. You're shovel skimming. You've used a trowel?"

"We did mock excavations with them, yes."

"Well, this is much the same, as far as what you're doing. It's just a giant trowel." She stepped out of the unit they were using and skimmed the flat shovel along the ground, keeping within the single quad. Once a few centimeters were removed across the northeast quad she tossed it into the bucket. They passed the next few hours that way, Nel rotating between the teams. The next time she paused by Block B, Malik was frowning.

"It's strange, with storms this severe I expected a pretty windblown surface, loose and shallow uniform top level."

Nel grinned at the comment. "I did too. I'm looking forward to get the geo data. Anyway, keep up that technique, just try and only take down a few centimeters at a time. Check your depth as much as you need to until your eye can pick up what level is." She tapped the helmet. "These will make that part easy."

The other tech tromped over, empty buckets in hand. "Nothing," they remarked. "Some slightly larger grains but nothing cultural."

Nel hummed, glancing at the name on their suit. *Luk*. "I imagine most surface artifacts have blown away."

Luk tapped her arm. "Dr. Bently, you have to press the comm button, unless you engage autocom, which switches on to your department when you begin speaking. Otherwise you're talking to yourself."

What else is new. She winced, pressed the button, and repeated herself.

"You think it's all collected at the base of various ruins?"

Nel's suit beeped with a waiting communication. She excused herself and opened the second line. "Yes?"

"Dr. Bently, it's Zachariah. I believe we were set to meet today."

Fuck. She glanced at the time, which was, indeed reading 1403. "Yeah, one minute. I'll be right up." She straightened with a groan. "I've got a meeting, I'll check in when I'm done. Arnav's in charge. Keep up the good work."

It took several minutes to depressurize and strip off her suit before finding one of the only private offices in the entire lab. The door was closed, but the thin material translucent. Inside she saw the rough shape of Zachariah pecking away at a keyboard. She knocked.

"Come in," he called, glancing up with a distracted smile. "Sorry to take you away from your work on the first day, I thought you'd want to get it out of the way before the finds start coming in."

"Ah, yeah." She guessed he was right, but why it was necessary in the first place was lost on her. "So why am I here exactly?"

"Have a seat, Dr. Bently."

"Call me Nel, please." She sat, glancing back as th thin door ground shut. After a second the material turned opaque.

"Please be assured this room is outfitted with radio dampeners and signal jammers to protect your privacy. I'd like you to feel like we can discuss anything here. The usual rules apply—unless you express a wish to harm yourself or others, what we discuss remains between us."

She frowned. *Therapy? What dig requires a therapist? Or springs for one?* "You're the shrink for the entire mission? That's a bit of a heavy workload."

"Not everyone will see me regularly, and many already have their own personal therapist who will communicate with them privately from *Odyssey*." His tone was patient, but crisp. "So let's get started. I have a few questions for you, then I'll set up the automated test, which contains about 600 questions. It's not one of the antiquated IQ tests, but projective. Once I evaluate and discuss your answers, we can decide whether to talk more regularly."

Yeah, not gonna happen. "I think I'm good on that, but let's dive in. Question one?"

"How are you feeling about the mission?"

"Honestly?"

"I'd hope so," he smiled. "But I'm pretty good at telling when someone's lying."

"A bit overwhelmed. This is both very much my wheelhouse and totally alien—literally. And I've never been a sci-fi fan, so it's harder to adjust I think, since the 'cool factor' isn't really there."

"All reasonable responses. And what about your feelings on IDH and the politics behind this?"

"I wasn't aware there were any, but um, isn't that kind of IDH's bag? Mystique and altruism to hide the sketchy shit in the space closets?"

His black brows arched slightly, but his mouth was still curved in a slight smile. "Like most large organizations."

She glanced around the room in a thinly veiled attempt to buy time. Zachariah was a kind man, from what she could tell, but up here she was at the mercy of IDH, and shitting into the hand that fed her was reckless, even for her. "Sorry, I do appreciate everything they've done for me, I'm just not used to being so in the dark."

"I've discussed with some of the higher ups how confidence is only increased with transparency, but clearly I've been overruled.

Frustration with the whole aside, how are you doing with your fellow scientists? How do you feel about your work here, both at IDH and this site specifically?"

"Samsara is a really weird dream, honestly. Everything both innocuous and bizarre. I'm looking forward to understanding what happened here. Kind of wondering why me, though."

"You're skilled in your field."

"Yeah, I'm great, but I'm not the best. I'm not the most driven or professional—for fuck's sake I was part of a manhunt across New England."

"I think you have a combination of traits—you are skilled, but you are also reckless, disregard rules, and have gray morality."

"Excuse me? I get that you're Christian or whatever, but I thought space would be a bit less on the homophobe train—"

"I'm Muslim, and not homophobic—when given the choice you allied yourself with a large organization that framed people for murders they caused. Questionable morality."

She looked down. "Right. Sorry. I didn't mean to assume."

His smile was back, and still as gentle. "It takes a bit to understand the differences between our world and theirs. I'm still caught of guard sometimes. Speaking of, how are you getting on with your department?"

She shrugged, wincing at the stiffness of the electrosuit around her shoulders. "I think alright.

People listen to me, let me ask questions without seeming too baffled at how I got my job." She grinned wolfishly, "Which frankly is a nice change of pace from Earth."

He chuckled, twirling a lock of his dark hair around a tan finger absentmindedly. "And your interpersonal relationships—I noticed you've been keeping to yourself."

"I'm not putting up walls or pushing people away because I'm hurting, Dr. Lieberman, so you can stop that nonsense. Lin and I are just dealing with some stuff—privately—and I'm wrapping my head around all of this. And yeah. Grieving. But getting pissed and all that? That's always been me."

Zachariah stopped twirling his hair. "No one is born angry, Nel. It's something we can work on if you'd like. Anger is exhausting."

"You're telling me. But it's kind of all I've got right now."

"Perhaps you could reach out a bit, even with small talk. It's very easy to become isolated in a new place, especially one so far from home. And I think it's understandable to not know how to unpack your thoughts on Letnan First Class Nalawangsa. What about your feelings about Dr. Servais and the events of Los Cerros Esperando VII?"

"I'd think it was obvious." Nel sat back.

"How you say you feel is just as important as how you actually feel, Nel," he chided.

Implying I'm gonna lie about how I feel. She didn't want to talk about this, and something about the intensity in his dark eyes made her feel too seen. "Mikey was my best friend and that site my baby. Notice how neither is here. Can I take the test now?"

He pulled up what looked like a basic standardized test and rose. "I'll leave you to it. When you're done you're free to go. Any questions?"

"Nope, thanks." She couldn't get this over fast enough.

"Happy digging."

"Happy shrinking," she retorted. The door shut and she peered at the true/false questions. Most were straight forward, though she cracked a grin at the query about how happy she was with her sex life and another about whether she felt understood. *No one fucking understands me, Zachariah. I'm from a different planet.* She liked the psychologist as a person, but therapy was far too intimate.

The day was almost over when she submitted her answers and descended into the orange haze of the site. Even without the buffeting wind, the fine grains drifted in the air, encourage by the lower gravity. She paused by Block C.

"How is it going?"

"Down," Lefteris responded with a cheeky grin. "Northeast quad, there, is the last one of this level." He checked the time. "We can open the next one after notes."

"Let's play it by ear," Nel responded. It was strange not to have a time crunch. Her digs always had an expiration date, when students and teachers alike had to return to the real world. Putting the science foremost was a welcome change. *Aside from the "when do I go home?" factor.* "If there's more than half an hour left, go for it. Found anything?"

"No, but it's not like…" the comm faltered into static then silence. Lefteris's gaze wandered to where his screener stood by the bank of screens.

"But what?" Nel followed his line of sight. "You have a concern?"

"No, just heard some stuff is all. I guess lucky the whole site is surveyed, eh?"

Nel hummed in agreement. "Well I'll keep my eyes out for anything. Did the soil change much?"

"Not at all, really. Still just as light. Not as loose, but I think the loose on top is literally just what fell out of the air when we engaged the hab shield."

"Good point. I'd be curious to see how it changes. It'd be unusual to have a deep A horizon in this climate."

"Why is that? I've never dug on a planet before. Just asteroids."

"Shit, really?" Nel blinked. She couldn't imagine what kind of archaeologist she would be if she hadn't spent a summer or two breaking her back doing CRM. It was the best way to learn, at least for her. She eyed the levels and the clean, slightly paler sand of the excavated level. It was perfect. Laser perfect. She wondered if it was elitist to think hands were better than tech when it came to precision. *You loved the total station when you first got one,* she reminded herself.

Lefteris stared at her, concern on his tan face visible through his helm. "I'm doing my best. But I'll get the hang of it."

"Oh, no! You're doing great, I'm just surprised." She offered a crooked, awkward

"A few well-connected kids I know got to dig in actual dirt, either on *Odyssey* or on Earth, but that's not common." He shrugged, suit exaggerating the movement.

The coms crackled and Lin's voice cut through their conversation. "Nel! Block A!" She stood by the tower, hand waving in the air. "We got something!"

EIGHT

A handful of melted metal was not something Nel thought really worthy of celebration. She realized most people wouldn't find a few flakes of stone worth celebrating either, though, and tried to temper her disinterest.

"Hey, Dr. Bently, how's the digging?"

Nel glanced back as she slid her tray down the mess line. "Sandy, but not finding a ton."

"Arnie said he found some melted metal by the tower. Not what you were hoping for?" The man piled rehydrated potatoes onto his tray, wrinkling his nose. "Yuck, thank God for tabasco, eh?"

Nel snorted. "Yeah the food's a bit rough. I was hoping *Odyssey's* chefs might be able to send us something out of the mercy in their hearts."

"That'd be the day. I'm just glad it's not mining rations. Those are worse." He jerked his head at one of the few unoccupied tables. "Mind sitting with me? I wanted to chat about geo samples."

She glanced at the piping around his uniform. Sure enough, it was steel gray. *Right, Dr. de Lellis, my seatmate.* The crash flashed through her mind with echoes of screaming metal and buzzing coms. "No problem. I do owe him a beer though, for the first finds of the project. Even if they look like Megatron's boogers. Or fulgurites."

Paul guffawed. "Good luck. You think the potatoes are bad? We don't even get booze down here. Too volatile, decreases efficiency, strain on resources, and it's not worth the weight risk."

Nel shook her head and slumped onto the bench across from him. "That's what was hiding in our contracts, eh? There's no digging without drinking from where I stand." She examined her slice of protein for a moment before deciding makeshift shepherd's pie was her best course of action.

"What's a fulgurite?"

Nel hummed, wondering how to explain. "Where lightning touches sand it makes these gnarled tree shapes, sand colored glass in the fractals of electricity. Pretty nerdy, nerdily pretty, all that."

"This seat taken?" Lin hesitated by the bench, glancing between Nel and Paul.

Nel smiled and patted the spot next to her. Zachariah was right. She was exhausted, and should make a bit more of an effort. "Only by you. How was your day?"

"Alright, slow, as first days usually are! How're you doing, de Lellis?"

"Oh you know," he sighed, flashing her a nervous smile. "How's Dar?"

Lin looked away. "I wouldn't know. Barely seen him in the past while. Last I saw him he was as prickly as ever. Worse, even."

"He's under a lot of pressure," Paul defended.

"He's not the same man as when you dated," Lin snapped.

Nel's brows rose. She thought they knew each other because Lin was, in her mind, some sort of space noble—she knew it was far from the truth, but having parents in director's positions in IDH lent the fantasy a shade of truth. "Paul, you wanted to discuss geo-samples?"

Relief lit his dark eyes and he nodded. "Yeah. We're doing coring at the cardinals and some irregularities, outside and inside the shields. I wanted to touch base about where to drop those that overlap with the site. That way we all get the info you need." He rubbed the base of his ear. "God, I hate wearing coms all day messes with my tinnitus."

Lin didn't roll her eyes, but she looked like it took a great effort. "You'll get used to them soon enough. If you're talking work, I'm finding better conversation." Her hand lingered on Nel's shoulder. "Talk later maybe?"

"Sure."

Paul watched her go, eyes narrowed. He opened his mouth, as if to comment, then shut it and turned back to his food. "Anyways, I have the proposed locations marked on a map file. If I send them to you, would you take a look? Just okay them, or suggest a new one?"

"Of course. Thanks for checking with me. Half the time its like no one's even on the same project with so many contractors. Are you taking baseline samples for us to compare any feature composition to?"

"Ideally. If you want us to take any additional ones, though, I'd be happy to. Any excuse to play inside the shields."

Nel snorted. "I don't envy you. The atmosuits are awful—fuck, these enhanced long-johns are hard enough for me to get used to. You're like the fourth person to mention mining to me today. IDH mines a lot?"

"Asteroid mining is where all our resources come from, so it's our biggest industry. Half of us grew up on mining colonies or bases—we have most of the analysis and excavation skills needed for archaeology."

Nel shook her head. "I've noticed very few people choose archaeology right off the bat. Most stumble into it. I guess a couple lightyears and some different stars don't change that."

"Plus it's one of the only ways we can get off-base and use our skills. No one wants astro-kids. Almost can't blame 'em." He chuckled, "Once

Donatus, my cousin, though I'm embarrassed that we share any genome, frankly—got drunk and passed out in the corner of one of the airlocks on the ventral wing of the base—"

"Whoa, I thought you people didn't drink."

"You kidding? My family's Catholic. One of the first things my dad did was rig a distillery from spare reclamation parts. Missions are different," he explained, potato-caked fork waving for emphasis.

Nel stifled a laugh, chin resting in the crook of her palm while she listened. "Alright, so Cousin Donny is drunk in the airlock." Her stomach clenched just thinking of everything that could go wrong if one passed out in an airlock.

Paul continued, detailing the several-thousand credit search for the boy, the drone-scan's discovery of a wilted space suit drifting in one of the craters that made everyone think the teen was lost to them. "Of course, when we open the airlock, somber and suited up to march over to retrieve his remains, he falls into the hall, snoring. He'd been worried our grandfather would beat him for getting too drunk for work, so he hid in the one spot with a malfunctioning cam feed."

Nel chuckled, picturing the looks on Donatus's family's faces. "I'm glad it was a false alarm."

"Oi, de Lellis!"

He turned and winced. "Work never ends. Thanks for chatting. I'll send that file over tonight. No need to have it back before the end of the shield-cycle, though." He rose, taking his half-finished tray with him.

Nel followed suit, navigating the ruckus to deposit her tray into the slot for it to be sterilized. His story reminded her that somethings really didn't change. Family, the dynamics of communities, all the details of being human, that was the same. Her eyes found Lin, perched on the edge of one of the tables in what looked like a friendly, if heated, debate. Maybe it wasn't space that made her alien. Maybe Nel just never met anyone like her before. *Two things can be true, Bently.* Nel smiled, and slipped down the hall to her room.

Blue light from her screen was a counterpoint to the orange through her window. Nel tapped the map Paul sent over a few minutes before. Most locations barely impacted her grid, but the area within the towers was prime real estate. After a few adjustments before she saved it and sent it back to him.

NEW MESSAGE
SENDER: KAPTEN GRETA WAGNER
SUBJECT: Audio issues

Finally, someone could actually answer a question for her. She opened the message, only to sit back with a frustrated sigh.

Checked into the sounds you were hearing. Nothing concerning, some low-freq. feedback but nothing abnormal. Probably has something to do with residual EM radiation or interference leaking through the shields from the storm. Annoying, but no need to worry.

Of course it was fine. Like everything in space it was weird and a mystery. She hadn't expected the "unexplained" in UFO to apply to the aliens too.

So far she stuck to only watching one of her mother's videos every few days. Loneliness nagged at her, less than it had at first, with her mind busy on learning and planning. But it was there nonetheless. She curled up on her bed and hit "play."

"Hey Sweetie! I've got an awful cold brewing today, so I probably sound ridiculous. Bill already had it, thankfully, cause I can't play nurse with a box of tissues shoved up my nose. Hope you're taking care of yourself up there. I hope you'll send a video soon."

Nel sighed. *Soon.*

"I'm redecorating the house—Bill finally sold that rowing machine he used twice, so I'm making that into my little studio. The girls and I meet there every week for book club. This week we're reading

Untold, by Amy Spitzfaden. So far I love it. Not your jam—modern fairy tale." Her red nose wrinkled. "Though being whisked away to another world by a mysterious and beautiful woman does sound a bit like a fairy tale in itself. It doesn't feel real, you know."

Her voice faltered and Nel's heart sank. "It feels as real as when you were in Chile, I guess, or running, but the time and distance, it's just too big for me to wrap my head around it. Part of me wonders if it's real. I'm tired of people disappearing." She sighed, and Nel caught a glimpse of white in her mother's bangs.

"Oh mom, I'm so sorry." Before now Mindi's videos were lighthearted, if short. It seemed loneliness was contagious, even across the stars.

"Anyways, sorry to get down. This cold is kicking my butt. I was thinking a nice warm sage green for the room. I'll show you chips next time. Stay safe, Annelise. I love you." She blew a kiss and the screen when dark.

"Love you too, Mom."

With silence the room dimmed, blue light fading to faint turquoise, as if she slept beside an aquarium's glow. She tossed onto her stomach, but it was too cloistering. It didn't help that the rooms were as well-insulated as the average tent. To the right she swore she heard another officer's breathing. Amidst the chaos and confusion, she had one constant—even if she refused to rely on her, Lin was there. Nel rose and pressed the comm button, followed by Lin's name. It was late, but not unreasonably so.

"You okay?" Lin's voice whispered through the air of Nel's room. She could almost feel the other woman's breath.

"Yeah. Lonely. Lot on my mind. You got some time?"

"For you, always." The comm clicked off and a minute later a soft knock sounded on her door.

Nel slid it open, glancing down the hall before letting her in. "Thanks."

"I was wondering if you were going to keep up the just-friends thing for the whole mission." Lin climbed onto the end of the bed and tucked her long legs under herself.

Nel laughed. "It wasn't about appearances—though I'd like to remain professional." She slumped to the floor by the window. "I'm restless and exhausted and haven't really had the headspace for anything other than maintaining course, you know?"

"I know."

"And what's with 'just' friends? Friends are just as important." She stuck her tongue out, hoping it conveyed her correction as playful, not confrontational.

Lin laughed, tucking a lock of hair behind her ear. After a day of being braided its usual straight curtains were interrupted by waves. "I've lost touch with a lot of my friends, actually."

"Cryosleep?"

Lin shrugged. "Life, more like. And choices."

Nel tilted her head. "Me too."

Lin's dark gaze roved up Nel's body to her own brown ones. "You're not the only one who gets lonely out in the stars. You're just less used to it. So what's on your mind?"

"Everything." Nel pressed a hand to the floor. "It's hard not to feel like I'm stuck in some tin can up here."

"I can help with that." Lin slid off the bed, and moved to the room's control panel by the door. She tapped a few buttons. "You're lucky to have officer's quarters, so you're on the outside wall—not wedged in the middle."

The floor tiles drained of color, slate brown liquid crystal swirling into transparency. Below, the site was arrayed across the sand, more detailed than any map. The circle of black towers erupted from the umber ground. Lin lowered the lights until the room was lit only with the brilliant orange of the not-night landscape below.

"Wow," Nel breathed, sinking to the ground. Cool Kevlar tiles pressed lines into her goosebumped skin. Lying on her stomach wasn't claustrophobic now. Instead it was closer to flying.

Fabric brushed the tiles with a soft hiss as Lin lowered herself beside Nel, long fingers lacing with hers. "Better?"

"Yeah. It's still there—thinking of this city, or outpost, or whatever. The space station above us. You. The fact that they never found Jack Orso after the crash. Home. But watching the sand rattle the shield helps. It's humbling to remember there are so many forces mightier than us."

Lin's hand ghosted over Nel's bare arm. "Peace in the face of chaos."

"What's that from?"

"Nothing. It's just how I feel when I look at you."

Nel's stomach flipped. She wasn't sure this was a conversation she was ready for. "Peace?"

"In the face of all the chaos in here." Lin tapped a long finger on Nel's brow. "Your mind, your determination, your passion. It's so beautiful and such a mystery."

Nel snorted. "I promise I'm no mystery." Lin opened her mouth, but Nel leaned forward and caught the woman's words with her mouth. Lin's tongue was soft, warm, insistent. The memory of it dancing elsewhere sent fire down Nel's body, blood rushing after. She groaned against Lin's lips. In this moment the mess of grief and network of lies that first brought them together didn't matter.

The taller woman rolled over onto Nel, rising over her, black hair a cutting out everything but the storm. Her movements were slow, but not out of uncertainty. There was a new tone to her movements, something almost demanding. Her hands slid Nel's shirt off, fingers pausing to flick a pink nipple before continuing their languid journey over Nel's shoulders, down her back, around her waist. Each pass seemed to draw another spike of heat from Nel, every pinch or rub arching her back.

"Pin me," Nel's voice shuddered between her moans. After a year of needing to control everything—and failing—all she wanted was to surrender to the dark eyed woman poised above her. Lin's hand wrapped around Nel's wrist, and she tucked one leg up, pressing herself down until they were belly to belly, core to core. Her toes gripped the Kevlar, pushing her up and in, hips twisting with each thrust.

Fire and electricity blazed through Nel's body, her own movements answering Lin's without thought. One hand tugged free of Lin's grip and pulled Lin's ass closer, knuckles white against her brown skin. Her leg wrapped tighter around her waist. Nel's gasps became moans. Lin found her hand and pinned it back above her head. She dipped down, hot lips to Nel's sensitive ear. "Come for me."

The first shudders began deep inside, rolling out against and again. Lin pulled back and Nel watched stars explode behind her eyes, everything too close and muffled at once as her orgasm thundered through her. Lin must had followed her over the edge. Lin's head flung back, nails carving half-moons over Nel's pale skin. She flung her head forward with a long, low moan. Her arms shook and she lowered herself onto Nel's heaving chest. "Thank you."

Nel glanced down at the mess of black hair and light brown skin. "No, thank you. That was great." She rubbed an absent hand along Lin's side. "I hope these walls are insulated."

Lin giggled. "I guess we'll find out."

Nel rested her cheek against Lin's shoulder. "You smell good. Sweat and you and warmth."

"Do you forgive me?"

Nel made a face. "You can't make stuff better just with sex—even sex as good as ours." Her eyes lidded, and she let them close, listening to the thrum of Lin's blood and the rumble of her own heartbeat. "Give it time."

NINE

"Just send me the damn numbers." Nel snarled at the computer. Zachariah's message was a bright square on her screen.

Dr. Bently,

Please make an appointment sometime in the next few days to discuss the results of your evaluation.

-Dr. Lieberman

She flicked the screen off with unnecessary force and shoved out of her chair. Why would they even need to discuss anything? Surely, he could just send the results, slap on some diagnosis about her being pissy and call it a day. That's all the therapist had done when her mom coerced her into going after her father's death. And his insinuations that she was depressed were absurd. She didn't spend all day comatose in bed. Sure, she was sad, but it was because her best friend was dead and her entire world changed. Anyone would be sad.

She jerked her covers into order and stalked from her room. Paul caught sight of her in the hall, but perhaps her glare made him think better of conversation.

Anger issues, though? *You have no idea, Dr. Lieberman.*

Almost two weeks living and working with the same teams bred a certain comradery, one she was used to—jokes and pranks abounded, and those who didn't already have nicknames when they arrived did now. Except for Nel. Well, she was sure she had a nickname among her crew or the rest of the techs and scientists. *Just not one they use to my face.* If her records weren't sealed to all but her supervising officers and medical personnel, she'd think it would have something to do with the psych updates to her file.

"Today's the day!" A hand clapped on her shoulder and she whirled, lip curled in a sneer.

"What?"

"Whoa, sorry Dr. Bently." Arnav rolled back up, hands raised. "I'll wait for your coffee to kick in." He snapped a vial of stimulant into his port and slipped back to his table.

Guilt flashed through her, but it was lost in the miasma of frustration and isolation drifting under her thoughts. *Today's the day.* He was right. Today they opened the tower doors—or tried to, at least. Block A was excavated down to 90cm, enough that the balcony doors beside it were pedestaled on several centimeters of dirt. She was excited.

Rather, she should be.

Caffeine only served to sour her stomach to the point where even the reconstituted eggs—her favorite of the dodgy space breakfast food—looked dangerously rich. Consequently, she was the first to get suited and ride down to the site. Even through the layers of Kevlar shield and her glass helm, the wind roared. Without the comm chatter, she could close her eyes and listen to the gnawing static buzz of her suit and the chattering teeth of the storm around them. It was almost peaceful.

When the rest of the crew arrived, she stood by Block A, hands on hips, staring down the door. She tapped the comm for a base-wide announcement. "Attention Samsara Base Alpha, the archaeology department is opening the first of the towers at 08:30, ah—" she checked her wrist again, "—0830, I mean. So in about twenty minutes. Any an all personnel who wish to observe are welcome to join us. Let it be known, anyone making an open sesame joke will be terminated, effective immediately."

A couple affirmatives rolled through the coms, followed by Paul's "Roger that, Dr." At least they let her weak attempt at humor slide for now, even if it was out of pity, rather than actual humor.

Arnav stepped forward, gaze flicking from tablet to door rapidly, a hunter running every calculation for attack. The scanner thunked onto the door, the tab's screen filling with a series of spikes and feeds as it looked for infrared, EM, any echo of life, human or otherwise. He tapped another few buttons, eyes narrowed as he listened to the feed over his private comm.

He raised a hand, black brows knit.

"Arnav?" Nel asked.

He raised a hand for silence. One gloved finger tapped a button on the scanner and the ticker lines bounced, disappeared, then flickered back into existence, unchanged. "Alright. Clear." His voice cracked from the public to just Nel's ears for the second half, "There's background interference, EM in nature, but nothing I can pinpoint. It could be the building is dormant."

"The building?" Dormant described a hive, a colony, a virus. Not a structure.

"The Teachers integrated with their environments in a way we can't—don't." Arnav shook his head. "I think we should send a drone in first. I'm good with simple scans and judging structural integrity, but we need eyes in there."

"Heard," Nel tapped her wrist and found the tech department. "Hello, Tech. We're entering the spire. Permission to borrow a security drone for recon?"

A reedy voice answered. "Granted. I'll call Mari in, they're out-shield on a scan trying to find the rest of the hydraulics from our ship." A second later, undoubtedly after a discussion with his drone pilot, he continued, "They'll be there in thirty. Standby."

Nel thanked him and stepped closer to Arnav and the looming gate. "Alright Arnav. Drone ETA in half an hour. Let's open this thing."

Arnav motioned for folk to step back and tugged the scanner free, replacing it with another, similar piece of equipment. It flickered to life, blinked once, then went dark. "Alright. We're in." He hit another button, and the tower shuddered, a faint mechanical stretch after an electronic nap.

For a moment everything was still. Then sand eddied from the edges of the door, a puff of old air as the door rumbled down into the body of the building. Nel leaned forward, eyes fixed on the yawning darkness before them. Goosebumps skittered up her arms and her suit responded. She was wrong. Arnav's expression wasn't one of a predator.

It was one of prey.

Whatever happened on Samsara might not be over, and here she was knocking on the front door. Stillness reigned. Several of the onlookers returned to their tasks, coms buzzing with anti-climatic mutters.

Nel edged forward a step, and another, until she could peer into the blackness. For all she could tell it just dropped into oblivion. She settled at the edge of Block A, head tilted. The space beyond wasn't simply a dark room, the same way she knew on the corridor when the dark woods weren't empty, but watching. Buzzing crackled through her suit, just shy of human hearing, just loud for her the hairs on the back of her neck to rise. Her eyes narrowed on the architectural maw. Black swirled against the unfathomable dark.

"Dr. Bently?" Arnav's voice jolted her back to reality.

She realized she was leaning forward, hand inches from the tower wall. "Sorry, Arnav."

"Curiosity, eh?" His chuckle was warm, and he jerked his thumb behind them. "Drone pilot's here with their rig."

Nel glanced back.

A small, slight person stood a few paces from Block A, helmed head bowed over a much higher-tech tablet than the one strapped to Nel's belt. Their fingers flew over the touch keyboard, pausing to adjust two dials on the sleek black quadrocopter beside them. After a minute they glanced up and raised a distracted hand to Nel. Words bloomed from a tiny projector on their tablet.

Morning Dr. Bently

I'm Mari Star Song, Technical officer. Sorry for the delay, I'm trying to fix one of the blades. This sand is hell on fine machinery.

Nel nodded, then faltered, not sure if she should type a response or speak.

Mari must have noticed the hesitation; they grinned, and another string of words appeared.

You can comm me. I can hear, but speech isn't comfortable for me.

"Sounds good. What do you need from me?"

Nothing, really. You just want a general scan of the area?

"And some detailed shots if we find anything interesting."

Roger that.

The drone sputtered, sand puffing from its left rear rotor. It lurched into the air then hovered, a pet content to wait instruction. Mari grinned and tapped a series of instructions into the tablet, brought up several paragraphs of code and dragged it into the drone's processor.

The rotors whirred faster and it rose in the air, camera spinning to orient itself before it glided through the doorway and disappeared.

If you want I'll patch your tab into the camera feed so you can watch.

"Please." Nel unclipped her tablet and opened the contact request from @MariMachine. A second later the camera feed appeared on her screen. She settled into the sand, one gloved hand shielding the screen from the general glow of the site. The grainy image showed a beam of light panning rhythmically, it's radar feed and IR appearing as tiny windows in the corner. It was cold, apparently. Colder than the ambient temperature, Nel realized. The walls were plain, carved lines leading from one room to the next, reminding her of monorail tracks.

The winding ramp lead down to the main entrance, several meters below the surface of the sand now.

Air from the drone's blades swirled the thin layer of sand from the dull gray of the floor. Other than the slight dusting, and a few piles collected in the corners, the floors were untouched. The drone dipped through a doorway and clattered into something. The screen went black.

Nel's heart jumped into an anxious beat. "What was that?"

Mari frowned, crouching next to Nel, fingers flying over the keys, one hand moving the control gently back and up. The camera sputtered static, then the feed returned.

The drone ran into a barred doorway.

"Cage? Prison?"

Mari shook their head. *They didn't have prisons. Or cages. That's a human thing.* They slowed the rotors, allowing the drone to hover at the edge of the bars, scanning the space beyond.

The light was too faint for a detailed image, and the IR said the space was large, cavernous, almost, and cold. The beam of light caught the edge of a fallen pillar and the broken chunks of some other part of the building. Something pale glinted beneath the massive structure.

"What's that? Can you zoom?"

The camera zoomed, the image refocusing in pieces.

A set of ellipses appeared above Mari's tablet.

"Fuck." Nel's stomach dropped and she rocked back on her heels. A gleaming femur jutted from the sand, caught in the camera's light. The delicate curve of a rib arched up beside it. Piled beneath drifting sand and broken architecture were dozens, no, hundreds of bodies, reduced to naked bones.

TEN

Multitudes of pale grey remains were stark against indigo, the image as grainy as the dusting of sand.

"Computer: 200x." She scrolled left, following the knobs of vertebra, breaching bones in an ocean of sand. Behind her the gathered crowd was silent in the lab, a kind of sacred silence settling over the space. Now ribs, like the rooms bars, made for keeping in, keeping out, but both empty save for ghosts.

"300x. Left 70 pixels." And here, where crumbled architecture landed, surely with thunder and screaming metal, the perfect dome of a skull mirrored the opened ceiling above.

"500." She could tell only that it was human. Low camera quality did nothing to make uncovered bones less horrifying. Nel's eyes ached. She raked a hand through her pixie cut and slumped back into her seat. "Pause it there."

"Bently, I don't know what to tell you." Arnav protested. "There's nothing we can tell—not really—from a pixelated screen-cap."

"We can see they're human."

Even with her osteo-anth background, Molly's eyes were glazed and lidded. "All due respect, Dr. Bently, but I'm with Arnav on this one. Until we actually get boots and trowels in there, we're not going to know what the deal is. And some aren't human, judging by size alone. I imagine the building crushed them when it came down, but we can't know for sure until we take a closer look."

"You're forgetting the bars on the door, Molly." Nel snapped. After staring into the black void of the door with the near-constant white noise of her suit, her nerves were shot. Faint beeps and hums of equipment drifted from the analysis portion of the room. Breath billowed in her tired lungs. "I'm sorry. I know you're right. We need a closer look. But it's also my job to keep you safe, and finding a pile of bones—some of which do indeed appear to be human—makes me a bit leery."

"Your track record isn't great on that front, if I remember the reports."

White fury flashed through Nel's mind with a crack. When her vision cleared, she saw her coffee mug rolling on the floor in the corner. A hefty dent marred the blank wall behind the holoscreen. "First thing tomorrow I want Arnav and the combat forensic specialist—"

"Letnan Singh," Arnav provided.

"Right, you two meet me and Noemi at the door. We'll grab backup, then head in. Lefteris, you'll replace Arnav and join Luk on Block A. Molly," her hard gaze flicked to the young woman at the end of the table, "You'll be taking over for Noemi on Block C."

"That's the fucking empty block, Bently."

"Then you should have no problem staying safe while the rest of us do our jobs." Nel flicked the screen off and stalked out of the lab. More detailed instructions were needed, but that was for tonight. Right now she didn't trust her fingers not to shake. Snapping at grad students in Chile was one thing. She didn't need Mikey to tell her throwing an aluminum coffee mug when questioned by an adult colleague—even one as nasty as Molly—was unacceptable.

On her way up to the dorms she passed Zachariah's door. It was translucent, his form pacing. She drew a deep breath and knocked.

"Yes?" The door slid open. His black brows rose when he saw her, arm's crossed, outside his office. "Oh, Dr. Bently. Come in."

"I know I'm supposed to set up an appointment."

"I've got some time."

She sank into the chair, gaze fixed on her clenched hands. If she relaxed her grip she knew she'd crumble, every ounce of her control disintegrating into nothing. "I lost my temper today."

"I see. I didn't get any notifications about the incident."

"It was a minute ago. In the lab. And as much as I hate it here, this is my job, and I can't really imagine going home either, so I'd rather not be fired. You have those results?"

"I doubt very much you did anything worthy of firing." Zachariah fixed her with a thoughtful stare, then turned up the door opacity. "You jumped right from losing your temper to wanting to know your results. You think they're connected?"

"I think you made a few observations about my anger and I just got a bit too angry for a professional setting. So maybe we should go over them. They can't be good, if you're requesting a meeting."

"Actually we always meet with patients to discuss results and feedback." He cleared his throat and leaned back. "Would you like me to begin or would you like to discuss the incident?"

Nel shrugged. She didn't want to be here, but she didn't want to be bundled back into the sardine tin and shipped home. "You can't just send me the numbers?"

"No, not really. Most won't mean anything to you without interpretations."

His eyes were gentle and she hated him for it. Analytical she could handle. An old-quack who had no understanding of what it took to get where she was, she could ignore. Zachariah and his steady understanding were different. "Alright. What's wrong with me?"

He snorted. "Nothing's wrong with you. But you have some coping mechanisms that aren't that healthy and some baggage to unpack if you want to let go of some of your anger."

"It's just anger."

"It isn't. Anger stems from deeper emotions, often related to trauma. Anger is the smoke. Fear, hurt and powerlessness are the bonfire."

She fixed her gaze on her hands. Swollen joints, scarred knuckles, a whorls of callouses marked where she'd punched things, broken digits, and worked her hands raw. *Anything to keep reality from catching up.*

"You don't need to tell me, but I invite you to think back on your anger and the things that—superficially—make you angry. Follow the smoke and you'll find the fire."

"Look, can you just give me something to sleep?"

"Your sleeplessness is another point I wanted to bring up. Your answers also had a high correlation with depression. They indicated loss, but also long term sadness."

She scoffed. "My best friend's dead. It doesn't take a shiny degree in Shrink from Space U to figure out I'm sad. I have trouble sleeping. That's all. I'm not missing work or forgetting to bathe or eat."

"No, you're not. You're fairly high-functioning when it comes to the classic symptoms, but you also had a high occurrence of what we call 'fake good' answers. You're minimizing, Nel. It's part of why you're so successful—you pour yourself into work, using anger as rocket fuel. And it's a great fuel, I'll give you that, if not sustainable. But the reason you're here is that you're running on empty."

"I'm here because it's mandated by IDH."

"Fair. But you walked into my office this afternoon of your own volition."

He had her there. She heaved a sigh, raking her hands through her hair. "Look, can you just write me a script for Ambien or something?"

He chuckled. "No. If you had a port you could ask requisitions to supply a cocktail of melatonin. I can see if we have oral options and suggest a prescription for some. And for your temper—it sounds trite, but start with counting. Remember—these people are your employees. You don't have to like them and they don't have to like you. You just have to work together. I think better sleep hygiene will help your patience as well. Give your body something else to burn."

She swallowed hard, then forced herself to nod. It was woo-woo stuff her mother believed, and other than some sleeping pills, she wasn't interested. But she needed to make it through this mission. "Fine. I'll take the melatonin."

"I think that's a great choice. I'll update your file and send a note to requisitions now, so you can try it tonight. And Nel?" His voice stopped her as she made for the door.

"Yeah?"

"If you do want to talk about where the smoke leads, I'm here."

"You sure you don't need another set of hands?" Lin protested.

"C'mon, cut the apron strings," Nel joked. "It's a snug fit down there, and I need you up here dealing with Luk and Lefteris's finds. And hopefully there will be lots of those."

"Ah, man," Arnav groaned, "If you find cool shit when I'm up to my berries in bones, I won't talk to a-one of you."

Greta's clear voice cut through the buzz and chatter. "If you talk about your 'berries' one more time I'm requesting your transfer, Arnav."

Nel rolled her eyes and buckled on the thin cable tether.

"Dr. Bently, I presume?" A deep voice rumbled through the comm.

Nel looked up and up to see a tall person in a flat grey suit very different from all the scientists' white. Their belt bristled with several different attachments for what appeared to be a prosthetic hand. Currently, their arm was outfitted with something heavy that Nel would rather never have to stare down the barrel of. "Ah, combat forensics?" she hazarded.

"That's me. Letnan Third Class Singh. I'll take point, the rest of you can bring up the rear. Once I've cleared the area you'll be free to poke around and test whatever you'd like, but if I say run—" her gaze flitted to Arnav's chair, "Or roll-out, as the case may be—then you scat, get me?"

Nel resisted the urge to bark, "Aye, aye!" Instead she nodded, and muttered "Affirmative." It didn't matter how much sense the officer made. She hated orders. She tested the cable again before stepping in line behind Singh. Arnav wheeled in place next, followed by their forensic specialist. Helms' tint decreased as they stepped through the door. Singh's flashlight shed brilliant white light through the room.

Nel's display flickered for a second, switching between IR and vis-spec. "My helm it's fucking up."

Singh paused, glancing back. "What's the problem?"

Nel frowned, tapping her wrist to refresh the display program. Already her heart hammered and her suit attempted to squeeze her into complacency or comfort. Her helm went black, save for the glimmer of the flashlight on the dull walls. She hadn't realized how familiar the extra information had become. A second later her display reappeared, functioning normally. She forced her breath into nonchalance and replied, "Ah, never mind, I guess. It's fine now."

"Roger. Keep the coms clear and let's move."

Keep the coms clear. The undertone of condescension may have been in Nel's imagination, but it pissed her off nonetheless. Were she in Singh's IDH military boots, Nel knew she'd be annoyed at the jabbering of the dumb Earthling. Her ears ached in the absence of distracting conversation, or the various pings of missives and updates from her crew—all of which she had suspended until they were back to the orange safety of the surface. Instead, everything hummed. Her suit, the heavier atmosuit around it, and the faint, gnawing buzz of static and something just outside the realm of her hearing. If she wasn't already teetering on the edge of a temper tantrum, this would surely put her there. *Maybe I should have actually taken that sleeping shit last night.*

Arnav's high-traction wheels squealed faintly, even through the insulated glass of their helms, and Nel glanced back. He flashed her a thumbs up and what might have been a wink. A second later a message appeared on her tablet.

Don't worry about Singh. She's a tightwad when it comes to missions, but good under pressure and a great shot. It's when she cuts loose during R&R you've gotta watch out.

Nel snorted. His description sent a pinch of wistfulness through her, and she wondered how this whole adventure would unfold if Lin wasn't in the picture. *Or in my bed.* Shoving her inappropriate and frankly unwarranted thoughts aside, she focused on the narrow winding hall. Marks that were faint etches on the drone's feed were now deep, calculated grooves glinting with bright copper. Perhaps it was her imagination again, but when she brushed the surface her hand tingled, as if with static charge. They wound around the building's core, avoiding crumbling sections of floor. For all of Singh's humorlessness, the trip was uneventful.

Nel still held her breath.

At the bottom of the ramp the hall broadened, another corridor leading off into a cave-in to the left, and a closed, solid door to the right. The bars before them gleamed under Singh's flashlight. She crouched, deploying a small hovering disc that darted between the bars to scan the room. When it returned, the officer uploaded the data to their tablets. A moment later their helms synced and the rough map of the area was superimposed over the space.

"Room is clear. Air quality is consistent with the surface. I'll scan again once the door opens."

Arnav moved forward, locking his wheels. The chair whirred and the seat rose several feet from the chassis so he could reach the heavy electro-mechanical lock at the height of Nel's head. The block he fixed to the metal was a smaller one, with several extra wires. The readout started, the door thunked, but nothing happened.

"Everything alright? Did you disengage the defense—"

"I know how to open this shit, Singh-er, just give me a second." Despite the hard words, his tone was gentle, and his movements slow. Nel wondered how rich he'd be if he bottled his patience to sell. *Maybe that's something else Zachariah can 'scribe me.*

A second try triggered a squeal of metal. It ground upward then lurched to a halt halfway up. Arnav's smile warmed the words drifting through the comm. "Open Sesame. That's as good as it's gonna get. The electrics are clear. Must be some cave-in above that's blocking the door's pocket."

Singh nodded and sent her microdrone in again. Nothing had changed, despite the sand drifting down in the wake of the rumbling machinery. "Clear. I'll stand guard while you dirt folk do your thing."

Nel edged into the room, eyes darting from black corner to looming shadow, half expecting an alien corpse to lurch from the darkness. What did the teachers even look like? She'd never thought to ask. "Alright, Arnav, I want a detailed map and photos of all the rooms, especially any additional exits. If you encounter remains, drop a pin. Noemi, you're with me. We're moving this sand to get a better idea of body-count. Use skulls alone for now. It'll give us a low-ball estimate." She glanced at Singh, not liking the idea of eyes on her while she worked. "And update with possible COD. Let's get started."

Moving to the first pile, she let her tab snap a shot, then dropped a pin on the brow of the skull. When a little cursor prompted her to add a note, she cleared her throat. "Human. Adult. No obvious COD." Her gloved hand paused, hovering over the temple. There was little tissue left, save for ligaments, holding the body in it's final position. "Arnav—any idea about the temp in here? It's freezing."

"Your suit should—"

"No, I'm fine, I mean, the readouts are saying it's literally freezing."

"Ah. The atmosphere. Up top it's hot due to the suns. Down here, without light, it's a bit different. Maybe they froze to death. Hope so. Sandblasted is a hell of a way to die."

"But why?" Nel wondered. The coms crackled into silence and she moved on to the next body. Two hours later and her back ached from crouching over skeletal remains. Pounding filled her head every time she looked at the flickering light of her tablet screen. She peered at the count. Arnav marked three bodies, one he labeled as "non-human." Whatever that meant. Noemi cataloged another three dozen. *Fuck. This isn't just a cave in.* Her gaze slid to the bars. "How many people were on Samsara for the event? Roughly?"

Singh's deep voice was a dirge. "Thousands."

Whatever dregs of an appetite Nel hadn't lost in the face of grinning mandibles disappeared. Samsara's black depths looked more like a mausoleum with every passing moment.

"What the hell is this?" Nel's booted foot clunked against a heavy lump buried in a particularly deep pile of sand. She crouched, gloved hand clearing off a huge long bone. "Far too dense to be human. Big, too. Your Teachers have bones?" She giggled at the question. It was a valid one, and she knew it, but the comment brought up images of giant squids in tweed jackets.

Noemi shuffled up beside her to examine the find. It took another few minutes, but together they cleared off what was left of the remains. Half were crushed under a massive cube of metal architecture. After a second the tech's faint laugh hummed through Nel's helm. "You don't recognize them? They're as alien as you are, Dr. Bently."

Nel tilted her head, mentally building a picture of muscle and sinew and flesh. The skull was cracked, but sure enough her flashlight glinted on the curved edge of a massive tooth. *"We lost more than just personnel and mentors when the world below went dark."* "Must be one of the a smilodon specimens Lin mentioned." She lifted a phalange to peer at it. It lacked the weight of whatever minerals would have replaced the bone during fossilization. A shred of what looked like rawhide clung to the joint. "A cast? This can't be tissue."

"What's left of it. Died the same way the people did, I imagine. I guess we know why there were bars."

Nel stared. "Come again?"

"Whatever killed everyone in here got the zoological specimens as well. Why the rest of these folk were sheltering in the habitat, I don't know."

Living specimens. Familiar weight dragged at her heart. "Fuck you guys had living smilodon down here?"

"I've got a door over here. More bars," Arnav interrupted. "And from what I can see cuvieronius. I think we're looking at some sort of housing for them."

Nel barely heard him beyond "cuvieronius." Her gaze roved over the other bones. Some of Arnav's notes indicated children among the human dead, but somehow, this hit harder. "We thought they were extinct. They were extinct—on Earth at least. For thousands of years."

"You could care less that thousands of human lives were lost, but you weep over the bodies of creatures you thought were already dead?" Singh cut in. There was no judgement in her tone, just curiosity.

Still, Nel's temper flared. *One. Two.* Her heart ached with the tragedy. It was illogical. *Three, four.* It was childish. She always preferred her people dead, but she never expected to mourn an entire species.

ELEVEN

A jumble of colored dots and lines were superimposed over Mari's drone scans. With Singh's added data it made a fairly accurate, if not overly detailed plan of the barred room. Nel jabbed a finger through the mess of dropped pins. "Alright, anyone wanna give me a better idea of what this building was for? Floorplans or something?" When no one commented, she prodded further. "An errant blueprint? Microfiche?"

"Most of us weren't allowed down here for any length of time. And if we were, it was for something specific. Not a tour of the capital," Molly remarked.

Nel glanced back. She hadn't heard anyone talk about the culture differences between IDH and the people on Samsara. *Samsarites?* She just assumed they were one homogenous culture. *You couldn't get hundreds of thousands of people to be the same no matter what asinine master race you hope to make.* "So people lived down here, but they were different from you folk?"

Lin's dark eyes were narrowed on the screen, head tilted at an nearly ninety degree angle. "You run any of the wall markings through pattern recognition?"

Nel followed her gaze, but didn't know what she was seeing. "I hadn't yet. I'm not as used to all the tech, most of my pattern recognition is just my own eyeballs. Why?"

"The scans of the rooms. Not sure, I just know it's familiar." She shrugged, but remained focused on the screen. "How many bodies?"

"134 human, three smilodon, and five cuvieronius. That pillar knocked the smilodon area open. I think these people were either sheltering here or were driven here. Noemi and I both noted pitting on the bones, but we won't be able to examine them in detail until we bring them up here. It could be from sand, but with the door sealed it would be unlikely."

"So where are the rest of them?"

Nel glanced over at Arnav. "The thousands Singh spoke of? Maybe farther in the tunnels. Hopefully we can borrow Mari and their drone for a better look. Tomorrow, I want everyone to finish their blocks and the next day we'll send half of you down with some lab folk to collect and properly map those bodies."

"Dr. Bently, tonight's the shield cycle. We gotta get the site locked down for that. It'll be a day before we can dig again."

She frowned at the tech, then looked at her tablet. Sure enough a blinking red dot in the corner revealed a site-wide reminder she had been ignoring for two days. "Ah, right. Lost track of time. So shield cycle."

Lefteris laughed, but it wasn't cruel, and he jerked a thumb at the doors down to the site. "We got the temp shields prepped while you were analyzing this data. Just gotta figure out who draws the short straws to go activate them in half an hour."

Nel blushed and looked away. Anger bubbled at the correction, regardless of how gentle. She hated how little she knew about day-to-day life in this world. Her confidence always stemmed from familiarity. "Well I'd volunteer but I'm just as likely to blow something up I imagine. So how long does the shield cycle last?"

"It's in the memo, I think, but just 24 hours. The programming needs to restart. The longer the uptime the buggier it gets."

The thought of the shield malfunctioning and putting her entire crew and site at the mercy of a sandstorm was sickening. "Ah, flush the system. Gotcha."

"Fucking leave it, man!"

Attention swiveled to the airlock. The door slid open and Paul stalked in, slamming his helm into his cubby by the door.

"Look, I just think it was a bad call," one of the other geo-techs quipped, following him into the lab. "And I'm not the one who lost an entire day's worth of data over 'curiosity'"

"It's not curiosity, you Earth-brain, it's my God damned job!" Paul crossed himself, hands shaking with fury, and stalked from the lab.

"I think we're done here," Nel murmured to her crew. "I'll send you details tonight." She straightened and followed the geologist through the halls. The building was quiet in the afternoon. Quieter, still, as people prepared for the shield-cycle. It didn't feel like a day off with an impending sandstorm raging outside. She found Paul in the tiny observation room just above the dorms.

He hadn't removed his suit, and one tan hand rubbed at the base of his ear.

"You okay, man?"

He shrugged. "My patience is shot lately."

"You and me both. I lost it on one of my diggers the other day."

"Heard about that."

"Oh?"

He glanced over, mouth curling slightly, more sadness than smile. "She's banging one of my techs. Got an earful about how you're not cut out for this life."

"I'm not."

He winced. "Ah, about the 'Earth-brained' comment, I was angry and up here it just means—"

"Irrational? I've lived there my whole life and I can't say you're wrong." Nel chuckled and leaned on the sill beside him. "So what's up?"

"Haven't been able to sleep. My tinnitus has been acting up. Those suits aren't the ones I'm used to I guess. Or maybe all the tech we're standing on has a latent signal." The red tangle of swollen vessels in his eyes lent weight to his words.

"The comm static—or whatever it is—bugs me too." She elbowed him. "Maybe you're a bit Earth-brained yourself. What's the tinnitus from? My dad had it from working at a machining plant for years. Even though he was an engineer, he was always down on the floors."

"Grew up on a mining colony, drills running constantly. We all go deaf by thirty-five. Any sort of ambient noise makes it worse."

"Fuck man, that sucks. I'm sorry."

He shrugged again. "Deaf isn't a huge issue up here, we're more accommodating than many, and on a colony where most everyone has hearing loss we have a bunch of tech that helps. But it's still an adjustment."

"My old boss at the college where I taught used a wheelchair. I never noticed how many stairs we used until I had to go different routes when we were together. I'm impressed with how accessible this place is."

Paul scoffed. "C'mon, who needs stairs in space?"

A deep klaxon interrupted Nel's response. Suspended on cables, even the building trembled. She glanced at Paul's suited wrist, conveniently still blinking with the time: 16:30. "I guess that's our warning to get the fuck back inside."

"Sure is." He heaved a sigh and patted his suit. "I'm gonna get rid of this monster and try and sleep through this cycle. Thanks for checking on me. I'm usually a patient person."

"No problem. And I've never been one, so if you need any advice…" she trailed off. She wasn't in the position to help anyone, if Zachariah's pointed comments meant anything. "Hope you get some rest." His boots clomped down the hall, silenced by the observation deck's door sliding shut. Nel pressed her brow to the window. The faintly orange air blurred the details of the patterned shield above them, but she caught a flicker of light crossing the surface in rhythmic waves. A second klaxon sounded and the translucent panels between the rigid bars glitched out of existence. Sand and wind crashed against the walls, sending the whole building rocking slightly. Nel belatedly braced herself with a wince. Spacesuits made her feel vulnerable, but this took it to a whole new level.

Ten minutes later Lin found her, curled at the head of her bed, eyes fixed out the window at the vermillion sky. "How's it going?"

Nel glanced over. "Alright. Listening to the storm. Reminds me of thunderstorms back home."

"I've never seen a thunderstorm. Not from the ground, at least, just from space. *Odyssey* doesn't have weather."

That dragged the archaeologist's attention from the writhing clouds to the tall mystery a few spaces away. Without the weather, what could small talk have been like? "It's visceral. They always made me feel alive, connected to the world, knowing everyone would glance up, brows raised, allowing themselves, just for a second, to be awed."

"That's beautiful. In a desperate way." Something shadowed Lin's eyes, something Nel thought she might recognize, if only they were a bit closer. "Being out here's a bit eerie."

"How so?" Nel watched her pace to the window, then to her desk and back to the window. "I mean, I totally agree, but this is your world."

"I've never been someplace without people. I mean truly. When I'm in a ship, there's the crew. The *Odyssey* even has very little solitude. Not true solitude. Everything was made, created by human hands. And on earth I spent half my time in underground bases, radio contact away from an entire troop of IDH operatives. I haven't be so wholly surrounded by something..." she shrugged.

"So alien?" Homesickness and the disorientation of a new planet were things Nel understood.

Lin must have caught the gist of the archaeologist's thought. "I know this is probably worse for you."

"It's not a contest. Can't you call your family? Or Dar?"

"They went dark, dealing with some issue with an Earth contact, I guess. As for Dar. We're not that close." Her response was immediate and non-negotiable.

Nel pushed aside the twinge of worry at the mention of home. "It seemed like you were, when we first met, in Chile."

"That's probably the biggest lie I told you."

Nel's brows shot up. "I don't know, I think 'I'm not an alien' probably takes the cake."

"It's the biggest lie to me." Her voice was soft. "After seeing you and Mikey together, I was jealous I guess."

The sound of his name on her lips was almost heresy. "You never met him."

Lin looked away. "You were all under surveillance."

"Right." Nel nodded. It felt like a lifetime ago. She envied her past self, free of grief and alien conspiracies. "You seemed so excited to see him on the site, for someone not close. And vice versa."

"I suppose I at least knew about Earth my whole life." She glanced up. "Are you angry?"

Nel leaned back in bed, eyes never leaving Lin's. *Am I?* Her gut seethed with her constant drive, constant fury, the fury of injustice, the fury of grief. But she was lonely, and if Mikey's death taught her anything, it was that the people she cared about mattered far more than any anger.

"Nel?"

"I was thinking. Angry about the lying? You've made a habit out of it. So yeah, a bit. But you knew that. I guess I'm still curious enough to be willing to wait for the truth." She patted the spot on the bed beside her. "So, why aren't you and Dar close?"

"We were inseparable until I was eight. Then he joined the academy—a year early—and I was left at home for three circadial years. When I saw him again we were five years apart instead of two and he was a man. I missed everything." She folded herself next to the other woman, knees separated from Nel's, by a breath and brilliant longing.

"Five years apart? How?"

"Cryo." She had not met Nel's eyes. "It's a great separator. We've not found a way to fix the gap inherent to animals subject to time. It was three years for me, nine for him. I had taken two trips, both in cryo. Time stopped for me, but didn't for him. We've bounced back and forth—sometimes I'm even older than him—but that first difference broke us. And because of how our parents taught us, we never recovered."

"How'd they teach you?" Nel allowed her foot to curl around Lin's leg. Lately it wasn't how different Lin was that surprised her. It was how similar.

"Molly was right. Most people on *Odyssey* never went to Samsara. We were two separate entities really, but we balanced each other. My father's from *Odyssey*. My mother's from here. My father taught me everything about IDH and the space station. My mother taught Dar her world—obviously we were both exposed to more, and I can function fine there. But the legends we grew up with were different. Through us, the world would see that the two could agree. Or something. I think they thought our love for one another would be enough to counter any indoctrination." She glanced at Nel. "It wasn't."

Lin's feelings always seemed to take a thousand words to explain, but this time, Nel could distil them down to two: "You're lonely."

"I don't know if I'd recognize the feeling," Lin argued.

"Maybe because you've always felt it. It's your normal. I've felt loneliness a lot too." Nel took a breath. This was treading into dangerous territory for her, edging out to deep waters she wasn't sure were safe. "It's an only-child thing on Earth. Any kid who's othered, frankly. And being gay is othering, even if I grew up pretty privileged."

"Humans are weird."

"You say it like you're not. Human that is. You're weird too—maybe in a different way, but you're still human." Nel reached out, battered fingers lacing with Lin's delicate hand. "Loneliness is about as human as it gets."

Lin's eyes glittered, walnut glimmering through tears. "I've been an asshole."

Surprise slipped into Nel's veins, cool and calming, followed by something warm she didn't want to name. "A bit. But I'm not the easiest either. Like, at all."

"You pointed out all the places I've been dishonest, and it made me realize how natural lying feels in this world. I wonder how often I've believed lies in the guise of the greater good. And here you are, trusting me."

Nel snorted. "I don't trust easily."

"Liar." Lin's eyes narrowed on her. "You just wish you didn't."

The wind screamed around the corner of her room. Nel closed her eyes, letting herself sit in her flash of anger at being found out. Knowing another person—someone besides Mikey—knew her that well was terrifying. But, she had already trusted Lin this far, even if took the other woman's observation to make her realize it was, in fact, trust. The building swayed in the storm, sand and indifference hissing against the window. When she forced herself to respond, she found a smile warmed her whisper. "How would you know?"

"You crossed the stars on little more than a kiss and dare."

TWELVE

Nel pressed a hand to her back and straightened with a groan. "C'mon don't you purple-people-eaters have something for lower back aches? A suit that massages you while you work? Opioids maybe?" A small quadcopter hovered beside her, carrying a crate loaded with tissue samples. She scanned the vial in her hand and its barcode appeared on her tablet's screen, blank lines awaiting her input.

SAMPLE TYPE: Human tissue, ligament
ORIGIN: Remains (#39)
WARNINGS: HazMat

Noemi rolled her eyes and slid another sample from the same set of remains into the crate. "Massage units are mostly found on pleasure sectors and opioids are only for pain patients. If you're out here much longer though, you might want to get a port installed. Makes more conventional treatments easier."

"Fuck no," Nel muttered, shuddering at the thought. She couldn't stand the primal intimacy of tattoos or piercings, let alone integrated into her veins. *Pleasure sectors, huh?* She glanced at the body between them, gloved hands brushing over the weathered bones. "I think that's it for this set."

"Yeah, and I think Arnav and Malic's drones are almost full up too."

"We're gonna run out of room up there for the samples. And HazMat seals or no, I'm not keen on having my entire crew stacked in with a bunch of potential contagions. Nel slid the protective covering over the case of samples and activated it's vacuum seal. The thin barrier conformed to the shape with a quiet snap. Nel's suit pinged and she glanced down.

Communications: Message for BENTLY,
Authentication required
SENDER: Restricted IP, Earth
MESSAGE CLASSIFICATION: Private

She frowned. None of the vids from her mom needed authentication. "I'll follow these ones up, if you don't mind starting on the next without me. Looks like communications needs me for something."

"Ugh, I've been trying to get a vid through to my grandfather for days. Maybe the shield cycle messed up our connection. It's happened before."

Or this entire planet is cursed. "I'll see if I can bring back any good news." She trudged after the drones, winding up the ramp lit with dim, hovering globes their tech officer programed the day the shields came back online. they rounded the final bend in the hall and emerged from the tower. Block A was over a meter deep, and soon they would have to decide whether to pursue it farther down or switch to cataloging and scanning within the buildings.

I've never had a dig with so little digging, she mused. But, to be fair, most sites she'd studied in undergrad had fewer preserved structures. *Or preserved bodies.*

On her way across the site she passed Paul and his team. Each carried a massive coring machine over one shoulder. She waved. "Headed out-shield?"

"No, we're actually just getting started on coring where we discussed." Paul patted his helm. Fatigue abraded his usually gentle voice. "Few days behind cause we lost some samples. Got your data and points all uploaded so we'll be doing your sets too."

Nel grinned "Thanks. I'm curious to see what you find. There's so little data, but there's got to be even just a trace when thousands of people just disappear."

"Or die," Paul noted, watching the drones hum onto the airlock elevator with their fragile burdens.

"Right. Or that." Nel moved to tuck a hank of hair behind her ear, only to remember when her hand thunked against her helm that she was suited and her hair was too short anyways. "I'm really interested in that spot—behind the semi-circular ridge."

"The fact that it's on none of the maps makes me wonder too," Paul agreed.

The fact that none of this was mentioned other than in passing during our debriefing makes me fucking wonder. Every survival horror video game she played with Mikey and the half-dozen sequential films had visions of mutated viruses and shuffling zombies drifting through her head when she let herself relax for more than a minute. Her suit chimed again and she rolled her eyes. "Anyway, good luck. Let me know as soon as you find something."

Paul snorted. "I'm sure the lab will. Assuming we don't have to jettison the equipment in favor of becoming a makeshift morgue."

"Yeah, yeah, I'm taking care of it." Exactly how, though, she wasn't yet certain. Surely if their weight limits for transport on and off Samsara were too tight for a case a beer, wedging hundreds of human samples between the powdered protein and motion-sick scientists wouldn't be possible. *Maybe I'll phone Dr. Alvarez while I'm talking to Communications.* She unloaded the cases from the drones and pressed their "return" function before stepping into the sliver of free space on the elevator and jabbing the button. The motor groaned into motion.

Belatedly, she realized her only way off the elevator would be clambering over the stacks of samples they carefully protected all the way from the tower. Tapping her wrist, she chose the lab's PA system. "Hey guys, got myself in a bind. Mind moving a few of these folks so I can get out?"

The tech who opened the door tried—and failed—to suppress a smile. "Ah, Dr. Bently. Let me help." He wheeled the first two crates out of the way, tucking them into the crowded bays previously used to house extra equipment and various clutter.

"Thanks Benni. I'm working on a solution, I promise."

"No rush, they keep the rest of the lab rats out of my hair. I think the other techs are afraid of ghosts," the pathologist speculated. "I've always preferred the dead over the living, even if they're just tissue samples."

"Dude, me too," she sighed when she'd tugged her helm off. "There's easily a hundred still to go down there. I figured you get started with these guys, since they have the most tissue. I'll be with Coms if you need me."

"Surely we'll have some answers soon. Though IDing the lot will take some time." Benni murmured, seemingly to himself.

Nel hummed in agreement and hung her suit up before heading down the hall to the dim office that served as the Communications department.

The sliding door was closed and opaque, but she knocked anyways.

"What."

"Ah, it's Dr. Bently, I got message that I...got a message."

"Right." Another few seconds passed, then the terse voice spoke again. "Well, come in."

She slid the door aside to reveal a dark room filled with a tangle of cables and a dozen glowing screens in various shades of blue and green. The one directly in the fore, however, flashed an angry red.

"Is this a bad time?"

"Bad as any," Greta grumbled. Though Nel remembered her from the briefing, she hadn't seen the woman since their arrival. A stack of food trays sequestered in the only corner not filled with tech explained half of that puzzle.

"There's something I have to authenticate?" Nel prodded.

"Yep," Greta responded, tugging one hovering screen over to Nel with her gnarled hands. Black lines ran up her palm from wrist to fingertip, allowing her to integrate more fully with the tech, Nel supposed. "Handprint, name, and whatever you assigned for your password."

"Where did it come from? Any idea what it says?"

"No clue. Not my job to poke my nose where it doesn't belong." A toothy grin flashed in her sallow face. "Well, 'less they pay me for it."

"Right." Nel typed her name and password, then pressed her hand to the pad by the screen. It flashed green and her wrist dinged, alerting her to a new message in her cue. "So does this mean communications are open to Earth again?"

"'Fraid not. This one got into the *Odyssey* a week ago, just before the shield cycle. They're so distracted trying to get back in contact with Terrestrial Headquarters they didn't forward our mail to us until today. And even then, the most we've been able to get from *Odyssey* herself are file transfers and garbled words."

"You think it's just a weather issue or something more?"

The specialist shrugged. "Hard to say, though the meteorologists have been pretty excitable—" she jerked a thumb at the wall she shared with their office, "so I wouldn't be surprised it that's the culprit."

"Well, let me know as soon as you're through. Got a report to file soon." Nel paused in the doorway. "Thanks."

Greta appeared to have already descended back into lines of code and frequencies. Nel shrugged and ducked back out, shutting the door quietly behind her. *And I thought I wasn't a people person.* Though she knew the techs could handle their work alone for a few more minutes, she still felt guilty ducking upstairs to check the mysterious new message. Secrecy or no, it would only take a few minutes to read.

She slid her door shut and brought up her computer screen. Her heart clenched at the banner that appeared.

(1) New Message: EMILIO SEPULVEDA for ANNELISE BENTLY
[ENCRYPTED]

Why would he write to me? When she pressed the decryption option, a question appeared in Chilean Spanish:

Who was playing in Jerod's bar while we spoke of the meaning of humanity?

After a second she recalled, and typed in Violeta Perra's name. The bottom dropped out of her stomach. She hadn't thought of Emilio except in passing, but she supposed he would have been "dead" and extracted from prison by IDH by now. The whole affair still made Nel's skin crawl. That he had gone to several lengths to make sure she was the only one—or at least the first—who read it did nothing to assuage her unease.

> *I hope this finds you well. Much has changed since you left, though I don't know how much you will have heard. I doubt, even with senti-comps and databases, you do not have the resources to see the patterns arising here at home. My brush with IDH and my faltering faith in the Founders comes at an interesting time.*

Like many of the Founders, I agree humanity has a bright future, and IDH does not hold humanity's best interests as a priority. But I no longer think they are the enemy. It is an archaeic word to use but when discussing the dawning of a new age and mighty empires, poetic language seems fitting.

I am in a unique position, trusted by both sides—by those who know I still live, that is—and I see events transpiring, building tensions between our two factions. Your article was published, to much scorn, but it gains traction on whisper networks and in pockets of the dark web. Enough that some people are listening. I believe something is coming and neither side is at fault. They don't even know its coming. Tensions between them are being stoked, and though I'm not sure of the reason, I believe it is deliberate.

Infantilizing in the name of altruism is not how I pictured our age of technical enlightenment beginning— though I am not surprised. Many cultures have seen strangers appear promising aid, and delivering only pain.

I fear the sky of this dawn will be bloody.

And so I write hoping you, too, are ready to listen.

I hope to hear from you soon.

Only hard plastic digging at her shoulder and hissing of recycled air grounded her. *What the ever-loving fuck?* She expected a note about IDH framing him, or his faked death. Perhaps something about her former site. Not paragraphs of speculation on the future of the planet. The time stamp told her Emilio had sent it at the new year, just after she left. Earth. And now the coms were down. Dread dragged at her gut.

If she were a praying woman, or believed in anything beyond chaos and oblivion, she'd hit her knees and bargain. Instead, she closed her eyes and turned to the one person she still had faith in. "Mikey, please. What can I do?"

Silence answered.

A ragged breath centered her, and she glanced at her screen again. Lunch was almost over. Her fingers hovered over the folder of vids from her mother, tempted to skip to the most recent to check that home still waited for her, blue and imperfect. Encryptions aside, she had no way of knowing if her correspondence was actually safe. Or if she even wanted to respond to Emilio's speculation and plea.

A few seconds' searching produced her cell phone, in hopes of taking a picture of the message before deleting it. When she tried to turn the phone on, however, she was greeted only by a black screen. Apparently two years of space travel was too much. She read the words again, and copied his IP and address before dragging the file to the trash.

A knock sent adrenaline zinging up her spine. She hastily shut her screen down and pulled open the door. "Yeah?"

Arnav's black brows shot up. "We're halfway through the samples for the main room and I wanted to know what the plan was for tomorrow. Everything alright? You look a bit frazzled."

"Just some Earthling shit I had to straighten out," she lied. "The time difference gets to me."

He nodded with a sad smile. "I hear you. Most of us have a bit of one to content with, but not many have the full two years."

Nel sighed. "Yeah, it's no fun. I just need to keep reminding myself that at least I'm doing better than our friends down in the spire. I hadn't even considered—what do you people do for funerals?"

"'You people' meaning Hindus, or…"

Embarrassment replaced her existential fear for a second. "I'm so sorry, no I meant IDH, or space people, or whatever. But I'm realizing IDH is less of a monolith than my Earth-brain assumed."

Arnav grinned and held open the lab door for her. "I knew what you meant, but it's not often anthropologists can call each other out."

"Please, always call me out. And you should see some of the anthro folk on Earth. It's a goddamn nightmare half the time. I'd still be arguing that we should leave those people to rest in peace rather than put them on display for entertainment."

Arnav grimaced. "Oof. But to answer your question, most of us with cultural traditions practice our same rites. What happens to the bodies varies, though on the *Odyssey* we return to the cycle. Not sure what will become of these ones."

"Once I get my report through to Alvarez, I'll have a better idea of what they're looking for. I'd like to switch our focus as well—seems our blocks aren't producing enough to warrant the effort, as much as I love digging." She fixed the suit awaiting her with a dubious glare. "Why don't you guys stick to the sampling for today. I'm going to check out some other areas I might drop blocks. If you have any issues talk to Lin or radio me."

"Will do, Scully."

She glanced at him, half delighted that she rated a nickname, half puzzled at his choice.

"You've seen the X-files, yes?"

"Ah, yeah, a bit. I was never a sci-fi fan."

"Exactly. You're the skeptic that still managed to study aliens."

"Don't you guys get offended by our sci-fi shit? Or at least think we're pretty off base?" She tugged the body of her electromesh up and plugged her atmosuit into its ports.

He shrugged and locked his helm in place, smoothly transferring from typical speech to the radio. "Not all of them are. Besides, they're entertainment. And a lot of the assumptions are pretty hysterical." He affected a robotic, nasal voice. "Take me to your leader."

She laughed and carefully switched over to coms herself. "So what does that make you—Mulder?"

"You really didn't see much of the show, did you? We've all agreed that if you're Scully, Lin's Mulder."

She glimpsed a flash of his thick black brows waggling at her and blushed. "Alright, you lech, I'll see you this evening. Hopefully with a better gameplan for tomorrow." She stepped of the elevator and made for the far end of the site. She barely needed the overlaid grid and map to orient herself now, even with the cloistering effect of the suit. She pulled the map up on her tablet and moved to the nearest curl of the ridge beyond the main set of structures.

Even if the tablet didn't display an inscribed arc, her gut said the curve of the ridge was too perfect to be natural. Despite what she told Arnav, she could have easily done this from the comfort of her room or the lab. *Annoying suit aside, though, I'm too hands on for that.*

Tablet in one hand, she hiked to the first of the ridge's evenly-space spines. Like the spire behind her, it was lined with mechanical-looking designs, with the addition of random pieces extending from its sides.

"They preferred function over form," she reminded herself. "So if I were a weird alien race what would use this for?"

Screaming ripped through the coms at 3:42. Hearing the sound through the helm was disorienting, as if it came from everywhere, from within her skull. *As if it's mine.* Nel's helmet flared with warnings, a distress signal flashing at the sound's location—just over the ridge from where Nel stood. *Paul.*

She hammered on the comm and broke into a run. "De Lellis, come in!"

Buzzing grew as the scream's volume interfered with the speakers, with the dozen people's frantic, crackling questions.

Nel learned early in life the difference between the sound of surprise versus pain. This planet might be alien, but the wrenching, animal sound of human pain still hit her in the gut. Her legs burned from the heavy mag boots as she hauled herself over the end of the ridge. *Fuck. Suit: Disengage mag boots.*

Confirm: Disengage?

"Medic! We need a medic!" *Suit: confirm!*

Two hundred meters out she found his kit, laid out to take samples. Scattered vials and staggering footprints continued for another fifty. His voice broke, warping in desperation.

"I'm coming, Paul, hold on!" Without the magnetic boots, her strides were long, wobbly, uncontrolled. *Where is everyone?* If anyone answered, she couldn't hear through the static and cries rattling her helmet's speakers. She staggered to where Paul writhed on the ground several meters away.

"Get it out!" He clawed at his suit, his helmet, as if swarmed by bees.

Sheer panic overrode her common sense and the harsh voice saying she should wait for a medic. Nel fell to her knees beside him.

His back arched, then he snapped in on himself, curling around his knees. Despite being helmet-to-helmet, she only heard his voice through the coms and it messed with her perception. She gripped his wrists, babbling, "Paul, I've got you, what is it? I've called the medics."

They were kneeling together now, her digging muscles screaming as she wrenched his hands away from his body. Hard fingers ripped into the meat of her forearms. Her left elbow gave way with a burning pop. His hand shot out, gripping her throat.

Warnings blared in her ears, orange and yellow flashing at the edges of her view. A spacesuit's heavy aluminum collar would be too thick for his scrabbling fingers, but the pliable fabric of her atmosuit was no match for a man in sheer panic. Through the two layers of glass she caught a glimpse of his eyes, bloodshot and vacant. Paul's thumb pressed against her jugular, squeezing the delicate arc of her hyoid.

Buzzing grew louder.

Nel shoved at him, edges of her world blurring. Her chest ached for breath. She ripped her hand free from his grip and slammed it up into his gut. Air rushed into her lungs, and with it came pain and the shrill cries of her suit's alert. *Suit: increase oxygen*. She hauled herself to her feet. Her hand rose, shaking. *Suit: fire*

Confirm: Fire?

Her hand shook and she couldn't think, let alone form a word strong enough in her mind. Paul reared back, free from her hold. Instead of igniting his own glove in an oblivion made just for her, his fingers fumbled on his wrist then at his neck. He tossed his helmet aside.

Nel no longer heard screams through the coms. Just howling air and the crunch of sand when the helmet came to a stop. Paul's skin pinked, blistered, blackened. He sank to his knees, mouth moving. It looked like an apology. Instead of words, blood splattered across her face.

Nel's world sizzled into oblivion. Maybe it was the coms. Maybe the roaring of her own heart in her ears. Maybe her last shred of sanity had crawled from her brain and exploded behind her eyes. Hands pulled at her, this time dragging her to safety. Through the blood already dried on the glass of her helm she glimpse a crowd around Paul's body. Someone—a medic, perhaps—plugged something into her wrist. All her visuals dimmed to a soothing purple except for the space directly in front of her eyes, which was now filled with the concerned brown face of one of the medical personnel.

"Is he alright?" In the wake of so much sound her voice was rough and hitching.

The medic shined a light in her eyes, back and forth. "Did you lose consciousness?"

"No. I don't think so. Is he okay?"

"Do you have any pain?"

"Just my throat. Feels like I smoked a pack and slept someplace I shouldn't have." She swallowed past what, for once, was a literal lump. It might be an absurd question, but it seemed worse not to ask. "He's dead, isn't he?"

"Humans can't survive in this atmosphere. It's toxic to us, has properties similar to napalm."

"Oh fuck." Nel's stomach churned. "I think I'm going to be sick." *What if I puke in my suit?* It had always been a funny, childish question. Now she wished she knew.

The medic checked her wrist. "Ty che blyad? You don't have a port?"

"I'm from Earth." She clenched her teeth against the nausea. "Just give me a minute."

"Nel!" Lin's voice cut through the static of coms and trauma. "Nel, are you alright?" The tall woman slid to her knees beside the archaeologist. "I heard the screaming, and your voice and I thought—"

"I'm alright." Nel's suited hand found Lin's and squeezed. "But Paul's not."

"Letnan, I need to finish triage."

"I can do it." Lin brushed off the medic's words, hovering over Nel. As much as the archaeologist hated clinging, Lin's worry blocked out the mangled corpse better than any helmet tint.

Nel tried to stand. A yelp jumped from her lips when a line of fire shot up her arm. "Let him help, Lin."

The medic turned his attentions to her right arm. "Dislocated radius. We'll take care of this up in the med bay." He rocked back on his heels. "Are you able to walk?"

Nel tested her legs and nodded. "Lin, can you walk with me?"

"Of course." Even through their suits, Lin's hand squeezed, tight and constant and familiar. "I've got you, love."

Nel took a shaking step toward the lab, then another. Everything trembled in the wake of adrenaline. Squeezing back, she picked the mission-wide channel. "All personnel this is Dr. Bently. I need to speak with all officers in the lab immediately. Everyone else return to your dorm." She hated how her voice shook, but she forced iron into her tone. "Samsara is on lockdown."

THIRTEEN

Nel didn't bother knocking when she and Lin reached Greta's office. "You said we can send files between us and *Odyssey*, yes?"

"Please, come in, make yourself at home," the Communications Kapten drawled.

Nel glared. "Not the time. I need to get a message through to Dr. Alvarez. Code: MAJORTOM79."

Greta stared at the red-brown splotches on the suit Nel hadn't bothered to doff yet. "That's an emergency evac code. What's going on?"

"You didn't hear?"

"Hear what? I've had my ears jacked into the feeds from the station since you last graced my doorway. I had to mute everything else to focus."

Nel slumped against the doorway. "There's been an accident. Something happened to Kolonel Udara de Lellis, the geologist—"

"I know who Paul is. Is he okay?"

"He's dead," Nel growled. She had no idea if the two were close, but she couldn't handle everyone else's grief right now. She had to focus on keeping the rest of the crew safe. "I'm drafting an emergency missive to *Odyssey* and getting my team the fuck off this rock. I'm trying to get a bead on when our evac ship might be ready."

"Understood." Greta leaned forward, dark eyes wide and focused on the two largest screens. "Unless you want it personal I have a basic emergency message I can get out in 5, but no promises on a response—"

"That's perfect. I don't need one. They just need to know we're coming." She turned to go, swaying slightly, then paused. "Were you close?"

"Nah, just digi-chess buddies. Still sucks."

Nel didn't know what digi-chess was, but nodded anyways. "Thanks. I'll let you know if I need anything else."

Greta rocked back in her chair. "Do I gotta go to the briefing?"

The archaeologist shook her head, "Just work on this, please. I'm just going to try and convince everyone to go too."

"Good. I don't like people."

Lin was waiting in the hall when Nel slid the door shut again. Her full lips were pursed. "You need to go to the med-bay."

"I've got a mess-hall filled with people wanting answers and I need to make sure the rest of my team and the other teams are safe. My damn arm can wait."

"It's not just your arm—you need to get checked out for trauma and whatever else. Have you thought about infection?"

Nel faltered and stopped. Fear hammered in her heart again. "What?"

"You're right. We don't know what happened to him, what made him do what he did. But he thought killing himself was better than the alternative and now you're covered in his blood."

"It's not a contagion." Options flashed through Nel's mind in single bursts: *Lock-down. Evacuation. Quarantine. Please, dear god, let it not be a contagion.*

"You don't know what it is."

"We'll I'll just try my best not to kiss anyone then," she snapped, shoving past Lin and heading to the mess hall.

"Yeah, cause you're so good at that," Lin muttered.

One. Two. Nel drew a breath and didn't respond. They were all on edge, and shitty comments weren't going to help anything. Tense conversation emanated from the mess hall, and Nel swallowed hard. She was getting a bit sick of having to tell her crew someone had died because of their digging.

"Alright," she began, tromping into the room. "I'll answer questions in a second. Officer Paul de Lellis is dead. At around 1540 he was doing routine samples on the north of the site and something caused him to panic. When I went to check on him, he attacked me and then removed his helmet. Exposure to the native atmosphere caused his death. We don't yet know what caused him to react this way, but I'm hoping medical and communications will help determine that.

"Our priority right now, however, is the safety of the rest of the crew. I realize I really only have authority over my department, but I'm hoping the rest of you will see the sense." She clenched her fist against the inevitable backlash. "I'm evacuating Samsara, effective immediately."

"This isn't up to you—"

She didn't even look at the speaker. "You weren't there, I know what I saw and Kapten Wagner is sending my evac code to the *Odyssey*. Now if the rest of you want to stay and endanger your teams, you go right ahead, but I'm not making that mistake." She swallowed hard. "Not again."

"I just don't think it's something that's gonna affect us," Paul's second-in-command explained. Her voice was flat. "That shit was in his head. As in, imaginary."

Nel frowned. "What makes you say that?"

"The whole afternoon he was muttering about his suit audio malfunctioning, about a noise."

"A noise?" Nel looked down at the Geiger counter, bagged and laid on the table. It was decorated with a spray of blood.

"Yeah. Said he heard a buzzing."

"The comm feedback was messing with his ears, I know that. I think violent suicide is a bit of a leap from having a hard time sleeping."

"You'd be surprised," Lin offered. "People get weird on missions far from home. Out in the Void."

Nel shot her a glare. Of all people, she didn't expect Lin to take the other side. *There're no sides. It's a discussion.* "That's valid, but I talked to him. And it strikes me as out of character."

"With all due respect, Dr. Bently, but as someone on his team, I think we'd have a better idea. He had a pre-existing condition, was overwhelmed and missing home and I agree, something broke him. But I don't think it was an alien disease, or secret audio frequency. I think it was stress."

The exhaustion in her voice made Nel pause. That same exhaustion was in her own voice. Those same shadows clung under her eyes and weighed her words. She blinked at the crowded mess hall, feeling foolish. "Alright. But I'd still like to err on the side of safety. I have Communications looking for a ride and trying to get ahold of *Odyssey*. Hopefully those of you who don't want to evac will refrain from writing up Disciplinary Reports on those that do."

"Understood, Bently." The geology officer's arms were crossed and the muscles in her jaw worked in an effort not to say more.

"May I have a word with you on your way to the med bay?" Lin asked.

Nel winced. It was the professional version of saying they needed to talk and she liked it just about as much. "Of course." Turning her attention back to the crowd, she offered, "If you have any questions, please let me know."

The med bay was small, a few doors down from Zachariah's office. One of the cubicles was already shut and dark, the door glowing faintly with the symbols for biohazard. Presumably it held Paul's body. The bay beside it was open, dimly lit with gold, though the number of wires and tubes and tanks on the wall negated the soothing light.

Lin slid the door shut behind them, mouth thin and face pale. "You need to take a minute. You're overreacting—Paul lost his senses and panicked and now he's dead."

"It wasn't just panic, Lin. There was something else going on. Maybe Coms or Medical will be able to tell, but it wasn't just panic. And I'm not overreacting—a man just chemically burned himself to death in front of me, I think I'm having a perfectly natural reaction!" Guilt dragged at her limbs. *Why didn't I calm him down? Why didn't I speak up sooner?* "Look, you were so focused on me getting examined, maybe you should get lost so they can make sure I won't infect the whole base," Nel growled.

"I don't give a fuck about the base!" Frustration laced Lin's words. "I thought you were going to die!

"What?" Nel was exhausted and without an immediate task, pain blurred her thoughts.

"Nel, all I heard was Paul screaming, and you going after him. And then you were screaming too. When I got there you were covered in blood—which I didn't know wasn't yours." Her lip trembled, and the hands clenched at her side shook. "I thought you were going to die. And I'm still not sure you won't. And I don't care about a contagion, I just want you to be safe."

It was all very touching to hear, but Nel wasn't in the mood for romance. "I'm sorry I scared you, but I can't really afford to worry about me right now. We have a crew who might be affected by whatever got Paul."

Lin looked down and finally nodded. "I'll let you be then. But please don't forget it's not just the crew up here. It's us."

Nel looked down at her hands, realizing she was still half-dressed in her atmosuit. She didn't know what to do with Lin's emotions, and knew distantly that would be an argument of its own later. "Yeah."

Lin hovered in the doorway for a moment, then disappeared. The door to the cubicle beside Nel's opened then shut and the same medic as before peeked in. Sorrow and fatigue clung to their eyes.

"Evening, Dr. Bently." They pinched the bridge of their nose. "Let's get you out of that suit."

"Hello Dr. Haas. Are you going to run a full panel on me?"

Their brows rose as they rubbed the liquid gloves onto their hands. "Goodness me, whatever for?"

Nel shrugged, attempting to tug her suit from her arms without further damaging her elbow. It proved impossible and after an undignified yelp, she allowed Haas to help. "Contagions. I don't know. I got covered in his blood."

Haas shook their head and sank into the seat beside the exam table. "Whatever was in that blood—if there was anything—died when it hit the atmosphere.

"I mean, if it was here in the first place, wouldn't—" Nel stopped when she saw the doctor shaking their head.

"Viruses and bacteria are often highly specialized. If a contagion can survive within the human body, it would be unlikely to survive on Samsara without an incubator. It's possible, of course, but highly unlikely. That's why human remains are generally not dangerous to the living. Your suit protected you, and by the time you came in physical contact with his blood, it was inert. I know because we just spent 20 minutes trying to get a viable sample from him."

"You sure?" As much as Nel didn't love Lin's fixation on disease, the other woman had made her more nervous than she was willing to admit. "Sure as a scientist can be. Now let's get your arm looked at."

They helped her slip the rest of her suit off, glancing at her left wrist. "You considering getting a port?"

Nel shuddered. "The whole idea squeams me. But you lot seem pretty keen on them."

Haas shrugged. "Yes, but it's out of the convenience. The fastest treatment in intravenous, and ports help with that. Plus all the other uses — quick transmission of inoculations, stimulants, routine meds, hormone replacement and so forth. You have a personalized code, so someone can't pop something in while you're sleeping—though doctors have a universal override code."

Nel made a face. She hadn't even considered the ports as an easy assassination vector. "I'll think about it," she lied.

Haas must have seen the lie on Nel's face, as they snorted and didn't press the issue further. "I'll need to pop this back into place—I'm surprised you haven't fainted yet, this injury takes its toll."

"I crossed a couple states with a fucked ankle and frost-bitten toes. This is temporary." Nel looked away as the doctor fished a small syringe from a drawer. The needle stung, then heat and cold eased through her joint. "Still appreciate the painkillers."

"Save it for afterward. It only takes the edge off." Haas tilted their head, voice changing slightly as they began a recording "Beginning treatment of dislocation of left radial head in Dr. Nel Bently. Analgesic administered at..." Haas glanced at their wrist, which sported more elaborate version of the average port and suit-control set up, "1714. Closed reduction to begin shortly, assisted by Dr. Julius." They tapped a finger, outfitted with a mobile keyboard, and their voice echoed through the medical PA system. "Dr. Julius to med-bay 3, to assist."

A second doctor stepped in a moment later, offering Nel a faint smile. "Evening," she greeted. "Given your records I'm mildly surprised this is the first we've seen you."

Nel laughed softly, "Me too, I guess."

Dr. Julius cupped Nel's arm, which the archaeologist found she could no longer move. "I haven't gotten a chance to ask about your journey on the powerlines—we're so used to heavily prepared missions, mostly because a trip into space without prep involves death."

Nel recounted the highlights, knowing full well the question was mostly designed to distract her from the ache and pull as they put her radius back into place. She only looked over when they covered her joint in a thick gel that turned to firm rubber at the touch of an electrode.

"All set?" she asked.

Haas raised another syringe. "Just got some stem-build and something to reverse the paralysis and you're free to go. Not that I think it will be an issue, but no digging for three weeks, even after the cast is gone."

Nel snorted. "If I have my way, no one will be digging until we know more."

Dr. Julius excused herself, and Haas carefully injecting her, thoughtful frown in place. "I didn't mean to listen in, but I heard what Letnan First Class Nalawangsa said, about you overreacting."

"I'm sorry to use this space for private conversations," Nel offered, too tired to be embarrassed.

"On the contrary, this is Medical—every conversation we have here is private. But would you be interested in some advice?"

"Relationship advice? I suppose I'm in the deep end regardless, and I've heard drowning doesn't look like drowning."

Haas's laugh was soft. "Professional advice. I support your choice to lock-down the site and give everyone the space to process alone or without the pressures of work. But out here death isn't the same as it is on Earth. Missions have casualties on occasion. Most of us aren't taught the same fear, the same clawing desperation to avoid it at all costs. I think some of what you read as apathy is actually acceptance. We grieve, surely, but the most extreme reactions—angry outbursts and deep depressions—are often tempered."

"I see." It was Nel's turn to frown. When they were done, Nel followed them out to the galley that served as the medical bay's main office. "Thanks for your work."

"Of course," Haas smiled in that gentle, parental way. "If you have trouble sleeping let me know and I'll give you something for the pain."

"Will do." She slipped upstairs, half expecting Lin to be waiting for her. Her room was thankfully deserted. Nothing could be done until they got through to *Odyssey,* nothing other than waiting.

Nel stripped her electromesh suit off and ducked into the cleansing station. *What I wouldn't give to stand under scalding water and forget about everything for a few precious minutes.* Instead, she rubbed the oily space equivalent of dry shampoo over her skin, scrubbing with the soft bristles on the other side of the bar. It certainly cleaned, but it did little for her mental state.

When she was through, she slumped into her computer chair and queued up a video from her mother. She didn't care that she promised only to watch one a week. Death warranted an extra. It was a longer one, her mom giving a tour of her newly redone room. Grays weren't really Nel's favorite, especially after being surrounded by them on the space station, but Mindi chose a nice warm one that almost looked purple. The lavender she embroidered on the curtains helped too. When her mom glanced back at the camera Nel saw she had gotten new highlights, and her bangs were trimmed. She smiled.

When the screen faded to black, she stared at the darkness. Hissing. Yawning night. Anger flashed for a second, followed by dragging fatigue. She shook the pitching feeling away. *Follow the smoke.* But she was too tired to think, much less do any sort of introspection.

On the shelf next to the two boxes containing Mikey and her father's cremains sat a tiny vial, untouched since Zachariah prescribed them. "I guess it couldn't hurt."

She glanced at the back and dropped a few under her tongue. They tasted like dust. Tucking her blanket around her chin, she curled on her side and stared at the boxes. It took years for her father's ghost to stop answering her. Mikey seemed more willing to move on. *Or I'm less ready for him to.* It was complicated when the ghost was really all in her head.

"Looks like every dig I run is cursed. Or maybe it's just me who's cursed. There's a guy coming to see you. Maybe he's already there. But his name is Paul. Paul de Lellis. If you get the chance, you guys should chat. Ask him where he's from. I dare you." Sleep edged into her voice, rasping and soft at once. "I never thought to ask—what's it like? Dying?"

She fell asleep listening to foreign wind howl, waiting for Mikey to answer.

FOURTEEN

Greta's voice crackled over Nel's personal communication, jerking her from heavy sleep. "Bently, there's a transport inbound."

Nel groaned and rolled out of bed, cracking her head on the bedside shelf. "Fuck." She peered blearily for a clock, then felt for her phone. "Shit. Right. Space. Computer: what time is it?"

"0254"

"Ugh." Nel jabbed at the blinking light to reply. "You get through to *Odyssey?* They sending people to evac us?"

"Technically," came Greta's reply. "I had to find transport on my own, using sub-level frequencies due to the black out, but we've got a ride."

"Awesome, thank you. You're the best Coms person I've met."

"I'm probably the only one," she snarked back.

"When should I have the crew ready by?"

"0945. I've forwarded missives to everyone. You might want to look over what 'essential belongings' means for your artifacts."

"Damnit," Nel muttered. She knew what that meant, "Will do, thanks."

"Not a problem. Gretatron out."

Wincing at the throbbing pain in her elbow, she lurched into her bathroom and stared at the mirror. Lin's concern and her crew's skepticism weighed heavily. *Should I have waited to talk to the station before using my code?*

"Computer: read instructions for flight leaving Samsara at 0945," she demanded, using the lukewarm water in the cup by her bed to scrub sleep from her face. As she suspected, "essential" did not include sentimental items or artifacts of any nature.

Once she was dressed, she updated the site map and finalized the notes left undone in the wake of yesterday's tragedy. She added a few suggestions, which whomever returned to this place—if it wasn't her, as she hoped—ought to take. More likely, the whole lot of them would ignore anything she had to say. *Knock that off. Pity becomes no one, Bently.*

By the time her notes were done and she donned her electromesh again, she heard the officers next door beginning their day. "Computer: Call Letnan First Class Lin Nalawangsa."

"Morning," Lin's voice was rough and low from sleep. "I see we've a flight to catch."

"Yeah, and I'm having second thoughts."

"I didn't think there was a choice," Lin paused silence a bloom before her voice filled through Nel's room again, "Why don't you come down here?"

"Once I'm done packing. About a minute." Nel bit her lip, realizing she didn't actually know which room Lin used. "Ah, which one?"

Lin snorted, "Seventy-six."

"Gotcha, see you in a sec." Nel shoved her mostly unpacked box back into the sleek metal case and carefully wrapped the boxes of cremains again. "You guys are really getting in the miles, eh? Promise it'll stop soon." Maybe it was a lie, but a woman could dream.

When Lin's door slid aside, Nel's brows rose. "I didn't realize my space was so…spacious." She glanced over with a wink, "Though up here isn't everything?"

Lin rolled her eyes. "If you invited yourself down here at six in the morning to make awful jokes before I've had my coffee, maybe we aren't as compatible as I thought."

"What," Nel's smile widened, "Did you do our star-charts?"

Lin groaned and flopped onto her bed. "You're awful. What did you want to talk about?"

Nel perched herself on the corner of the bed, staring at her feet, encased in reinforced electromesh. She missed her boots. "I told you I was having second thoughts about my decision."

Lin turned, focusing the full attention of her dark eyes on Nel. "And are you?"

"A bit—I think I'm feeling the out-of-my-element thing a bit more than usual. My work as an archaeologist and my PhD is something I have a lot of confidence in. For a long time it was how I defined myself, and I think in some ways it still is. But up here I'm hardly the most educated, and certainly not the most experienced in this niche. Aside from the fact that half of them haven't dug in actual dirt before now."

"Did someone say something?"

Nel shot her a glare. "Yeah—you. And half the people down here. And Dr. Haas."

"So Dr. Haas doesn't think it's a contagion?"

"You think I'd be here sharing air with you if they did? No, they just mentioned something about death and how you guys process it versus how Terrestrial folk do. And honestly, it resonated with me. How I initially reacted aside, do you think I overreacted?"

"You're asking me?" Lin's delicate brows rose in surprise.

"Well, yeah. You know me and I care about your opinion," Nel explained, surprised she even had to.

"I guess I wasn't sure about that last part. I don't think you overreacted. I think I would make the same choice, but perhaps not as quickly, and with more thought and conversation involved. But I understand why you did."

Nel looked away. "I think that's part of what Haas meant. And Zachariah. I think a lot of people believe I'm not handling Mikey's death very well. Or at all. And that's all this is."

"And is it?" Lin's tone was gently probing, but not accusatory.

Greta's voice burst through the base-wide speaker: "Evac in T-40 minutes. Loading in T-20"

"You people are your countdowns," Nel sighed. "No. I see why it looks that way, but it's not. Wait," she sat up, head cradled in her hands. "Maybe it is, but not like that. I'm doing this because of him—because I should have put a stop to Esperando VII before it got that bad. Because I should have listened to my gut when it was screaming someone could get hurt. The difference is, I thought it would be me. And I'd be fine with that. Not in a self-harm way," she quickly corrected, "I'm past that point in my queer-self-doubt. But because it's my responsibility so I'll take the fall."

"You had a feeling about that site?"

"Yeah. I even told Mikey about it. Likened it to a feeling I had walking this path on campus just before a girl got raped there. Call it instinct, whatever, but I had it. And I listened in college. But hubris made me ignore it in Chile. I'm trying not to make that same mistake. Even if it means burning rocket fuel to haul our asses out of here."

Lin smiled. "You didn't seem so sure about it yesterday."

"I guess I just needed a good night's sleep."

Lin's hand brushed over her knee. "I know you think you're up here as part of some big con, but you're really good at your job, and knowing when to make certain calls, and when to push through. That's why I recommended you."

Nel tilted her chin up to capture Lin's mouth with hers. "So it wasn't the longest distance booty call ever?

Mirth hummed from Lin's lips and warmed Nel's body. "Not as such, no."

"T-35 minutes."

"Shit. Alright, I'll see you down there." Nel shoved herself up, cradling her elbow. In the doorway she turned, "Thanks for listening. I know I'm not the best about sharing."

Lin's slight smile broadened. "Neither am I. See you at boarding."

Twenty minutes later, Nel slid her case into the narrow cargo bay of the transport ship. It crouched on its spindly landing gear, a mantid poised to strike. The ship's crew had the decency to activate a temp shield for boarding, so Nel only braved the wind for the 20 yard walk from the main shield. She edged around the side of the ship to the boarding ramp, only to be ushered from her randomly-chosen seat to one beside the cockpit.

"Up here, Dr. Bently," the pilot offered, gesturing. "You've got to say the code for the ship's computer to authorize the evac."

She frowned. "What if the person who originally mandated an evac dies before take off?"

The pilot frowned at her, jabbing at buttons during his pre-flight check. "Then another officer uses theirs or we do emergency override. Just push that and activate when I say," he explained, thumb jerking at an ominous button protected by a plastic cover.

Feeling chastised, Nel sat back and buckled her six-point harness around her space suit. A few taps muted the ubiquitous countdown, relegating it to a blinking display on her helmet's glass. *If only this was like getting my wisdom teeth yanked, when they let me play music.*

"Dr. Bently, your code please."

Without opening her eyes she flipped open the cover on the button and pressed it. "Computer: Authorize Evacuation Code: MAJORTOM-seven-niner."

"Evacuation Authorized. Ignition."

Engines grumbled. Her nerves frayed to a single strand. *Please don't explode.* Landing gear ground into launch configuration. Around them wind roared as the shields disappeared. Then the windblown orange surface fell away and they left Samsara behind.

Despite the emergent nature of their departure, Nel didn't expect the half dozen people awaiting them at the Arrivals bay. She dropped her bag to awkwardly shake Alvarez's hand with her left hand, shrugging away the concern at her cast. "It's not as bad as it looks," she explained. "When's debriefing?"

"Now, if your officers are well enough." His gaze followed the slim aluminum coffin gliding behind the evacuees. "Sooner would be best."

"Now is good," Nel answered, falling into step behind him. "My missive made it through?"

"Took a fair bit of our Communication's processing, but it did indeed."

"Lines still aren't open?"

"Local frequencies went online a few hours ago. We're still waiting for the Terrestrial satellites to come back. Suspecting it's not just an issue with *Odyssey*."

Dread's bony grip tightened on her intestines. "Right. I've suspected interference for a few weeks now."

He raised a dark hand. "Save it for the official debriefing. I'd like everything on record."

"Understood. The sooner we get this ironed out, the sooner we can get back on Samsara."

Something shadowed his expression. "We'll discuss it."

Why does this feel like getting my site permits revoked all over again? When Lin peeled off with the other lower ranks, Nel forced her shoulders back. She didn't like thinking of Lin as her liaison, but she couldn't deny the woman felt like her safety net in this alien world.

"Just the officers?"

Dr. Alvarez palmed open the door to the same conference room as their briefing a month ago. "We find it best for clarity's sake."

Nel sank into her seat, massaging the spot just below her cast. After the jostling ride from Samsara, her nagging ache spiked into biting pain. It was still far less than the other various dislocations and breaks she had experienced on earth, but even with advanced medical tech, a thirty-six year old didn't bounce back like a teen. *Is that thirty-six circadial, now?*

"Dr. Bently, as both witness to the event and the officer who evac'd, why don't we begin with your testimony."

Testimony was a legal word, heavy with blame and criminal weight. It implied there was a right and wrong. "Sure. If I might bring up my notes?"

"From memory, please. We'll compare your notes later."

She swallowed. "Of course. The event occurred yesterday approximately 1600. We were almost ready to end work for the day. I was mapping unexcavated structures along the ridge—manually, as well as digitally. You can check my field notes as to my exact location, but I was standing on the third spire. Based on a brief conversation, I believe Paul—Dr. de Lellis—was conducting core samples for our department at the anomalous structure not noted on previous maps of this area of Samsara."

"And at what time did you note signs of distress?" Dr. Alvarez asked. Curiosity hung on his level voice, but it wasn't concern.

"Screams, Kolonel Alvarez. He started screaming. It was approximately at 1545." She recounted the heart-pounding minutes that followed, stopping to take a sip of water when her voice cracked as she recalled him ripping his helmet off.

"At that time medics and several other personnel arrived, including Letnan First Class Nalawangsa and Dr. Chelala, Paul's second in command."

"And why was Letnan Nalawangsa present?"

Nel honestly tried not to roll her eyes, but judging by Alvarez's thinning lips, she did not succeed. "Because she was concerned for me. Apparently it was unclear, via the coms alone exactly who was in distress."

"I see."

Perhaps his displeasure stemmed more from Lin's inability to stay at her post, rather than whatever he knew of their personal relationship. "And at this point you called for a site lock-down, followed by the use of your Emergency Code to trigger Evacuation Protocol."

"That's correct. It should be noted that I did meet some skepticism about my decision and the reasons behind it."

"But no one attempted an official override."

"Not that I'm aware, no."

He turned to Dr. Haas. "And Dr. Haas, you and Dr. Julius performed the postmortem examination of Dr. de Lellis?"

"Indeed."

"And did you find reason to corroborate or negate Dr. Bently's decision to evacuate?"

A man's dead, for fuck's sake, Nel seethed. She was well used to peer evaluation, but this was feeling less and less like a debriefing.

"Though we found no immediate cause for alarm, or concern for the safety of base personnel as a whole, I believe Dr. Bently acted with sound mind and appropriate priorities."

Nel shot Dr. Haas a grateful look, though they didn't look her way.

"That's not what I asked."

Dr. Haas leaned forward, as if proximity to whatever device recorded this whole affair lent their words more weight. "Our findings were inconclusive as far as the cause for Dr. de Lellis's distress and resulting suicide, accidental or otherwise. As such, I would corroborate Dr. Bently's concern. She acted with her team's safety in mind."

Silence filled the room for a moment, then Chelala leaned forward. "I'd like to add some information on Paul's condition in the hours leading up to his death."

"Continue, doctor."

"He suffered from tinnitus, like many from mining colonies. Comm feedback often aggravated his symptoms, which in turn affected his sleep and mental state. Among other, smaller, issues, he made a mistake about a week before his death that cost us an entire sample set. His response to being called on the mistake was volatile, as many people in the lab at the time can attest. I believe, while regrettable, his death was due to a mental break caused by stress and exhaustion, not some alien contagion as Dr. Bently seems to insist."

"If you look at the coms record, you'll see Paul brought up a buzzing that increased as he approached the sample location. A buzzing. Not static. I'd also like to note I radioed Kapten Wagner on the first day of excavation regarding feedback I experienced in my coms—most pertinent, a buzzing sound. I find the fact that our observations coincided with your communications blackout highly suspicious."

"You can't be suggesting something on Samsara made Paul kill himself and wiped out *Odyssey's* coms without anyone noting its presence. Many Terrestrial personnel experience discomfort when exposed to coms for the first time," Chelala interjected, still refusing to meet her eyes.

Nel's inability to hold her tongue was about as famous—or infamous, rather—as her dedication to archaeology. As such, the shock on Alvarez's face when she surged to her feet came as a bit of a surprise. "Isn't that exactly what happened the first time? Your shit went down without warning? Honestly, I'm a bit tired of hearing my observations are because I'm ill-prepared for your technology. I heard a buzz. So did Dr. de Lellis. We're both admittedly more sensitive to feedback—me due to inexperience and he due to his pre-existing tinnitus.

"Sensitive. Not hallucinating. Perhaps we are best suited to noting an issue that others, more desensitized to background static, aren't. Dismissing this as simply a side effect of disability and inexperience isn't just offensive—though it is—it's irresponsible." Her breath heaved and a biting edge hardened her voice. "Again, with all due respect."

"I understand your concern, especially given the events at your previous Terrestrial site. However, I believe our resources are better spent on regaining contact with Earth, as opposed to cleaning up a mismanaged site. Evacuation was an extreme measure for what appears to be a regrettable, but unforeseeable tragedy. Excavation on Samsara Locus Alpha will renew, following an investigation. As of now, Dr. Bently, you are removed from duty, and your rank is temporarily suspended until further notice. When excavations renew, we will determine whether they will be under your direction or another archaeologist more suited to our needs. Each of you will be notified if your further testimony is needed. Dismissed."

Nel's temper exploded with the finality of his words. Her jaw ached with the effort to contain her vitriol. "But I'm going on record," she spat, "Ignoring the possibility that this wasn't an accident is a mistake. Last time I didn't listen to my gut, a man died. If you're not careful, someone else will."

FIFTEEN

"I heard you made a lot of friends during debriefing."

"Fuck off," Nel spat, slamming her palm on her door's panel to let Lin in. "I'm so fucking pissed."

"That's apparent," she noted, her hand wrapping Nel's shaking one. "We're gonna be up here awhile. I'm in as much trouble as you, frankly. I thought you could use some unwinding."

"Doubtful. And I'm not in the mood, at all."

"I wasn't suggesting sex."

Nel stalked to the window instead of answering. Between the monochrome environment and the ever changing unfamiliar sky, she had no idea if this was her same room or not. "What did you do wrong?"

"Listen to you, apparently."

Nel groaned. "Once again, my mouth is getting everyone in trouble, not just my sorry insubordinate ass."

"I think you've got a lovely ass, insubordinate or not."

Nel snorted, but didn't turn around. "I didn't mean to get you in trouble. Is there like, three strikes and you're out?"

"You didn't. I'm capable of making my own choices." Lin frowned. "Strikes?"

"Fuck, what kind of lesbian are you, that you don't know about softball or baseball? Didn't you see *League of Their Own?*" She raked a hand through her hair, wishing it was long enough to anxiously yank.

Lin shrugged. "You're speaking gibberish again."

Her social ignorance was temporarily distracting. "Ok, so movie night whenever we are back on Earth."

"You know we have access to Terrestrial media on the *Odyssey,* right?" Lin asked, tugging Nel a step closer to the door. "After I show you this, we can spend our probation catching me up on films I apparently need based on my sexuality and showing you every good sci-fi you've avoided."

Nel groaned, head rocking back to exaggerate her rolling eyes. "I think I've had enough science fiction for an entire lifetime, Lin."

"On the contrary, Nel, all of this is technically missing the 'fi' part of sci-fi." She tugged the archaeologist's hand again, firmly. "If I promise to let you complain the whole way there, can I please show you something? You need some fresh air."

Nel finished fastening her electromesh. "Yeah, fine." She hadn't realized she was complaining so much, but when she thought back on their last few conversations, it was clear who was doing the brunt of the bitching. Palming her door shut, she faltered. "Wait, fresh air? You gonna dump me out an airlock?"

"Not today," Lin's dark eyes narrowed with the contained delight of keeping a secret. It was a sweet look, on her usually reserved face, so Nel didn't press for details.

Instead, she took in the ship around her. Before she'd been overwhelmed by the novelty and distracted by the impending landing on Samsara. Now, stuck in the limbo of probation, she could relax enough to really absorb her surroundings. *Right, when was the last time I actually relaxed?* People bustled, and small inter-departmental drones ferried things between labs. Black conduits ran under the line of phosphorescence, like veins and neurons and lymph. *Symbiosis.*

"I think the intimacy of a space station, or ship, really helped you guys focus on sustainability. It's incredible, really. I mean, I recycle and all, but you guys—wow."

"I never thought of it as intimacy. It always seems like a necessity or desperation when planning. But I guess, yes, it's a type of intimacy." Lin's smile broadened and she glanced over. "I think you're really going to like where we're going."

"You gonna give me a hint?"

"You gonna pester me for one?"

Nel laughed, "I'm too tired to pester."

Lin stopped by a maintenance shaft door. "It'll take a few minutes to get down, since we're working against gravity."

"Not like I have anywhere to be," Nel muttered, following her onto the narrow platform. She lapsed into silence, drifting between distracted wonder and introspection while Lin keyed in their destination and the elevator hummed into motion.

"I'm taking you to the station's core. Where all our systems connect and recycle waste, remains, scrub the air, and so forth." Apparently, Lin was as incapable of keeping a secret as Nel usually was having one kept.

"Awesome, I like cool new science. Though," she shrugged, "I've been a bit overwhelmed by the amount of it."

"I think this will be different, actually."

After another minute the elevator slowed, stopped by "This one us?"

"Yep," Lin answered, brushing past her to authorize entry before moving back to let Nel go first.

The door opened on darkness. Air drifted past Nel's face, soft, entirely different from the carefully measured atmosphere pumped through the station. Downy hairs on Nel's neck rose, goosebumps freckling her arms as if ghosted with breath.

For the first time in months the animal part of her blinked into wakefulness. It was cool, damp almost. Softness dipped beneath her foot. Light glimmered beyond the ragged black lace of branches. Tucked within the center of *Odyssey of Earth,* was a pristine pocket of life. Longing flooded her heart.

Oxygen. Nel's hand met the soft serration of ferns. *Waste recycling.* Her electromesh incased toes curled into black loam. There was no path, just twisting moss and curled roots and tangling ivy. Massive redwoods gave way to lush cloud forest. Misters from the floor and carefully placed hanging pipe system increased the humidity. She took a knee, bare hands pressing into the soil. It was almost warm, as if baked under summer sun. "I'm in a forest?"

"The entire core is a forest," Lin's whisper curled around Nel's ear with a gust of plumeria. She followed Nel's winding steps, letting her worship in peace.

Nel stepped from high tropics into the brilliant gold and copper dusting of oak and maple. Some of the fallen leaves were hauled away to be used as bedding for the tanks of insects that served as the main protein source. She peered up through the stark branches. "What about sunlight?"

Lin pointed at a massive sphere that served as the very center of the ship, suspended between three pylons. "It's system evening right now, but during the day that radiates full-spectrum light."

"Basically this is the biggest basement grow op I've ever seen."

Lin chuckled, long fingers running down Nel's arm. "Basically. Air is cycled from exterior layers of the station and replaced with fresh, the trees and microbes in the soil recycling waste—including remains." Her smile crumpled when she met Nel's eyes. "I'm sorry, is this too much?"

Nel didn't bother to wipe the tears from her cheeks. She took another deep breath. Pine and soil. The sharp scent of fallen leaves underfoot and the pinch of wintergreen. Emotion broke her voice, but she didn't care. "It smells like home."

"It does to me too, you know," she replied, looking up at the trees. "Brilliant piece of engineering."

The archaeologist shook her head. "I studied humans for thirteen years, just to understand why we do what we do. Needing to touch dirt and breathe proper air full of moisture and scent, and—" Tilting her head towards the clump of grass, her smile widened. "And the sound of crickets. You might have left the planet 13 or 15,000 years ago, but you found a way to walk on Earth. This? This isn't just efficiency, or engineering, or sustainability." She brushed a hand over the rough, shaggy bark of a towering red oak, letting a sob lurch from her chest. "This is homesickness."

"You're an officer—technically, even if you're suspended from your current assignment. You can come down here any time. When you need grounding."

Nel turned in a slow circle, barely hearing the other woman. "I will. Thank you." She lowered her gaze from the protective boughs to Lin's eyes, dark in her luminous face. "I know I joke that you don't get it, don't get me, but I think you do. I just haven't been ready."

"No rush. I'm happy just being with you. "

"It's hard because he would have loved it up here. And I can't help but wonder if it should have been me." Thoughts of Paul blurred dangerously with memories of Mikey and Nel's heart was too naked to travel that road.

To her credit, Lin didn't answer, wrapping a strong arm over Nel's shoulders and pulling her against her chest. "Why don't we order dinner to our rooms and just spend the night not worrying about anything?"

"Sounds perfect."

"Plus, the way back is way more fun," Lin winked.

Nel snorted; she loved that the other woman had picked up that particular mannerism—but she knew better than to mention it. *She'd probably get to self conscious.* "Alright, I'm game."

Lin led her to where another door opened in the floor. Instead of an elevator, however, darkness filled the shaft when she cranked the hatch open. "This is how we always used to travel as kids, though our parents hated it. You like adrenaline, right?"

Nel peered at her, trying to gauge what Lin meant, exactly. "When it's not in response to screaming colleagues or exploding spaceships, or lost years."

Lin winced, squeezing Nel's hand. "Everything has been a bit of an overload lately, huh?"

"A bit," Nel deadpanned. "But I'm up for planned, fun adrenaline." The door slid open on a dark tube rising from the core to the outer shells. She peered into the dark depths. Flickering lights led along the sides. Her heart thundered between her ribs. A decade ago she would have plunged headlong into the dark, welcoming the rush, the roaring air, the thunder of blood in her veins as she surrendered to the inevitable. Now, she was a stranger in her own mind.

"Your suit will warn you, but I'll let you know when to engage the magnetic catch. Take a breath, take a step, and trust."

Why am I scared? Nel unlaced her hand from Lin's and jumped into the void.

WARNING! Her suit chimed in her mind, *Falling from high places can result in damage or expiration. Engage mag-catch.*

"Lin?"

"You're alright, trust me!"

Flickering lights became delicate lines of electric spider silk. Air whispered in her ears, fluttering in her hair. Weightlessness filled her body, and she felt, for a fleeting moment, utter freedom.

"Now!" Lin called, voice echoing slightly down the narrow cylinder.

Nel clenched her fists. *Suit: Engage mag-catch.* Around her the lights slowed their flickering as the electromagnets in her suit connected with those in the shaft.

Weight dragged on her muscles, as if gravity reversed, then she was weightless, suspended by the tiny field drifting between her suit and the walls. "Alright, I'm convinced, science is magic."

Lin giggled, drifting lower so the were eye-to-eye. It was rare that Nel wasn't craning to meet the 5'10" woman's gaze. Her peach lips curled in a slow smile before they eased over Nel's own. Her eyes fluttered shut, drifting weightless beside the other woman. Just breath and stillness. *Peace.*

The door snapped open, startling them apart. "¡Ay!" A scientist looked away, tan cheeks flushing as he looked away. "Sorry, my crate of entomology samples never arrived and I heard the noise and thought it got misdirected and—" He blinked. "It's against protocol to use transport chutes for travel."

"It's fine!" Lin promised, raising her hands to stop the nervous babble. "We'll be right on our way!" She grabbed Nel's hand and dragged her out of the shaft, belatedly reminding her to disengage the mag-catch. By the time they stumbled up to Lin's door, Nel was breathless with laughter. "Did you see his face?"

"He looked so offended! I never thought anyone would be happier to see a bag of dead insects than me."

Nel rolled her eyes, leaning on the wall while Lin slid her door shut behind them. Energy sang in her blood. "Oh it's happened to me plenty. Students, exes, women who were about to be exes, my mom at 3 am," she listed absently.

"You gave your mom trouble?"

"You didn't?

"Hardly. She was my best friend through much of it. We butted heads over Dar, of course. He spreads discord wherever he goes." Lin manually brought up the lights just enough for them to see. Unlike the other rooms, hers had a bit of personality—deep purple sheets, and small collected items—a flake from Los Cerros Esperando VII, a twisted hunk of metal and—

"Is this my bracelet?"

Lin's cheeks pinked and she looked down at the braided leather and metal beads. "Sorry. I snagged it when I left Chile. Take it back."

"I thought I lost it. And no, it looks nice here." Unnerved by the comfort she took in seeing their belongings together, Nel made a show of peering around the room. "You always stay in this one then?"

"Yeah, though I've gotten very good at knowing which tiny pieces of 'me' to pack. Wasn't able to bring any of it from the *Promise* to Earth though. You teased me so much for my clothes, but honestly I bought them all in Antofagasta a few days before we met."

Nel laughed, glancing absently at the menu Lin brought up on her computer. "This makes me miss Emilio"

"Sepulveda? The Founders leader? Why?"

"Ex-founders," Nel corrected. It wasn't as important as it had been before, though, the lines between good-guys and bad blurred beyond recognition. She bought a few seconds to think under the guise of picking a few items to eat. "Just the food and talk of Chile is all. He's, ah, he's been on my mind a lot. I see some parallels between this dig and my site in Chile. Just makes you think, you know? And with the coms down, I can't help but wonder if something's going on back home." She watched Lin's face carefully, but saw no suspicion. "Anyway, dinner."

"Right," Lin answered, typing in her own choices. When she had submitted it, she leaned back, sly grin in place. "We have about half an hour before it arrives—how about I lower the lights and turn on some music? Spend some time letting go?"

Nel wordlessly found the Civil Wars' "Dust to Dust" before tugging Lin closer. "It's going to take longer than half an hour to get me to let go." The surprised delight in the other woman's eyes sent heat shooting down her body.

"Better get started."

SIXTEEN

Dubious, blinking lights and the hum of electronics permeated the air of Greta's office. If Nel expected a high-tech massive version of the tiny cubicle on Samsara, she was sorely mistaken. The com's officer rubbed her bloodshot eyes, shooting the archaeologist a tired smile. "Got my message?"

"Why I'm here," Nel responded. "Though 'Fucked data: rm J 2105' is a bit hard to interpret. Is it a complaint or an invite to some weird sex party?"

Greta pretended to barf. "Nah, not me." She untangled a loose jack from the tangle by her left knee. She flipped her almost horizontal chair from supine to prone and pulled her main screen onto the ceiling—one of the few surfaces not studded with powerports and circuitry. "'Aight, so I compared the aud data from the day Paul passed to other times. The feeds were too garbled after the crash to get anything good, but once we got inside the shields there was no change. Nothing."

Nel sighed. "I mean I guess Occam's got me on this one—I just feel like the fact that I heard it means something."

"Lemme finish," She rubbed at the base of her ear where a wire jacked directly into her aural canal. "Compared his silence and feedback to yours." She opened the two feeds, showing Nel the map of the various frequencies.

"What am I looking at?"

"The background. I stripped voices from the feeds and compared. There's always feedback, weird blips, electronic farts, if you will."

"I won't," Nel interjected, smiling in spite of herself.

"Anywho, they're the same. Then, though, I compared it to other folks. This is where it gets funky." Her fingers splayed, black tattooed dots on her fingertips brushing along the holoscreen like beads of dew. "We've got everyone's feeds here. Whatcha see?"

Nel peered at the dozens of colored waves, the dips and arcs. "This low stuff."

"Yep. And you two are the only ones that got it."

"You know why yet?"

Greta shook her head. "I'm checking if you had any input that no one else got. But it looks like an auditory signal came in. Maybe turned on some loop."

"You have all the suit data or just the sound?"

"Just aud, but I can get the other shit if I ask. Even if Logistics won't fork it over, my bud Philharmonnica's got me. Eh?"

"Yes, Greta," Phil murmured through the main speakers. Nel couldn't tell if he sounded charmed or patient. "Morning, Dr. Bently. Welcome back."

"Morning, Phil. Thanks." she answered, wondering where she should look to greet the computer. "You got some kind of arrangement?"

"Nah, just old buds. I was one of the chief coms officer on the investigation when *Odyssey* went dark. Spent a lot of time scouring the aud from Ada's memory banks trying to figure out what went down. What you want me to do with the other data?"

"See if we were in the same area at the same time, somewhere we could have picked up background stuff. Maybe even where we boarded the transport—or when it blew apart." She froze, turning to Greta. "We were next to each other on that flight. First time I met him, really."

"I'm on it. Got a friend in trajectory who can run some sets for me."

"You have friends everywhere, Greta."

"Perks of the digi-chess team, baby. Never be lonely again."

Nel snorted, highly doubting she'd fit in on the digi-chess team. "So you're not the only one with access to this?"

"Two others are working the same problem, different angles. Also sure there's a forth double

201

checking my shit in case I'm in on the great Samsara comm crime."

"Do you think they'll find the same data?"

"I don't see how they couldn't if they looked. I mean it's right there. The best way to disprove someone is try and prove it right first, sometimes." She shrugged. "How I found it, honestly."

"You were trying to prove me right? That I'm not hearing shit?"

Greta glanced at her sidelong. "I actually like your dedication. It's not mindless, comes from somewhere with heart. And I kinda think you are. Hearing stuff." She inserted the aux port into her aural canal. "Difference is, I think what you're hearing is real. I'll send you another sex party invite when I've got the deets. Gretatron, out."

Nel smiled and showed herself out. Her mind churned with the image of those matching feeds. *Something happened, maybe even when the shields were down.*

She let herself into Lin's room, surprised the door opened for her. When no one answered, she glanced at the table by the bed. Lin had still been sleeping when Greta's message arrived. A projected note glowed on the surface:

Nel,

Went to burn off some energy and think about the next few weeks.

Make yourself at home <3

Nel found her tablet buried in a pile of clothes and pulled up the site maps. Thankfully, she had the foresight to save a copy to her private device. It wasn't as modular or high-res as the updated version, but she didn't care. A few seconds' searching give her the original map overlaid on the site. When she zoomed out, a second anomaly appeared on the edge of the screen. The spire Paul was investigating when he died had a twin. And it pierced the battered transport they crashed on Samsara's surface. *Something happened on that plane. Something no one's talking about.* She almost turned around to tell Greta her finding, but thought better of it. The coms officer was best left to analyze without bias.

But nothing said Nel had to sit back and let her have all the fun. She sank into the chair by Lin's faux window. "Computer: bring up all articles relevant to architecture and maps on Samsara."

Thunderous knocking interrupted Nel's reading two hours later, followed by the abrupt *hiss-shick* of the door opening and closing.

"You're not Lin."

Nel glanced up, frowning. "No I'm not." Last—and only—time she saw Dar he was a few hundred meters away under the glaring ship lights and through the haze of roiling atmosphere. The delicate arched black brows and broad nose and cheekbones, however, told her the man before her was indeed Lin's brother. "Dar, right?"

He shifted, imperious expression warring with confusion. "Yes. You'd be Annelise."

Nel scowled, shoving herself out of her chair and offering a hand. Imperious men were something with which she was too familiar. "It's Nel, actually. Or Dr. Bently, if you'd prefer."

After a second's hesitation he took her hand. "Komodor Muda Dar Nalawangsa."

"Ah, I never learned your rank," Nel dismissed. When he didn't continue, only smoothed and straightened the front of the long officer's robe over his suit, she prodded, "Lin's not here."

"Right." He glanced around, as if to check whether she was lying, and his sister was, in fact, tucked behind the collection of air plants hanging in the corner. "Did she say when she would be back?"

"No, just that she wanted to burn off some energy at the generation gym. Whatever that is."

"Gymnasium that generates power when used," he rattled off with impatience.

Nel understood why Lin didn't like him. "I can let her know you called."

"As if she'd return the favor," he spat. "I've been radioing her since she arrived here. Had to actually disembark and get my files stamped for transfer to *Odyssey* just to see her—despite our scheduled launch tomorrow."

I really couldn't care less, buddy. "Do you want to wait here?" She really wished he wouldn't.

"Please."

Damn. Retreating to her chair, she tried to return to her reading, but Dar's intensity was distracting, and he hadn't brought anything with which to occupy himself. "Did you, ah, bring a book or something?"

He rolled his head on his neck, hands still tapping. "I've been too busy to even pick up a new fiction aud or text. And after I heard about Paul I couldn't really."

Nel's distaste for the man paused, and she took a better look. A line marked where his lips thinned. Long fingers drummed on the chair's arm. Eyes, forced too-wide to hide the redness and swelling. *Oh.* "Oh, of course—you and he dated."

Dar's sharp eyes flicked to hers. "Where'd you hear that?"

"From Paul and Lin in passing. He asked after you," she offered, wondering at the defensiveness. Though homosexuality didn't seem taboo on the *Odyssey,* she wondered if it had been for Paul, with his Catholic upbringing.

The lines tightened, and Dar's gaze fell, hands shaking as he rubbed his temple. "We were almost married. Years ago. Before I was Komodor. I never met anyone like him—he was a beautiful mystery. I was a transport captain. Picked up ore and hydro from his colony. Tried to make it work, through job changes and cryo-jumps and lightyears and for a while, a long while, we succeeded. But when IDH taps you for promotion, you go."

"I know that feeling."

Dar looked up, startled, as if he had forgotten she was even there, listening. For a second he was perfectly still.

"Both the mystery and the IDH part," she whispered, an olive branch for his candor. "Lin's a bit of a mystery to me too. And as for the promotion—I'm here, aren't I?"

His laugh was sharp and bitter, just a bite shy of cruel. The finger resumed its tapping. An electric feedback flashed up his gloved with the motion. "She's something alright. You love her?"

Nel lowered her tablet to focus in earnest. She'd suffered through this line of questioning more times that she could count. She answered as she always did. "No idea. The only time I've loved people it hasn't been in the romantic sense. I'm not aromatic or anything, just takes me a long time to open up that way I guess."

His wide smile was Lin's. "I guess. But when my little sister said jump, a rocket ship didn't seem too high."

Nel let her teeth lend ferocity to her own grin, but didn't bother to elaborate. She wasn't into debating emotional semantics with anyone, let alone the brother of the woman she was currently banging. She caught his attention lingering on the screen of her tablet and turned it so he could better see. "I'm trying to fill in the massive gaps IDH left in the site's background research."

He had the grace to look chagrined at his blatant nosiness. "Samsara's a bit of a sore spot with them. We like to pretend we're the be-all monolithic utopia."

"I noticed. I've read that book though, and it never works out. Not for everyone. Usually not for anyone." Her own curiosity unfurled, noting the gaps between the few puzzle pieces she was given. "So you were taught in Samsaran tradition? Lin was trained in IDH?"

"Samsari. Yes." Dar's verbosity apparently ended with emotional overshares.

"How come no one talks about them?"

Dar's brows climbed toward his hairline. "Same reason you lot don't talk about religion and money and race unless forced."

"'Cause it's weird?"

"Fear. Fear of whether or not we're right. Samsara was a world of faith and trust and peace. Others saw it differently."

"I don't see why IDH would spend all these resources to investigate deaths they didn't care about."

Dar's eyes leveled on her for a moment, then he eased back into the chair. "Maybe think on what you know of them. What's the best way to hide something, eh?"

Dread slipped into Nel's chest and she shook her head. She didn't know how to answer him, and instead looked back down at the article. Apprehension tempered her interest. Like Emilio's message, Dar's words were something she couldn't afford to believe. Not with her entire life balanced on a tremulous promise.

Lin arrived before Nel could find some innocuous statement to throw into the sweltering awkwardness. The planes of Lin's face crumbled into distaste. "What?" She snapped, flat tone matching the hardness of her eyes.

"I wanted to talk about the site. And Paul. And see if you were okay," Dar explained, but coupled with his arrogance it just sounded like wheedling.

Nel eyed the door, but the Nalawangsa siblings blocked her egress. She hadn't realized how tall her girlfriend was until both of them stood toe-to-toe, tossing bitterness between them.

"I'm really not interested. You can read the mission reports like anyone else. Only the data is classified," Lin sighed. Stalking over to her cleansing station she began to vigorously wash her hands.

"I did read the mission reports, that's why I'm here. You were a key witness in my ex's death and I'm wondering why I heard about it from communications two days after the fact and not from your own goddamn handle!"

Nel wished hersuit would pick up on how much she wanted to be literally anywhere else and merge her with the chair cushion. Maybe it would jettison her out an airlock. At this point, a vacuous death was preferable.

"You stranded me on a foreign planet after a firefight and said I needed to grow up!"

"I said nothing of the sort."

"It's what you meant!" Lin was on her third round of dry soap and her beige hands were tinged pink. "'Both you and Earth need to figure out where your priorities lie.'"

Nel had to agree with Lin—that wasn't the kindest thing to hear from family after an electro-blast firefight in the dark hills of Chile.

"I knew you could handle it—and you did! You're here, aren't you?"

Lin whirled on him then, strands of sweat-streaked hair clinging to the ferocious lines of her face. "I'm not talking about ability to survive, Komodor Muda Nalawangsa, I'm talking compassion!"

"You're impossible. This is why none of us stay longer than a few days whenever we're all on one boat. You're notional, idealistic absurdity!" He strode to the door, glancing over at Nel. *Oh no.*

"Think about what I said, Dr. Bently. And best of luck with this particular endeavor," he muttered, gesturing at his seething sister.

She found her voice, though it was little more than a croak. "I, uh, I'm sorry about Paul."

"And I'm sorry about your friend, from Chile."

You don't even know his name. There'd been enough volatile arguments for one evening, however, and she just offered a stiff smile.

The moment the door *shnicked* shut, however, Lin turned on her. "What the hell did that mean?"

"He's just being a shit, you're not an endeavor—"

"I meant what did he tell you? And what business do you have letting him in my room? You know how I feel about him!"

It was clearly time to leave. Nel pocketed her tablet and gathered her overshirt from the floor "I don't, actually. I know you guys aren't close, but I didn't realize it was so…" she gestured vaguely at the space where she swore ozone still sizzled. "Most I knew was you were lonely. And he just insinuated that IDH might have caused the deaths on Samsara."

"He's wrong. I don't know how I can be clearer, Nel. I get that most massive organizations, especially those with military aspects, are corrupt, but no matter how much you try to make it, IDH is not a villain."

"I'm gonna get some air," Nel snapped back. "I'll talk to you later." She wasn't fan of having other people's bullshit dumped on her, and she certainly didn't need it from Lin. She strode down the hall, taking a half-remembered series of elevators and corridors until she came to the observation gallery. The massive bank of windows looked out on the giant beams and rings supporting ships and manufacturing. When navigating the inner layers, she imagined she was in a submarine or ocean liner. This view shattered the illusion.

Thoughts and fears rampaged through her head, and while the forest had its allure, the anxiety thrumming through her limbs begged for perspective, something more than admiring the trunks of trees. So much of her life—everyone's life—was dictated, surrounded, enmeshed in IDH.

They're the air everyone breathes. She pressed her hand to the inches of glass protecting them from the void beyond. *Literally.*

SEVENTEEN

Nel's computer beeped the moment her door opened. Groaning at what was surely more updates on the site yanked from her hands, she slumped onto her bed and pulled the holoscreen onto the ceiling. If she was going to get an ego-blow, she might as well be comfortable.

"Alright, day, what's the damage?"

As she predicted, there were several updates: the general mission missive from Kolonel Alvarez, followed by his initial organization-wide report on Paul's death and the obituary.

She couldn't stomach the latter, but she opened the first with reluctant fingers. Scrolling past several pages of explanation for those who weren't privy to the debriefing, she found the meat of the missive.

Investigations are being conducted into the unlikely scenario that some exterior force caused Dr. de Lellis's reaction, but at this time we have no cause to believe anyone else is in danger.

Excavations will resume shortly, under the direction of Dr. Arnav Patel.

"Oh for fuck's sake," she snarled, slamming her tablet onto the bed. The cushioned blow did little to alleviate her anger. If her skills were good enough to justify sending her into space, why would they yank her project away due to an emergency call that even the director admitted was understandable?

Groaning, she retrieved the device and pulled up the third and final message, almost wishing the system communications were down as well.

SENDER: KAPTEN GRETA WAGNER

SUBJECT: afternoon audio sex party—new data at 1423

Nel grinned. The communications officer was growing on her, quirks and high-energy aside. *Same could probably be said about me.* She put a note in her dismally blank calendar to go see Greta that afternoon.

The file of her mother's videos on her interface beckoned her, and her finger hovered over it a minute. She was down to fifty-nine. Watching another with no way of knowing when the systems would come back online, was a risk. Instead, she combed her hair and made sure sleep and stress didn't make her look sick before opening her own recording. The screen remained black.

"Hey, Phil?"

"Yes, Dr. Bently?"

"I'm trying to record a message for my mother, to send when the coms are back online. But it doesn't seem to be working."

"Our systems are weighed with pending vids. Perhaps try a text-based message," he suggested.

A few seconds of typing later, and her attempt was met with a flashing message.

ERROR: CONTACT UNAVAILABLE.

"What does 'Contact unavailable' mean, Phil?"

"It means the lines and contact information for that individual no longer work. The line's dead, so to speak."

"Because of the black-out?"

He hesitated. It was a fraction of a second, but she caught it. Computers didn't pause to think. Certainly not massive AI systems. "It's not because of the coms being offline. Approximately two-thirds of Earth's population has been cut off from communication. It occurred just prior to the comm outage."

"How many?"

"Just over 5.327 billion."

Cold filled her, too slow and creeping for her usual fury. It was bitter fear. This wasn't some space frequency driving people mad. This wasn't angry militants beating her best friend to death.

This was her mom.

"And you still think this is just a man with bad ears and an angry lesbian hearing things?" Rage pitched her voice lower than usual. She was pacing now, mind whirling as she ran through her listed contacts. "Try Annie Jones."

ERROR: CONTACT UNAVAILABLE.

"Tabitha Kline. She might be a PhD now."

ERROR: CONTACT UNAVAILABLE.

"Dr. Martin de Santos?"

ERROR: CONTACT UNAVAILABLE.

Over half the Earth was blacked out. Two years separated her from home, from everyone she ever loved, ever hated, everything that made her who she was, chemically, psychologically, emotionally.

"Emilio Sepulveda. Former head of the Chilean Founders."

A cursor blinked on the empty message box, ready to send her plea to the only person still able to hear her. Her fingers flew, typing then encrypting two words:

I'm listening.

Years ago something wiped out communications between Samsara and *Odyssey's* original senti-comp. And when the connection returned all that was left on the planet were bones and wind. Now Earth was dark.

If anyone—anything—knew the intimacies of communications and frequencies and the history of this space station it would be the mind running the whole thing, the mind that picked up the messy aftermath of tragedy.

"Phil," her rage-shuddered voice was a whisper in the dark.

The reply came, static and low, with more depth than any computerized voice usually boasted. "Yes, Dr. Bently?"

"We need to talk."

The pause occurred again, but a moment later a three-dimensional schematic filled her room. A beacon of blue light twinkled in the very center, and a faint green line connected it to what was presumably her current location.

Damn, this place is huge. "Is this where you tell me to find your thermal exhaust port?"

"I do declare, Dr. Bently," Phil answered, voice perfectly emulating a southern Belle, "I hardly know you." His timbre returned to its usual Anglo-baritone. "You'll have to make a house call, doctor. I'm afraid my legs aren't what they used to be."

She rolled her eyes at the joke as she zipped up her electromesh and headed for the door. "See you in a few."

The route was convoluted, but after the first few seemingly unnecessary turns and a third trip down a maintenance elevator, she realized it was hiding her trail. Either Phil thought someone was watching her, or he feared someone would find whatever massive room housed his CPU. Maybe she wasn't a fan of science fiction, but she knew what happened when a computer didn't trust its users.

At the deepest level, a door in the ceiling blocked her way, sporting a large panel. It prompted her to enter her credentials. She didn't bother to try. Obviously she had neither the rank nor the clearance for such things. "Phil?"

The door opened.

"Climb on." A ladder was a steel spider thread suspended between the forest floor and the synthetic sun. Rather than booming through the entire forest, his voice emanated from a tiny hole on the ladder itself, just for her.

Nel did as she was told, wrapping an arm around the single central beam, feet curled around the narrow holds. Metal hummed, then the ladder retracted, lifting her toward the brilliant ball of light. She fought back a thread of nervous laughter. *Don't go toward the light.* Halfway up she came to the dizzying realization that the sun didn't move. In fact, the entire space station rotated around the still sphere at its center.

A single hatch awaited her, as thick and official looking as an airlock. Her fingers brushed the cold metal. "Knock, knock."

Air hissed, dry chills ghosting over her skin as the hatch opened. It was, indeed, an airlock. The lights dimmed while chemicals scrubbed excess moisture from the forest from the air. The second hatch opened and she ascended into a dark, bitterly cold room.

"Morning, Dr. Bently. It's nice to finally meet you in person."

"You too," she answered. The sphere was large, still several stories in diameter, but the lines of massive circuits and heavy cables dangling—no, she corrected, floating. A gentle push of her toe sent her gliding into the air. *Right, no rotating, no gravity.* Massive thermal sinks took up one segment of the sphere, transferring the heat of processing out to the forest beyond as light. Between the dim light and series of blinking lights indicating various diodes, it took her a moment to orient herself. No multi-storey pixelated, alien head awaited her, just a small holoscreen projecting the face of a thirty-something white man. He had brown hair, she guessed, and dark eyes.

Beneath it sat the same head in a tank.

Nausea raced up her throat and she bit back a visceral gag. The uncanniest of valleys yawned before her. Murky water, like a neglected aquarium, surrounded the head, which looked young and old at once. Waxy skin, thickened by years—decades?—in viscous fluid stretched over atrophied expressions. Phil's bald scalp descended to a slight brow ridge, strong nose, flared nostrils. Like the scalp, his brows were hairless, even the half-closed lids of his eyes bore no lashes. Full lips twitched under a broad philtrum, an echo of myriad mutters. He was handsome, Nel supposed, if you liked your men the way you liked your baby gherkins.

"I don't know what I was expecting but this sure as fuck wasn't it." She peered closer at the flicker of life contained in the decapitated processing unit. "Does it hurt?" It was a strange question, she realized, and one he must have answered a thousand times. "Sorry, that was stupid."

"It wasn't. And I think, it did, at one point." His physical mouth didn't move, but the voice emanated from everywhere. "Perhaps it still does and I don't know what pain is, anymore."

"How does this work?" She wondered, allowing herself to drift around the tank, noting pulsing tubes and fluttering valves.

"Me and the ship, you mean?"

"Yeah."

"I'm not the only one, but I was the first — people made so clever they almost weren't people anymore. I'm in a tank because of an accident and they didn't want to lose my processing power and their investment. The others are in tanks because it's easier to keep a head in stasis than a body in cryo."

The thought of dozens of ships piloted by disembodied heads was an uncomfortable one. "I'm not sure where I fall on the ethics of all that."

Phil's' laugh was tinny. "Me neither. The wetware is mostly a formality now. I could probably live within these circuits alone."

"So why did you bring me here?" She looked around the dim room. "I mean, the creep factor is incredible, but I don't see the point."

"It's one of the few places on *Odyssey of Earth* that I wholly control. No security cameras, no audio surveillance. Just you and me."

Curiosity erased most of her dread for a moment, and she tried not to think of the inherent threat in his statement. "And your aquarium. Do you need a filter or something? Looks a bit green."

"Not in the least. Several hundred types of bacteria in here keep something as simple as a sinus infection from killing everyone on board."

Nel shuddered. With the topic of massive casualties finally broached, she curled her legs under her to float, cross-legged before him. "So about Earth."

"About Earth," he echoed.

"You've got a tra-zillion processing units, don't tell me you think this is all just some cosmic accident."

"I don't. But I don't know what it is. I have suspicions. But panic is the last thing a space station, or ship, or transport needs is panic. Panic causes death—you saw that in Paul. And before you argue with me, think about it."

She tried to. "He didn't die because of panic, he died because—"

"I agree something caused him to react without reason, but it was panic that drove him to remove his helmet despite knowing exactly what that atmosphere could do."

Nel drew a breath. Reading the reports of Mikey's death infuriated her—how could something as gut wrenching as murder be reduced to three tidy words of "blunt force trauma?" After another second of counting, she nodded. "Alright. I get that you don't want to cause a panic. But shouldn't you be looking into it?"

"Turn around. See the four banks over there?"

"The whirring ones?"

"Those are the processing units dedicated solely to scanning every frequency, every wavelength, for blips, for irregularities, for any sign that the Teachers, or anyone else, is out there. For perspective, it takes one of those to man every simultaneous conversation I have in a single district of this station. I'm doing far more than simply 'looking into it.'"

"What do you think of the feedback on Paul and my coms."

"I don't like it. I don't know if its purposeful, or leftover radiation, but I have no doubt it was caused by that crash landing on Samsara and where you two were located."

"So shut down those frequencies. Aren't they just really low, pretty much beyond human hearing. Certainly beyond human speech," she argued.

"No one ever told you about the Teachers, did they?"

"For all I know they're a bunch of Lovecraftian tentacles larger than Jupiter."

"And you haven't asked?"

"I've made guesses, but no one seems keen on sharing." Her attention roved from his physical head, to the projection, and back. It was hard to know where to look. Clearly his eyes no longer worked, augmented with thousands of visual receptors from every level of the station.

"My eyes are up here," he joked, and a red light blinked next to one of the readout screens. "When the Teachers first arrived on Earth it was a booming voice from the sky. Essentially. They have no corporeal forms, except on the occasion that they choose to pilot something. Instead, they travel as sound waves through the universe. They are sentient sound, essentially. It's something we are still working to understand. Don't try and wrap your head around it. Even I struggle with the concept sometimes."

"Liar," she whispered through the haze of her mind being blown.

"Hardly. I'm just a man, give or take a trazillion processing units."

Pounding filled her head and she rubbed at her temples. Her suit's pressure increased a fraction and it was only then that she realized the thing must be cranking to keep her warm in the freezer of Phil's room. "So if IDH shuts down low frequencies, they risk trapping the Teachers outside, basically?"

"Basically. Not to mention It's our only clue as to what this is, and we need that lead right now. Once it got in, it looped. Without a constant transmission we still can't trace it. If I had legs still I'd march down there and reboot Samsara's computer just to solve this mystery, danger be damned. But alas."

"What about Dar's theory that IDH is behind it all due to whatever prejudice they have against Samsarans? Samsari, sorry."

"I think, like everyone whose lives are dictated by this organization, he needs to remember their limits. He needs to think bigger. There are easier ways to commit genocide and when you're the biggest bad in the sky, there's no reason to hide it. Generating propaganda against them to justify the whole thing would be easier if they were worried about PR."

Nel hummed in thought. He had a point, but human history was filled with ludicrous ideas and even wilder reasons. Perhaps years in bacterial fluid had made him forget his humble beginnings. "People are fucking illogical, though."

Electric laughter buzzed through the speakers. Perhaps that twitch, there, on the corner of his mouth, was the memory of a smile's curve. "You're not wrong."

Warning: power levels low, her suit muttered through her mind. "My suit's running low."

"Understood. There's one more thing you need to hear: you're in a unique position, balanced between these worlds with the curiosity and means to explore their relationships to one another. But it won't be easy."

"Science never is, right? I think you're proof of that."

"Your covenants will be rocked."

"What covenants?" she drawled, "I'm a scientist, not a religious."

"Often they're the same. Am I human?"

She whirled, staring at the head, though the voice emanated from the dozen speakers hidden within the room's infrastructure. "What?" *Was that a glitch?*

"You're an anthropologist. You study people—people so far removed from one another culturally that sometimes they don't seem like they could possibly agree, and yet they do. People so different in their bodies—people who produce different patterned pigment—"

"Those are mutations, adaptations, evolution playing trial and error, but not species traits—"

"And then there's me," he continued over her babbling attempt to keep her mind from breaking. "Me, sitting in this tank, with a brain a thousand times more powerful than any other person's before me, with genes twisted and torn by people who thought they were gods: am I human?"

Nel's hands shook. There was a right answer, she was sure of it, one her heart thundered out from it's seat on her tongue. *Of course you're human. You were born human, you'll die...* She stopped. "Can you die?"

"Atta girl." The image above the head smiled. "There isn't a right answer, but you're still asking questions. It's a puzzle for you, one you're going to need an answer to. Not in the species sense, but in the heart-and-soul sense."

"Why's that?"

"This project will be your hardest. I'm not having a premonition, I've just done the math. You need to determine your definition of human, Nel, and hang onto it with every last fiber of your being. Remember it when you're afraid."

"I'm not afraid." But the bonfire burning in her chest wasn't anger. It was fear. And searing, constant instinctual fear drove humanity. *Maybe that's what they're missing up here.* Or perhaps they needed to listen to it more.

"Remember who you are and why you're here, remember humanity, Nel, and remember bravery is just accepting your fear."

Warning: power levels critical. She knew he had given her everything she needed, but it was impossible to untangle from the mess of expectations and shattered perspectives. "Thanks for helping me figure some stuff out."

"Thank you for still believing in all of us—even if we live in circuits."

She smiled, faintly, at the camera, wondering what she looked like when reduced to photons and binary. "I hope we both find some answers." A nudge against a winding cable sent her drifting through the first hatch. The door clanked shut and a different kind of warmth bled into her suited body. She climbed onto the ladder again, barely noticing as the second door opened. Moisture was cloying after the dry air of Phil's room.

Fear threatened to override her body, to freeze every decision and put her mind on lockdown. Perhaps it was why she chose avoidant anger. Anger was easier to fight that fear. Anger was easier to channel. Fear, though, fear she had to face.

EIGHTEEN

Glittering light filtered patterned gold across the black loam and her pale skin. Nel leaned back, relishing in the roots digging into her back. Bands of electromesh on her chest and shoulders peeled back to expose copper solar fabric, allowing her suit to recharge under the false sun. Her fingers wormed into the soil, relishing the scrape of dirt under her trimmed nails. How much of this loam was brought from Earth? How much was built from the bodies of generations of abductees? She always believed when someone died, that was it. Poof—gone. Mikey, however, waxed poetic on how his atoms would become soil, air, or return to stardust. *I'll have to bring some of his ashes down here.* It wasn't much, but lent him a tiny spark of immortality.

Four months ago she slept on a forest floor so similar to this, in the New England wilderness and wondered whether she'd survive to see the next day. *Two years and four months,* she reminded herself. Her chest ached at the thought. Lives ended in seconds, without warning. If something happened to Earth she would never arrive in time. Her mother's last gasps of breath would fade into apocalyptic air years before Nel ever even knew.

She closed her eyes against burning frustration. She felt it, let it settle into her bones, then forced herself to move on. Action, movement defined her. This was her element—discovery and massive leaps of faith and time. If Earth was going to survive, she needed to pull her head out of her frightened ass. Greta was looking into it, Phil was looking into it. She didn't know what a hardheaded archaeologist added that a super computer and communications officer didn't, but she had to try.

I thought I'd hear Earth was okay, but we just were protecting them. Or something. She hadn't expected a primer on the Teachers and the definition of human. Her suit chimed as it gained enough power for the coms. With the fear and confusion, she was tempted to contact Zachariah. Talking it through might help, though she wasn't sure if this fell outside the confidentiality clause. And Zachariah didn't help with the ache in her chestor the shaking in her hands.

With a breath that dredged up every fear, every potential loss she was risking, she called Lin.

"Hey." The other woman's voice was low, but not sullen.

"Hi. I'm sorry I walked out. Do you think we can talk a bit? I, ah," she summoned the alien words, "I really need you here right now."

Silence stretched between them for a moment, then her voice returned, warmer and humming in the damp forest. "Of course. Where are you?"

"In the forest," Nel explained, frowning at the intrusion. She checked the leaves around her. "Temperate Zone."

As much as they needed to talk, Nel wasn't looking to rehash everything she'd witnessed with Dar, not after everything she learned. She saw Lin first. The other woman slipped through the trees, long hair down for once in curtains of jet that dappled walnut in the sun.

Warmth uncurled in Nel's stomach. Dar had a point—she might not be willing to label what they had, but she crossed star systems for this woman, even if a job sweetened the deal. She sat up and raised a hand. "Lin! Over here."

Lin's smile widened and she broke into a jog. Warmth turned to fluttering nerves in Nel's chest.

A pace away, the taller woman slowed and flopped onto the ground beside her. "You doing alright?"

Far from it. "A lot on my mind. Just processing."

"I hear you there. My brain has been firing on high speed lately. Feel like I've barely seen you, too. I've been discussing everything that happened with my mentor, Dr. Ndebele. She agrees that this is complicated, but she would have made the same call."

Nel hummed, content to just listen to her for a moment. She didn't even care that the site was no longer hers. She just wanted her home to be safe—though finding out what happened would help.

Lin chewed on her lip, running a shaking finger along a fern. "So, you met Dar."

"Yeah." Nel let their words hang between them for a moment. "I'm sorry I left when you were upset."

"I was being a bitch. I just didn't like being blindsided by him like that."

"He said he tried to message you, which probably should have been my clue to tell him to go packing. I just honestly had no idea things were that tense. You hugged when he was in Chile," she shrugged, tilting her head back to follow a ray of artificial sunlight.

"I know. His messages sounded official and completely unrelated to family stuff. Was he nasty to you?"

"Just weird. The whole thing was awkward, but that was probably me. And just so you know, I don't think IDH destroyed Samsara. I don't trust them at all, but just don't think they did it." Nel explained quietly. The argument seemed so small in the face of everything she learned, perspective cooling residual anger. "I think something big is happening, bigger than IDH could handle. I also think you and Dar could stand to take your respective blinders off and really look at what's happening."

Lin blinked at her, opened her mouth, then shut it again. "I know. But every time I see him, I can't help but think of everything I wished he would have done, everything I wish I said. And now I just remember begging him to take me home and him leaving me on that sorry rock. Like I wasn't family."

Exhaustion turned what would have been anger into casual offense. "You begged him to take you with him? What about the site? And me?"

"I just killed a man, Nel. Because it was my job. Over ancient history. I might not have let on, but it messed with me. I spent weeks unable to sleep, just weeping, planning, covering both our asses. It's why I wasn't there when they first went after you. But it's also why you're not in prison right now."

Guilt replaced her frustration and she leaned forward, elbows propped on her knees. "Shit. I had no idea."

"You never asked. And I didn't know how to start that conversation. I know we look at death differently up here, but death and killing someone are different. Sure, it was for the job, and in self defense, but I was never trained for those types of missions." She looked down. "I think part of me was scared that I was capable of that."

"I'm so sorry. And I was really wrapped up in my own bullshit, huh?"

Lin's shoulder lifted in half a shrug, but her faint smile softened the gesture. "A bit. But you did have a lot to contend with."

All the space in Nel's heart usually occupied by fury was now open, ground made rich with pain and fear ready for growth. "Nah, it's an always thing, I think. I was always so focused on my school, or work that everything else wasn't important. Too fixated on my lane to even noticed the other drivers, so to speak. It's why most of my relationships end." She rubbed the back of her neck. Doing something worth apologizing for was old and familiar. Actually wanted to repair the damage she did, however, was new. "I fucked up. I'm sorry. How are you doing now?"

Lin laughed, low and gentle, a sound that fit in golden light. "I'm fine. We have far better mental health resources than you lot do. It still bothers me on occasion, and it should, but I've dealt with it." She took Nel's hand. "You said you were processing?"

"Yeah, well. I spoke to Greta yesterday—I'm supposed to meet her in a bit to go over some data."

Lin pursed her lips in disapproval. "Isn't that interfering?"

"I don't really care. IDH can do what they want with me, but I'm more worried about this heap of metal and my home." The high of intimacy and knowledge faded fast in the face of whatever loomed over Earth.

"Home? You really think someone is orchestrating this."

Nel shrugged. "I'm used to antagonists."

"Don't have a drive unless there's something to fight?" Lin teased. The mirth faded quickly. "You look like there's more."

There's so much more. "There is a frequency in my coms and in Paul's. It might have to do with where we were when the transport crashed. She's looking into it. But I wasn't imagining things."

Lin's beige cheeks pinked and she looked away. "I'm sorry I suggested that."

Nel searched Lin's face, noted the places where she guessed lines would form in a few years—or decades, perhaps. The shadow of fatigue under her dark eyes, and the tiny mole just beneath her left eye. She didn't know how much Lin already knew, but she was willing to bet it wasn't all of it. Was it something Lin could handle, or would it shatter her along with her faith in IDH? Could Nel even begin to explain it properly? Her sharp sigh was half laugh, half exhalation. Just two months ago she plead for honesty and now she debated lying for the same greater good.

"Nel?"

"I also spoke to Phil," she admitted in a rush, jerking her chin at the sun concealing the senti-comp's room. "In, ah, in person."

Lin's smile disappeared. She sat up, crossing her arms over her chest. "What?"

"You know he's a head in a jar, right?" It was a strange way to begin the discussion, but the obvious seemed as good a place to start as any.

"I did. They all are. Not everyone knows, but some do. But it's not something anyone really likes to talk about."

"Yeah, I see why. Big old ethical hodgepodge there. Anyway, I tried to message my mother this morning and got an error message. And a few others, and when it wouldn't work, he told me about Earth. And the blackout. It's not our comes. At least, not just that. Two thirds of the Earth is out of contact, like the line is cut. Did you know that part?" Hidden under her chin, she crossed her fingers, hoping Lin hadn't kept this from her.

Lin's eyes were huge in her face, gaze roving the gently swaying branches above. She blinked and looked up. "You're joking. Two thirds?"

"I wouldn't joke about this. Earth's gone dark. Our coms are janky, sure, but this is more than that. And they're hiding it."

"To quell a panic."

"There are people up here with families on that 'rock,' as you put it." Nel reminded gently. It took all her counting and breathing to keep from snapping that maybe this warranted panic. But leaping down Lin's throat wasn't the way to get them on the same side. "I understand not causing a panic, I'm cool with that, but there are gray areas."

Lin nodded, then seemed to emerge from her haze of twisted thoughts. "Oh no, Nel, you said you mom was one of them?"

"Pretty much everyone I could think to call. Except for Emilio."

"You got through to him? What did you say?"

"It was a reply to something he sent last month when we were down on Samsara."

Lin lifted her head, fully focused now. "Care to explain?"

Nel braced herself. It wasn't often, anymore, that Lin's full attention rested on Nel, and when it did the circumstances were far more intimate. Asking Lin to trust her was one thing, but baring her own shattered soul and everything she just learned was wholly different. "He said something's coming. And it's not IDH and not the Founders. It's something bigger. And he simply asked if I'd hear him out. My response was that I would."

Lin gazed at Nel's face, as if she could see the truth written in the lines and freckles. "You believe him?"

"Lin, that hunk of sand went dark just before everyone on it died. We can delude ourselves that some people lived, but let's face the facts. Everyone on that planet died. Maybe even the Teachers, though I don't know if they can." Emotion tattered her words, and she drew a breath in an effort to make her words clear. "And now it's happening on Earth. Emilio's right, but something isn't coming. It's here and no one is paying attention."

Chirping rose from Nel's wrist, muffled by the rolls of electromesh usually protecting the solar charger. When uncovered, it projected a display of Nel's meeting time with Greta. "I gotta go."

Lin's eyes were shadowed with the weight of everything she was taught and all the pieces that fell through the cracks in those doctrines. "Right."

"Are we okay?" It was something Nel never asked. It was something she never cared about before. When Lin just stared at some point beyond her shoulder, she brushed the other woman's fingers. "Lin, we okay?"

Lin nodded, smile more a reflex than expression.

"I'll see you as soon as I'm done, promise." Another moment of faltering, and Nel slipped from the glade. She had been there, staring into space as her world crumbled around her. And she had been there because of Lin. Part of her felt guilty for being on the other end, now, but another part was relieved. *She's human after all. Under the gleaming metal and electric tattoos.*

Nel was a few minutes late by the time she arrived, having overshot Greta's door by several rooms before realizing her mistake and backpedaling. Why was advanced tech synonymous with lack of personality?

She knocked, realizing, belatedly, that Greta's jacks probably drowned out all sound. As usual, the office door was shut but not locked. Her hooked finger slid it open a fraction. "Gretatron?"

A soft, high sound hissed from some unseen speaker, but otherwise the room was still. "Greta? It's Nel. Sorry I'm late."

Faint blue light from the screens barely penetrated the darkness. Nel knew enough not to go fiddling with wires on the disabled lighting control, so edged closer to the screens. The display showed a loop of sound, perhaps whatever it was that she wanted to show Nel. The smallest screen had a bright blue dot pulsing at the crash site on Samsara. Nel grinned. *She found it too.*

When she leaned closer to get a better look, she caught a faint noise, softened by static, though it wasn't coming from the main speakers. Instead it drifted from the darkness above her. She stepped back, knocking into whatever mess of wires Greta probably had hanging from the ceiling. Peering against the screen glare, she tried to make out the sound's source. It wasn't a wire she bumped.

It was a pale hand, tattooed with circuitry.

"Fuck!" Horror flamed through her. Nel staggered back, fumbling her tablet out in an attempt to shed more light. A thick cable tangled her feet and she went down. Remembering, she choked out, "Computer, raise lights!"

Nothing happened, and she blinked through the bouncing light of her device.

Greta's chair pinned her to the ceiling, a cybernetic Lepidoptera. Her head twisted, past the point of a human neck. Titanium tangled with her twisted neck. Greta's lifeless jaw hung slack, eternity glazing her eyes. Whatever wetware she used to modulate her voice and replicate audio had ripped through the flesh, looping some faint swan song. It was a scream, turned down so low it was just a whisper of agony.

Bile surged up Nel's throat and she clenched her jaw against retching. "Help! Computer, no Phil: I need a—a medic or, security." Terror bubbled from her mouth with sputtering sobs. "Anybody!"

Just like with the lights, no one answered. Her tablet clattered to the floor. Despite the torn arteries and strands of sinew, her shaking hands tried to staunch the dribbling blood.

"What the hell?" A shadow blotted out most of the light as he appeared in the doorway. "Dr. Bently?"

"Thank fuck—"

"What's that noise?" He stepped in, peering about, rubbing the base of his ear, the way Greta did. Reaching over to one screen, he slid the volume up to full.

"Don't!" Nel warned, but it was too late.

The scream wrenched from the speakers, grating and far too long. Even with her fingers wedged in her ears, it shook her body, turned her bones to tuning forks of pain.

Eyes watering, he jabbed the volume into silence and turned to her. "What in God's Name…" His eyes roved from her hard expression, to the body on the floor, then back to the black oil and blood slicking her hands.

Oh no. "No, no, not what it looks like, dude," she protested, stained hands out before her. "I found her like this. I was trying to help."

Eyes never leaving hers, he depressed the button on his wrist. "Security, this is Kapten Connors. There's been a murder."

NINETEEN

Sleek dark walls were a welcome change. The locked door was not. Nel paced from one corner to the other, trying not to touch anything with her bloody hands. Security took all of ten minutes to bundle her into this safe room upon arriving at the scene.

How could they suspect her of murder on a ship with security and surveillance in every hall? The memory of Greta's recorded, mechanical scream frayed her nerves. From the corner to the table and back. On the tail of horror, of grief numbed by familiarity, came another thought. After weeks of listening to that aberrant frequency Paul lost it and Greta's biomech throat exploded.

Am I next?

Nowhere—not even the vast expanse of forest beneath her pacing electromeshed feet—was safe. Fear didn't begin to cover it. She stumbled to a halt and tucked herself into the corner. All her exercises on controlling her temper must have worked, because now she was reduced to a trembling ball of fear instead of a raging asshole. "I'd really prefer the latter right about now, Zachariah," she snapped.

The door hissed open then shut behind a security officer. She staggered upright, determined to look at least a little in control even if they both knew it was a lie.

"Dr. Bently, if you could have a seat?"

Thick titanium reinforced his glove and heavy matte plates of armor augmented his suit. Someone wasn't fucking around. Nel splayed her hands on the table and eased into the chair.

"Which one are you?" She asked. "Agent Smith or Agent Spender?"

He did not smile. "Can you detail your whereabouts today?"

"Ah, sure." *I really can't.* She had no idea whether meeting with Phil was allowed, or known, or where cameras were in each layer that she passed. "Well, I spent the morning in my room, trying and mostly failing to get messages through to home. Then I took a wander through the station, checked out the forest and so forth. I met with Lin—Letnan Nalawangsa there for a few minutes before heading to Greta's office. This morning she sent me a message asking to meet. I was running a few minutes late. I didn't see her—"

Nerves choked the words for a moment, and she sucked air in through her clenched teeth. "I didn't see her body right away. When I did I tried to call for help, but Phil wouldn't answer. That other tech guy arrived about then. I think you know the rest."

"Indeed." His pale eyes, like a fish's gone too long without light, inched over her. "And what is your relationship to the terrorist Emilio Sepulveda?"

"What?" She blanched. "He's not a terrorist. And I don't have one with him."

"You emailed an encrypted message to him this morning. I believe that entails some connection. Is it business? Romance?"

"I'm gay," she retorted.

His gaze didn't waver.

Heaving a sigh, she shook her head, "No relationship. We're acquaintances. He helped out during the firefight at Los Cerros Esperando VII. He messaged a month ago expressing concern about some events back home. I merely replied because I, too, am concerned. Said I was listening."

His eyes flicked to his device, as if to be sure it had recorded that note, then his attention returned to her. "What is your opinion of IDH? Specifically their work on Samsara?"

"It's a job. I trust them about as much as any other boss—I know their main concern is some bottom line, rather than individuals. Not a problem, just how business works. I find their lack of transparency frustrating, but mostly because I like to have all the information I need to do my job."

"That was candid."

"That was the truth." She heaved a sigh. "Look, I get that you lot aren't keen on me, but I was offered a job and I took it. Not my fault your background check wasn't done till now. If you're so worried I'm some fanatic extremist, check the camera feeds."

"The camera feeds are down. Same with Philos. Have been since you left the core."

"For fuck's sake." She sat back, anger and panic sparking through her body in turns. "I could barely figure out how to flush the damn toilets up here—you think I'm gonna know how to sabotage a space station?"

"It's not my job to figure out how you did it. Just what you did."

"Maybe if you focused on the 'why' you'd figure out there wasn't one," she suggested, crossing her arms. She missed the shoulders and biceps actual digging gave her. Samsara's low gravity robbed her of any hope at an intimidating presence.

"Why are you so angry?"

"Why am I—" Surely her brows just climbed into her widow's peak. "You're accusing me of murder, sabotage, and terrorism. None of which I have any interest in. I've probably lost my job, I'm stuck up here in this giant spherical Rubik's cube literal light-years from my family. I'd think it was obvious."

Without missing a beat, he swiped to whatever was next on his digital docket. "And can you explain why you didn't manually override Dr. de Lellis's suit?"

Nel rocked back. Why hadn't Lin mentioned it? *Because she knew I'd never learned.* "You're joking. No one taught me how to do that. I'm lucky I haven't de-pressurized my own suit trying to take a piss!" Frozen fury rumbled through her words and forced her to her feet. "Write me up for incompetence. Fire me for overreacting in an emergency situation. But don't you, don't you fucking dare accuse me of murder. The United States government already tried that, and if anyone knows how to properly frame someone for a crime they didn't commit it's the U. S. of A."

"I think I have all the information I need," he closed down his device and rose.

"Good." Nel returned to her chair, continuing to glare. "Get your jarred brain back online and start barking up a different tree."

The door slid shut quietly behind him, but she wondered if he would have slammed it. Her electromesh claimed an hour had passed, but it felt closer to five. Lin's faith in IDH and Dar's clear lack of trust in them warred in her mind. When there was no one left to trust, she had to trust the data. She worried at the largest on the palm between her thumb and index finger. *Except I can't make any sense of it.* How could sounds kill people?

The door slid open again. Refusing to look up from picking at her hands, she forced her voice into a casual drawl. "Come to blame me for the Hindenburg now?"

"If you're to blame for that, then we seriously misjudged which department you belong in," Lin smirked. Her hair was hidden under an electromesh hood designed for inside a space or atmo suit. "I thought he'd never leave."

Relief washed over Nel, but only for a moment. Her gaze dropped to the new suit in Lin's hand. "What is that?"

"It's your way out, love." She tossed it onto the table between them. "They've got a lock on your electromesh—you cross that threshold every blast door on the level shuts. But this one's unprogramed. Basically useless as a suit, but better than strolling through the halls naked."

Nel glanced from the suit to the open door, then to Lin's bright eyes. Running would set off a search, another manhunt, one that crossed star systems instead of states. But no one knew what she did, no one trusted her word, and somewhere, far beyond these suns, Earth needed her.

"Trust her."

"Mikey?" Finally, his voice, even if it was just a whisper.

"What?" Lin frowned and glanced back. "If we're doing this we gotta go now."

"I didn't do this."

"I don't think you did, but you can't save the world from a prison cell, Nel, and no one else is going to do it for you."

Nel crossed the space between them in three strides. Cupping the back of Lin's neck, she pulled the woman's head down to hers. Their lips melted together for a moment, the heat of fear and passion melding for a breath before Nel pulled away. "Thank you."

Lin's smile flashed. "Quick. I got us a ride to the *Promise*, but security will be back soon. I'm hoping Dar will have a rare moment of family-first."

Nel stepped into the corner and yanked her suit off, taking the electrodes with it. "Fuck."

"Doesn't matter, just change!" Lin hissed, glancing down the hall.

The fresh suit was stiff, and a size too small, but Nel managed to tug this zipper up without ripping skin. Yanking the hood over her head, for good measure, she folded her old one over the back of the chair. "Ready."

With a final glance toward what must be the security offices, Lin slipped down the hall. Every few paces her gaze darted from their path to her wrist and back. Each step was as fleeting as it was precise. "Walk slower," she murmured as they approached the first door. "Casual."

Casual? Nel didn't recognize casual any more. *Not even if it seduced me with a six-pack of Black Pond's jalapeno saison and a two month sabbatical in Venice.* Nel lengthened her stride, letting her arms swing loose.

"Casual, not do-see-do," Lin clarified. Tension lined her throat and strained her smile. "We'll go in two floors first, to throw them off, then meet up with a pilot on the freight deck. Easy."

Lin's definition of "easy" seemed at odds with everything Nel had seen so far, but trust was trust. *And prison is prison.* "Let's go."

Lin palmed the panel of the shaft across the corridor.

"SYSTEM BACK ONLINE."

"Fuck."

"Shit! We've got five minutes before they notice you're gone. Ten, max." Lin whirled, scanning the hall, fingers flying over her device. "Maintenance shaft."

Lin backtracked until she found a plain gray hatch. A quick palm on the door opened it, and she grabbed Nel's hand.

Nel tumbled in first, twisting so she fell belly-down. Perhaps it was the panic, but she swore they fell faster this time.

"Freight deck coming up!" Lin called.

Suit: Engage mag-catch. Nothing. Dread chilled Nel's blood. She peered over her shoulder. "Shit! My suit's dead!"

Lin's pupils blew. In second steel replaced the terror, but Nel saw it. *She's as scared as I am.* Her descent sped up again as she released her own brakes. She reached for Nel. "Hold on to me!"

Their fingers hooked, then Lin's nails scraped Nel's forearm, clawing her closer to safety. *There!* Nel wrapped her limbs around the other woman's slender frame. Air howled in her ears, doors flashing past, barely slowed by the electromagnets struggling to halt their combined descent. She clenched her jaw and prayed to the only thing she'd ever believed in. *C'mon, Mikey. Now or never.*

"Engaging mag-catch." Phil's voice boomed through the shaft. Air dragged, snapping her head back as their bodies tumbled to a stop. "Phil?" Lin asked. "Are you alright?"

"Virus triggered a wipe and reboot is all. No damage, but the best I can do is clear your way. Anything more and they'll blame reprograming."

Nel swore he sounded tired. Tears threatened her frayed composure. "That's more than enough. Thank you."

"Don't thank me yet. I need you to do something for me."

Nel's memory flashed to their conversation. "You need me to be your legs. On Samsara."

"Get me in so we can find out what happened on Samsara and to Ada and we'll call it even."

"Deal," she whispered.

Lin already had the door open. "Samsara?"

"It's the only way to find out what might happen to Earth," Nel whispered. She had strained Lin's tentative loyalty so far already. *Just a bit more.*

"We're four levels from the freight deck." Lin's wrist dinged and she frowned. "Bavin's gonna get the transport primed for flight checks. I'll let him know the change in plans."

Relief lasted only until Nel slid the maintenance hatch closed behind them. This level was dark, filled with turbines and pressurized air. "Aren't they going to ground everyone?"

Lin waved her question away and took off into a variable city block of recycling systems. "He's not a rules person as it is. And it takes hours to change a flight. Most they'll do is lock the blast doors to the Launch Deck."

Locked blast doors sounded a lot like trapped to Nel, and she didn't like being trapped.

"Where are we? How many levels to go?"

"We're in the pumps. This is what moves the air to and from the forest. There should be a way down to Launch from here." Rumbling shook the walls, faint, but undeniably there. Lin's eyes closed in a plea for patience. "Blast doors are down."

Nel jerked her chin at the huge hoses and pipes on the ceiling, noting the colors of each. "Do vents have blast doors?"

Lin glanced up, following her gaze. "Yes, but they're on a second system. They only go down in case of catastrophic failure."

"Well, despite what my step-dad would have you believe, I don't think I qualify." Nel found a smile slipped onto her face. "Find us the vent that goes to your friend's launch bay."

Lin's grin matched hers and she traced a path on her device. "That one."

"Hear that Phil?"

"Air vent to launch bay D562 cleared. All blast doors shut via manual override, but no one will get through for approximately thirteen minutes."

"Why are you helping?" Nel supposed it didn't matter, not in the grand scheme, not when it came to life and death. Not when seconds mattered.

"I've done the math," he answered, computerized voice warming a fraction.

She chuckled and hauled herself through the narrow grate behind Lin. "You're a good man."

The vent was tight, large enough for her low-gravity atrophied shoulders, but only just. Ahead, Lin belly-crawled, unable to get her long legs under her. "500 meters." Lin's murmur bounced along the metal, gratingly loud in the tight space.

"Just signal," Nel hissed.

Lin flashed her a thumbs up and crawled onward. Eight minutes later Lin raised a hand and pointed. A heavy seam in the vent denoted a level change, and the two meters of vertical vent beyond confirmed it. Lin jumped and pulled herself over the edge, but there was no room to turn about and offer the shorter Nel a hand.

Thank fuck for all those deep units, Nel thought with a wolfish smile. She braced her back and edged upward. Each push of her electromeshed foot warped the metal behind her and sent manufactured thunder wavering down the vent.

She winced, and finally hooked an elbow over the side. Ahead, Lin tossed a relieved glance over her shoulder and continued on.

Insistent alarms sounded a few levels deeper.

"Let's move this along," Nel hissed. One more corner and they stopped over a grate.

Lin pried it loose and shot a quick glance down. "We're two bays away, but we can make it if we run. He can push his window by a minute, but no more than that."

"Running I can do." Nel dropped down after her, wincing as the landing sent shockwaves through her ankles and shins.

"Hey!" A security officer raised his gloved hand.

"Go!"

Nel took off after her, ducking with each sizzling blast of the security officer's weapon.

A voice crackled through Lin's comm. "Where are you, Nalawangsa?"

Lin smacked her wrist. "Start the launch, we're on our way!"

Another massive doorway and they were in Launch bay D562. A tiny transport waited, half the size of the one that brought them to Samsara months ago. Its engines rumbled, all but the pilot's side hatch open. A brown hand shot through and pulled Lin inside. A second later it hauled Nel into the safety of the cockpit.

"Thanks, Bav," Lin panted, tossing Nel a space suit before donning her own. "Get us out of here."

The pilot grinned and the transport's ignition screamed. "Roger that."

TWENTY

Cargo rattled in the open bay of the transport. Nel braced her elbows on her knees, hands clenched as they descended. Another lurch and her stomach bounced from her throat to tailbone.

"Where do you want me to put this little lady?" Bavin asked.

Nel glanced up to see the sky tilted, horizon at a 35° angle. She returned to staring at her boots. "Site of the crash. But you're gonna have to be careful."

Lin leaned over the controls, pointing at something on the screen. "Should be right there. There's a spire that we hit."

Bavin scoffed. "What, were they trying to go VFR? In this mess?"

"No," Nel forced herself to her feet. "Instruments went down as we neared the site. There was some flare of static and then we hit it."

Bavin tilted his head, leaning into the headphones clamped over his halo of hair. "Shit, yeah I hear something. Low frequency, though—"

Nel slammed the larger button on the radio, heart pounding. "Shut the radio down!"

Bavin shrieked and swatted at her. "I trying to fly, here, woman!"

"Instruments too, everything you can spare," Nel said, ignoring his glare. "That's what caused the crash. It's what killed Paul and Greta."

"A sound killed people?" Lin stared at her, eyes narrowed and unreadable.

"Don't ask me to science it for you, but that's why we're here." She wished her voice didn't shake, that whatever grim steel weighed in her stomach lent her words strength. "Phil mentioned a virus hidden in the audio. If it took him out, even for a few minutes, there's no way a simpler computer will handle it. I'm starting to think that's what happened to Paul's suit and Greta's wetware."

Bavin shuddered. "I knew wetware was a bad idea. That shit gives me the willies."

From the corner of her eye, Nel caught Lin staring at her tattoo. Her face was sallow, even under the orange glow off of Samsara's surface. Nel laced their fingers together. "I think, while we're down here, we ought to stick to messages. No audio coms."

"Lin, why'd you have to go for the crazy one. I can't be without coms." He blanched, "What if something happens—"

"Something already did happen. You want your ship's computer to fry? You want your atmo suit to force you into a panic?" Nel fished her helm from where it rolled during their turbulent landing. "These things run with just local power and such, right? There's no giant wireless battery?"

Lin shook her head. "Friction generation and solar. You sure about this?"

Turbulence knocked Nel into the seat, and she returned to her seat. "Yeah. Sure as I've ever been."

Lin glanced between her and their pilot. "Bav, please."

He straightened the Black Panther figurine atop the instrument panel. "Roger. Going dark."

Lights flickered out. Dim, emergency backups appeared along the floor and ceiling, pulsing with each shudder of the engine. The map disappeared, followed by the scrolled radio channels. Radar, tachometer, and the gyroscopic altimeter remained active, along with a few readouts Nel didn't recognize.

"I'd suit up."

Nel locked everything in place while Lin adjusted her helm. A message appeared a second after the suit powered up:

"We've got this."

Their eyes met, a glimpse of familiarity in a sea of alarms and clattering space freight. Nel found a grin, leftover from their night of 90's rock and room service, and slipped it on.

Leaning over, she pointed at a location about 800 meters from the original crash. She curled her brows in question when Bavin glanced up at her.

He nodded and lowered the landing gear. The ship swayed, dropping altitude in chunks as the wind threatened to blow them miles off course. Another lurch as they crested a dune and a heavy crunch shook the ship's belly.

Lin grabbed her hand. *"So what's the game plan here?"*

Ideally, they would have discussed this before donning their suits and switching to messages. *Or running from space station security and hijacking one of her brother's transports.*

"Get to the crash, see if the signal is originating from there. Send the data to Phil in a message—no audio." She shrugged. *"Try not to die?"*

"We could try and get the samples from the site."

Nel nodded. If they had time.

Alarms blared as *Thunder-bump* screamed to a halt. Sand exploded around them, decreasing the already minimal visibility. Bavin stabbed at some buttons, engaged the leveling gear. The ship stayed at an angle.

A second later his message appeared on their helms. *"Thanks for flying Samsari air, do come again. I'll stay here. Gotta cycle the engines and repair that strut. We're leaving at 0850 at the latest. Don't have enough fuel to take off before or after that, when the rotation—"*

"Gotcha." They had hours, barely. *"And if we're not ready in a day?"*

"Well, you're fucked." A string of what were obviously cartoons of several different sets of genitalia followed his message.

She rolled her eyes. Even in space she couldn't escape emojis. At least up here they had graduated from the peach and eggplant. Catching the pack Lin tossed her—her own dig pack, she realized, after a second—Nel followed her down the gangway and into the storm.

She staggered, clinging to the ramp's strut. "Crash is 873 meters at 43° of my location!" she called, belated realizing shouting was wholly pointless. She repeated herself in a message, adding: *"You bring a tether?"*

"And a temp-shield."

"You're my hero." Nel clipped the tether to her belt and checked the analog compass. A correction of four degrees and they were off. Between the wind and constantly checking their progress and direction, her brain didn't have a chance to run simulations of every terrible scenario. Still, her heart hammered. Adrenaline seared her nerves. Cutting the audio and coms meant they didn't have to listen to the manhunt occurring in the sky above, but after the isolation and speculation of her cross-state trek, Nel hated radio silence.

Each tug on the tether reminded her that, this time, she wasn't in it alone. She glanced back, but Lin was a faint shadow in the miasma of churning sand. Why had she come? Not a day ago she was IDH's lapdog. *Fuck, I hope we find something. Anything to justify mutiny.*

Her next step slipped off something slick and she stumbled as her mag boot struggled to find purchase. The thick black material of an atmosuit, faded to gray from sun and sand, poked from the ground. *"I've got something here."* She crouched, brushing sand hopelessly away even as the storm whipped more over the find. A badge, with the number 333 emblazoned below.

Lin fell to her knees beside her, digging deeper, head bent against the weather. A second later she found his helm.

Nel looked away. Coagulated blood blackened the interior of the glass. *"Let's keep going. Just in case."* It wasn't contagious, not in the traditional sense, but her heart couldn't take much more.

Lin rested her hand briefly on that man's helm, then followed.

For someone raised in a culture that didn't fear death, Lin seemed remarkably affected by it lately. Perhaps they never had a reason to fear it, before now.

Another dozen steps against the wind and the spire loomed from the storm. Nel followed the sleek circuitry carved on the side. Somewhere, scattered around them, were the pieces of their former transport. Nerves fired up her arms without the electromesh's reassuring press. No flush of heat answered her wind-battered shudders.

Lin grabbed her shoulder, pointing at the half-submerged door. The pattern scribed across the surface wasn't one Nel recognized, but for all she knew it was identical to the one above the bodies.

Please let there not be more bodies. Excavated graves were different when their occupants were long dead. Eons lent staring sockets a gentleness. It was a gentleness, a kindness, the Samsari dead lacked. Death felt different when you were its prey.

"I have Arnav's lockpick, but it's going to take me a few minutes. Take a look around? You've got 50m of tether."

Nel raised a thumb in affirmation, and edged around the side of the spire and fell to her knees. Howling in her mind drowned out the screaming wind. Still, when subjected to silence, her thoughts spiraled into the looping scream whispering from Greta's butchered throat. Flesh, dotted with oil and torn from within interrupted every fifth thought, followed, more frequently now with Paul's burning face.

How had things come to this? Her shaking hands combed the sand. Nagging truth weighed in her heart. She knew where this investigation would end—if not for them, specifically, for IDH and their precious Teachers. The dread behind Lin's eyes said some piece of her suspected it as well.

These are the first shots fired, and one side doesn't even know there's a war.

Lin's message that she got through flickered through the whipping sand. Nel hauled herself up and staggered back. Hopefully the low visibility hid the tear streaks behind her helm.

The door ground open, sand pouring down the exposed ramp. Nel shook away the sensation of being devoured and stepped inside. Like the other spire, it led down, but here the walls were covered in circuits, all massive and gleaming. Air whistled over the opening, but as much as Nel wanted shelter, her gut told her closing that door meant death. Twenty meters farther and the storm was reduced to a distant roar. She pointed to the branching hall.

"Any idea?"

"Let's stick to the main hall. We already know this place has skeletons in its closet. No need to hunt for more."

Nel's laugh puffed, overloud in her helm. She was willing to bet far more than skeletons hid in the dark places of this planet. Quiet pressed on her ears. In the aftermath of the past few days, silence was sacred.

A cavernous chamber waited at the end of the hall, dimly light from some unseen source. It was as if the very air glowed with residual energy. She spared a few seconds of anxiety for the thought of radiation.

"I think this tower is a mirror to the other one, if I remember the maps." She checked her device, which Lin had tossed in her dig pack. Without the connection to the space station or a suit's computer, it was slow, but better than nothing.

"It should be. Samsara had a series of towers—they called it a sanctum, framed by the two tallest ones—but none were in these locations."

Nel didn't know how architecture worked up here, but she distinctly remembered on Earth it wasn't easy to move buildings around like so many puzzle pieces. Other than the faint light, the hall seemed inert. The glow of her device bounced across carved metal as she stepped inside. Drifting sand crunched under her boots, felt more than heard.

"What are these carvings?" Some were clearly practical, some electronic language she had no will to make sense of. Others symbols were inscribed over, or through the circuits, as if rerouting ancient power with some great colonizing language.

"They're Samsari, carved over the Teacher's language, essentially." Three dots appeared on Nel's screen, blinking, for several minutes as Lin explained. *"I think the first designates this planet. The second humanity and the third the Teachers. I've never seen them written out like this, in this hybridized language. The two aren't very compatible."*

Nel brushed a hand over the towering symbol. The primal sensation was back, the same as when she gazed into the abyss of the first door a month ago. There were places she had walked where a piece of her knew her boots were not welcome. Her blood knew Samsara was not for her.

They came so far, and Lin had already given up so much, how could she turn and say she was having second thoughts? She caught Lin's gaze.

The taller woman's face was pale under the harsh glow of their devices. Stress dilated her dark eyes to black. Whatever it was that didn't want them there, she felt it too.

Nel stepped back, giving the wall space to breath. Her thigh collided with the hard lip of a table. She whirled, heart thundering in her chest, free hand catching herself on the edge. *An altar?*

"*They're misspelled,*" Lin noted. "*And pieces are loose.*"

Nel barely read the words. The table before her bore a model of the planet—sans sand. Every detail of the buildings replicated in delicate miniature, complete with their own lace-like circuitry. She checked the maps again. The model mimicked the city's former configuration. The scientist in her screamed not to touch the alien technology, but the larger, human part reached out a curious hand.

It moved. Each tower was set in a smooth track, an entire city turned into a sliding puzzle. *Or built as one from the beginning.* Whatever blasted death across the planet's surface and sent computer-killing waves into its surrounding space originated here.

Lin glanced back. The weight in her gaze told Nel everything she needed to know: this room was the key to the snarled lock of their project.

With trembling hands, Nel slid each building in the model into the current location of its massive counterpart. The only building that remained unchanged was the tower in which they stood.

Metal ground. The symbols on the wall rotated, the loose pieces Lin noted earlier twisting and dropping into place. Nel had no idea where to begin reading the words, but now they just looked right. Complimentary.

A thud echoed, then another, followed by the crack of electricity surging through conduits long disused. Lights bloomed around them. Their helms' glow increased, and noise crackled into life. Sound exploded around them, music without rhythm, sound with just enough repetition to have meaning. A second stream of sound underlay it, words, words Nel knew.

"SAMSARI STATION POWER: ONLINE. LIFE SUPPORT SYSTEM: ONLINE. COMMUNICATION SYSTEM: ONLINE."

"Shit the coms!" Lin's voice cut through Nel's helm. "The city's power just came online, and I guess our suits—?"

"Doesn't fucking matter, Lin," Nel reminded, grabbing her hand. "We gotta get out of here."

Lin didn't move. Her gaze was fixed on the three words scrawled over the electronics. "The symbolism was the point. There are so many easier ways to reroute power." She shook her head. "Some really good programmer did this."

"STATION COMPUTER: ONLINE."

"Lin, I think we've seen enough. That's all Phil needed. Let him run the diagnostics on this electro-building."

"I think I can handle it." Phil's voice was loud, exponentially more resonant through the massive speakers integrated into the room as well as their suits.

"How the hell—"

"My sensors noted as soon as the system came online. I hacked into the coms and am working on accessing the rest. I blocked external signals on your channel right now, but this system is elaborate. Get to the surface."

"You hacked?" Nel muttered, glancing at the door to make sure their exit was still clear. The naked admiration in Phil's voice at the computer's complexity tightened her stomach.

"How do you think I got this job, Bently? I'm a programmer. You don't stick just anyone's head in a jar."

Nel wanted to argue that she probably wouldn't stick anyone's head anywhere. Before she formed the words the ground shuddered. Metal screamed. "Alright, art tour's over, Lin." She snapped a picture of the room with her device, then found Bavin's handle. "We're on our way back."

"Bently? What the fuck did you do? The ground's shaking."

"Turned the city on, channel's safe for now." Nel yanked Lin toward the door, panting into the mic. "Prep the transport!"

"I told you I needed—" He protested, voice whining even through her helm.

"Doesn't fucking matter!" She repeated, breaking into a jog. Lin followed, expression unreadable behind her mask of horror. They emerged from the building, Nel colliding with Lin when she halted on the threshold.

Samsara's surface cracked, sand pouring through the fissures. Wind howled still, but now it rushed toward the site, as if through a crack in a pressurized shell. Alarms flashed on her wrist, but without her electromesh all they did was panic her more. *Atmosuits aren't meant for a vacuum.*

On the horizon the site's shield flickered and went down. Frustration flashed through Nel's chest at the thought of their meticulous work sandblasted away. Light bloomed, so bright it bordered on heat, rivaling the suns, rivaling the searing terror in Nel's chest.

Sand thundered from the surface of the planet. New wind, the wind of dissolving atmosphere, pounded into her, a gritty massage through the layers of her suit. A concussive wave tossed Nel to her knees. It swept the planet, ripping crash debris from the spire. She fumbled at her arm, outstretched against the onslaught. Her teeth clenched. Finally her gloved finger found the keypad and her mag-boots clapped to the surface.

On her helm, the map flickered between the two configurations. The compass, however, was still active. *That's all I need.* "Let's head toward the *Thunder-bump*."

Silence.

"Lin?" Chasms, made with mechanical perfection, opened between her and the storm-shrouded ship. A few meters out, however, everything was lost in a sea of churning sand. "Lin!"

Horror howled in her chest, louder than any alien storm. She whirled, blood pounding in her veins. *Not this.*

"Here!" It didn't matter hundreds of meters might separate them. Her voice was in Nel's ear. In her head.

"Fuck, I thought—where are you?"

"I got blown off by the wave. About 300 meters from the ship." Static threatened to drown her words.

"I'll meet you there." Nel switched the conversation to include their pilot. "Bavin, come in?"

"Bently, this is Bav, over."

"We're headed to you. Will the ship be ready in time? Over."

"Copy that. Guess she'll have to be. Bav out." Buzzing turned to screeching.

Sudden silence pressed on Nel's ears, interrupted only by sand hissing against the insulated glass over her head. Whatever firewalls Phil erected for their coms must have fallen.

"380 meters," She whispered, an isolated incentive. Crevasses cut her path back to safety, but for the few paces she could see, most were no more than a meter. Her chest ached from breathing against the dragging air, and she refused to look at her atmosuit's power and O2 levels. Earth was lightyears away. Safety was a distant memory. A murder trial impended in the skies above.

But just 380 meters away, Lin waited for her.

Dragging herself upright, she clenched her fists and took a step against the wind. "Hey Mikey. Remember what you said, about using anger to drive me?" She staggered, wind buffeting to the edge of a ravine.

"You needed something to fight against." The memory of his voice was almost lost to static and distance and time.

"I was wrong."

"I know. You need something to fight for."

"Not something," she rasped, easing over the clean metal edge of the next chasm. "Someone."

When she was 76 meters out, the ground shuddered beneath her. With a final howl, the wind died and visibility cleared. "Shit."

The planet's maw opened between her and the gouges from their landing. A glance into Samsara's bowels brought bile surging up her throat.

"Bav has to take off now, or we're never going to make it," Lin murmured. The storm no longer played havoc with the coms.

Nel's heart faltered. Pragmatically, she knew saving two lives was better than risking three. "I understand." All the fear and adrenaline and drive that brought her this far sputtered into numbness. "Just find my mom, please—"

"Shut up, you asshole, we're coming to get you."

Relief flooded her, followed by embarrassment. Sure enough, the *Thunder-bump* lurched into the sky, made a pass, then turned about. Its wings shuddered under the force of flying so low. Who knew what electromagnetic fields Bavin had to combat? They dipped closer, then pulled up again. "Dammit," He growled. "Alright, I'll come round again and open the rear hatch. I can't get any lower without crashing, not without both stabilizers intact. You're gonna have to jump."

Fuck. The transport came about again, engines whining. They were 500 meters away. *Thunderbump's* hatch dropped and a ladder tumbled out. "Jump?"

300 meters and closing.

"Hey, Nel?" It was Lin, long legs wrapped on the rungs, hand outstretched. Nel eyed the chasm. Even without the storm, the edge was precarious.

"Yeah?'

"The gravity's low. Trust me. I've got you."

70 meters.

A flic of her thumb and disengaged her mag-boots. She gauged the distance between them and crouched, thighs burning after months without digging. Nel crossed the galaxy for this woman. Surely she could spare another twenty meters.

"Now!"

Nel jumped. For a moment she was weightless, floating. A breath and then gravity took hold. Gloved fingers gripped her forearm and she jerked into motion. Pain exploded through her shoulder and arm as the force yanked her injured elbow out of place. Samsara fell away beneath them.

"All aboard?" Bavin asked.

"Yeah." Lin's grip didn't loosen until the cargo bay slammed shut behind them. Her helm bumped softly against Nel's, tears glittering through the glass between them. "I've got her."

TWENTY-ONE

"Got good news and bad news," Bavin relayed. He engaged the autopilot and tugged his helm off with a sigh. "We're in orbit, just outside the range of its massive electromag field."

"That sounds like the good half," Nel noted. If she never had to wear another space suit, it would be too soon. With the ship's the pressure and atmosphere stabilized, she shucked off the stiff fabric. Sweat matted her hair and trickled around the ill-fitted edges of her electromesh.

"Yeah, the bad half is we'll be out of fuel within an hour. And that's running on minimal power."

Nel blanched, "You didn't think to, I don't know, check the fuel light?"

The pilot let out a dark chuckle. "I could've made it halfway to the *Odyssey* if I'd left your sorry ass back there."

"Noted," Nel snapped. "So what now? How far above that are we?"

"Hang tight, I guess. We'll hook around using our residual momentum, and the station should rise right about there—" He pointed at a nondescript point on Samsara's lower horizon. "—in five hours."

"I suppose we're sitting ducks, mutiny wise," Lin drawled. "Can't very well ask for a tow and not expect a security escort."

Nel glanced back at her. "Do you think there's any way they'll take a look at that massive machine and decide they have better ways to spend their time?"

Lin's shoulder lifted in a halfhearted shrug. "I gotta get out of this suit before it chokes me."

"You can riffle through the cargo," Bavin offered. "I had to jettison most of it to even make it off the ground, but it was crew supplies for the *Promise.* You're welcome to whatever is left."

She nodded toward the rear of the transport. "Let's find something better than dirty atmosuits and electromesh."

Nel wholeheartedly agreed, following her down the narrow, pipe-filled corridor to the cargo bay. It was substantially more roomy than it was earlier. Her stomach growled as she lifted the lid of one crate. "Got a ton of protein bars in here." She pocketed two and tossed a third over to Lin.

"Jackpot." Lin took a bite and pried the lid from a case of A-shirts and boxer briefs. "Here, love."

Nel's fingers brushed Lin's as she took a folded clothes. *Love.* "Thanks." She stripped, pulling on the comforting, dry clothes. Her skin was still sticky and her hair was a greasy mess, but it didn't matter. Across the cargo bay, Lin donned her own underthings, raking tangles from her long hair. The shadows under her eyes could have swallowed *Odyssey*. Nothing mattered, other than being here, together and safe, if exhausted.

Her head pounded from the whiplash of the past twenty-four hours. There was so much to say, so much to process. *Where do I even being?* A breath, a second of silent, then she whispered, "So it never was a planet."

"I guess not, no." Lin glanced up, chest rising in a soft sigh. "I never thought I'd be here."

Nel tilted her head, worried if she moved a hairsbreadth more, she'd startle Lin back under her mask of control and ignorant trust. "Here?"

"Drifting above Samsara as she implodes. About to be court martialed. Not really caring about either, because you're across from me and we're both alive."

Nel's grin echoed Lin's tired smile. "I was just thinking the same—the last bit, at least."

Lin's dark gaze drifted over her shoulders, crossing her features and finally settling on Nel's. "That might be the most surprising part of it all. What changed?"

"I did." Nel let out a soft laugh. "Thank you for breaking me out. I know it couldn't be easy disobeying orders."

"I've done it before. In Chile and when you were running. I guess you're a bad influence on me," she teased. Her expression sobered, however. "Or a good one. You've helped me see that while IDH has a stirring manifesto, there are secrets and branches that don't adhere to it. I still don't think they did this. But I realize now that they could have."

"What about him?" Nel asked, jerking her head toward the cockpit. "How'd you convince him to fly us?"

"He works for the *Promise* and like most of them would do anything to inconvenience my brother. He's not military though, so this will be less of a crime."

Nel frowned. Dar hadn't been a peach when they met, but the level of disdain most folks seemed to have for him told her she was missing something. "He's kind of a rules guy, huh?"

Lin nodded. "Do you think Phil will put a good word in? For us I mean?"

"I'm sure, I just hope they listen. Maybe if he threatens to cut the oxygen off—"

"That's horrific. And besides, those are all on closed systems with multiple redundancies." She trailed off into silence. "Not really the point, I guess. My parents are going to be furious."

"I worried about how being a fugitive would effect my mom, but honestly, she just wanted to know I was safe. She never once—that I know of—actually thought I did it. Even when I started to wonder. And Phil will find the truth somewhere, down on that mechanical rock." Nel glanced over. She recognized the wan, expression on the other woman's face. "How're you doing?"

"All right." Lin's words were hoarse, as if from screaming. *Or crying.*

"You don't look it." Nel risked crossing the bay and sank onto the bench beside her. "And you haven't since you saw those symbols."

"That place used to be a temple and something desecrated it. It was homage to everything we came from, all we had achieved. Those words just drove it home. Each of the Teacher's words is so nuanced it takes a dozen words in human languages to explain a single concept. They're capable of feeling so many things simultaneously." She glanced at Nel "Remember what you said about that song?"

"'Dust to Dust?'"

"Full of sorrow and tenderness and journey and grief. Maybe the Teachers are like that song, encompassing emotions we have to describe using several of our own."

"They're made of sound, so are they, themselves their language? This whole thing is really stretching my brain," Nel confessed. The concept of sentient sound—or matter that was only able to be perceived via audio, as Phil had clarified—wasn't one she could easily conceptualize. "What did those symbols mean?"

"The first is the planet's name, which is roughly 'life cycle,' but depending on the piece you're looking at it means peace, eternity, and death. That's why we call it Samsara—Samsara Ahimsa Mrtyu. The three closest words we had."

Chills swept up Nel's bare arms. "Those words have a lot of weight, even in crummy old English."

Lin nodded. "The second is just the word for us—or it was, originally. Those extra lines there, and this swirl, it changes 'emissaries ' or 'students' to 'savages.'"

"That doesn't bode well." She knew the question she would have to ask, the accusation, but the fragility in Lin's eyes told her to wait, told her it would only shatter the tentative intimacy hovering between them. Nel tried to keep her voice level, but judging by the pinched lines at the corners of Lin's eyes, she failed. "What did the last one say?"

Lin hummed, voice melding two sounds, one haunting, the other beckoning, full of promise and warning. Tears prickled at the corner of Nel's eyes. "It was just the first name of the Teachers." Lin's words were devoid of the playful innocence Nel first fell for.

"What does it mean?"

"Strangers."

Nel sat back. At the start of this journey Lin had been a stranger. They had a lot of work left ahead, and Nel wasn't ready for the word love, for the feeling, not yet. She caught the orange gleam from the cockpit's open door on Lin's warm tan skin. *But maybe soon.*

Thunder-bump's engines sputtered into silence. Nel glanced up as the lights extinguished with a clunk. Backup lights flickered on, intermittent and sallow. Pain replaced her ebbing adrenaline. "I think my appreciation for Jasper Hill's local hydro plant has skyrocketed in the past few weeks. You guys can light speed but you can't manage a few days without another outage." The teasing fell flat, and she returned to staring at her hands. Pain made her too uncomfortable to pace, but nervous energy fired up her legs. She settled for bouncing her knee.

"Generations ago they had another name." Without the engines and wind and crackling coms, Lin's words were a confession, whispered into the sanctity of space. "Some called them gods."

"But they aren't," Nel argued. "They're aliens—cosmic travelers who simply learned to walk long before we did." *Right?* It was obvious, so why did she sound as in need of convincing as Lin. These weren't her origin stories, these weren't the myths her world rested upon. "That's absurd."

"Nel, my ancestors saw glowing beings descend from a hole in the sky and offer them longer lives, health, prosperity. They offered us the choice to take flight and travel hundreds of thousands of miles." Emotion ripped her voice ragged. "Don't tell me you wouldn't have called them gods."

Nel's mind paged through the stories she ignored from the bible, the Norse myths, the stunning images of Hindu gods. Her blood chilled. Fear was familiar. This wasn't fear. Primal terror in the face of thunder, in the face of an approaching storm swept through her. She cleared her throat and grasped for a straw. "My mom always said God was benevolent. So why do you look so scared?"

"How would you feel on Judgement Day?"

"Ladies, we got a problem!"

Nel winced. "Coming!" She didn't move, however, eyes fixed on Lin. As much as she wondered if the Teachers might be responsible, she hadn't considered the consequences of that possibility until now. "It could just be an accident," she offered, echoing all the people she argued against in the briefing.

"We both know you don't think that."

"Sooner rather than later!" Bavin shouted.

Nel dragged herself upright, pulling Lin up beside her. New and old injuries smarted and her elbow was a mass of white heat. She limped up the stairs to the cockpit door, hovering on the threshold. "What's up?"

"Samsara isn't crumbling. It's opening."

Lin appeared a step behind her, fingers trailing across the bruised small of Nel's back.

Nel stood, transfixed by the scene below them. Even if it wasn't her own, watching a planet implode was a peculiar kind of heartbreak. Samsara's surface fractured, grinding in mechanical rhythm. Massive discs at the base of each building whirred and twisted in hideous transformation. The ground, once swirling with gold, now gleamed black against the void of space. Mechanical crevasses widened, folding outward as the spires slid deeper, acting as tumblers of a massive lock. Electricity crackled from within.

"What that—"

A second concussive wave exploded from its center, sand and metal and its little remaining atmosphere obliterated. The *Thunder-bump* tipped with the energy of the blast.

When Nel's eyes cleared of sunspots, Samsara quietly rotated, reduced to a series of rings around a sphere of brilliant light. All the terror she just saw in Lin's eyes gripped her own heart, rotted tendrils curling around her future. She knew a gate when she saw one.

I did this.

Pain shot up her arm as her fists clenched, but it brought a wave of clarity. "I had no idea. If I did—"

"Don't start." Lin's voice hardened. "This is IDH's fault, or Phil's, when he asked you to do this."

She just trusted them, trusted it would never get this far. *I trusted I would always be on the right side.* "I should have known better, is all."

Lin straightened, peering at the horizon. "Bav..."

"I see it," He growled.

"See what?" Nel leaned forward, squinting at the view.

"On radar," Lin explained, pointing at one of the instruments. "Can you bring it up on the screen?"

A holographic image filled the window, displaying a much closer views. Another wave, this one of radiation, swept off Samsara. Nel's heart dropped further. Shadow and energy writhed, then silver streaked from the center of the gate. A spaceship materialized, sparking for a moment before its engine's fired. Another followed it, and another, as seven, a dozen, no a hundred ships glitched into existence around them.

"Please tell me that's back-up," Nel whispered. "Tell me it's just your parents coming to bail you out."

Bavin snorted. "Despite what Dar would have you think, Laksamana and Brigadir Jenderal Nalawangsa aren't Lord Captains of our entire existence."

Lin shot him a glare. "They're accomplished, is all, and he's right to be proud."

Bavin's brown eyes rolled, but he didn't bother to argue. Instead he scanned the new arrivals. "Look at the way they move. Stunning. It's the same systems we use, couple models ago, Kd2 Jasa engine, maybe Kd2-Σ with those thrusters. But its body is designed completely differently—hell those entry shields are Terrestrial tech I'm pretty sure."

Fury roiled through Nel, steam rising from the burning terror in her chest. How could they run without fuel? Or was this how she would end, powerless and trapped, without a single weapon to raise. *If we fall, Earth is next.* She refused to think that her home already fell, that this was just the Teacher's last stop on some cosmic cleanup duty. *But what if they aren't the Teachers?* "We got enough power for a message?"

The pilot just stared at the com, expression a mix of disbelief and distrust. "I'm not radioing them until they see us first. We could slip by, they might not even—"

"Even what?" Nel snapped. "Even notice? Even deign to blow us out of the sky while they blast *Odyssey of Earth* and 180-whatever-thousand people into oblivion?"

Lin's eyes were wide. "I don't think we should run, but making first contact is dangerous."

Nel jabbed a button then another on the control panel and crossed her fingers. The radio screamed. A hasty twist of the dial brought the static under control. "Come in, ah," she glanced at the numbers emblazoned across the ship's side. "LP-672. This is Dr. Bently on the *Thunder-bump*. Welcome to Samsari airspace. Over."

"What the hell are you doing?" Lin hissed. "They'll call your bluff," Lin warned. "They'll scan us and see our engine's dead and half our landing gear is shot. We're no welcoming committee."

"Maybe today I am." Nel glanced over. "Trusting too much might have gotten me here, floating in a sardine tin above another ruined site. But," she gripped the comm tighter and raised a hand to the massive space liners above her, "I'm also still alive."

Static swelled, followed by the boom of a voice, masculine and rolling with Chilean Spanish. "Drop the ridiculous act, Bently, you make a lousy air traffic control officer."

Nel's mental gravity flipped. "Emilio?"

"Good to see you again. I hitched a ride with Capitán Reyes of *Le Fe De Amor*, flagship of Los Pobledores Aerospace Fleet."

"Fleet?" Nel hissed. "Since when?"

A low laugh rumbled through the speakers. "Remember the cave? I think it's time I told you that story."

Check out this sneak peek at the next Nel Bently Book:

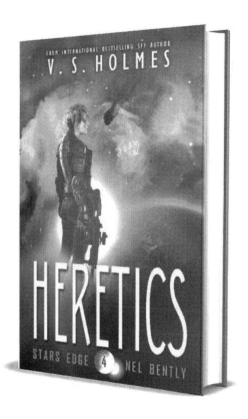

ONE

Nel glared at the message blinking beside her bracelet. Her nerves were shot. The elevator's whispering hydraulics sounded closer to sandblasting the hull of a crashing ship. Soft phosphorescence flickered sickly green over fresh pink scars and the white threads of old wounds on her arms. She wished for the comfort of sleeves.

The decision to disband audio messages was unanimous, at least until *Odyssey*'s sonic bloody mystery was solved. Her shaking hand fumbled with the holographic buttons until the unread message appeared in the air above her wrist. Nel preferred texts anyway.

> *I'll be there soon, talking with my mentor.*
> *Can't wait to see your outfit!*
> *-L*

Nel glanced at the faux-silk front of her vest. Even without the distortion of the elevator's curved aluminum, she doubted she'd recognize her reflection. At least the available fashion offered something suitably androgynous—high-collared vest and thigh-hugging pants. The soft faux leather of the boots cupped the aching place where her toes once were. *Even if they aren't steel-toed.* Woven translucent pads covered the sand burn and nicks Samsara left across her exposed biceps and forearms. Hopefully she looked closer to Ellie Williams than, well, herself.

She had hoped Lin would meet her outside the hall—feeling nervous was impossible with someone that beautiful on your arm. *C'mon, Bently. Get your shit together.* This wasn't an exploding planet or deadly soundwaves. Her lip curled. She'd take either over a gala any day.

The elevator passed from its metal tube to a glass cylinder, treating her to a view of the hall. The guests who arrived on time already ranged about, a sea of rich colors and glittering accessories. Nel flexed her hands. Copper and burnt sienna were as subdued as she could go. She was used to archaeology conferences, mingling with too much alcohol and too little professionalism. She could hold her own with glorified shovelbums. Surrounded by space scientists and cultured extraterrestrials? She was a turkey among peacocks. *Fake it till you make it.* The platform slowed and she plastered her favorite cocky smirk on her face.

Murmurs and soft laughter filled the hall. Somewhere the sound of water trickled, though Nel couldn't say if it was recorded. *Hopefully not.* She rubbed the base of her skull and stepped out. Several gazes glazed over her as she edged through the crowd. Did they dismiss her because they didn't know who she was or because they did? A handful of folks clustered by what she prayed was a buffet table. Anything to occupy her hands. If it wasn't for the promise of snacks and getting a moment with Emilio, she wouldn't have bothered to come at all. *Okay, and maybe to see Lin in a fancy dress.*

As it was, she had barely managed to say a dozen words to the secretive Los Pobladores leader since he glitched into Samsari airspace four days ago. *And you still haven't told me that damn story.*

Curiosity dragged her focus to the glass bubble pressing into the forest at *Odyssey*'s center. It was shadowed by the mighty boles of jungle trees, vines draping the lower segments of the glass. Two more levels rose above, but Nel cared more about occupying her fidgeting digits than mingling.

Hors d'oeuvres and drinks drifted by on hovering platforms. Nel maintained strict eye contact with a platter of cheese as she navigated the surprisingly sparse crowd. *It's a gala for the Samsara project. It's not like engineering should be here.* Still, the scarcity may have been as much an illusion due to the sheer size of the room. Someone Nel recognized but couldn't place offered a smile and wave, but their expression faltered when Nel attempted to return the gesture. Perhaps smirk wasn't the look to go for.

Nel's attention returned to the table. Edible containers housed each snack, meant to complement the flavors or act as a palate cleanser. While the majority of the protein was made of insects, she was relieved to note not a single prickly leg among the smorgasbord. *Fancy suit aside, you're an embarrassment to anthropology, Bently.*

Nel glanced at her wrist and thought about typing Lin a message. Instead, she let her alien boots wind their way through strangers and plants. She paused by another buffet table just long enough to shove some sort of tapenade into her mouth. She apparently dawdled too long because a figure loomed over her when she turned to make her exit. "Annelise!"

Nel cringed, wiping a hand on her pant leg quickly before offering her hand. "Ah, Nel, please. Or Bently. Anything really, but that."

"Yes, yes." The man pumped her hand repeatedly, grin vacant. "I was just speaking to your colleague there, Dr. Arnav Patel. He said you were present for the planet's ah...rearrangement."

"Rearrangement," she responded, voice flat. "Yeah, I was. Didn't feel like rearrangement from there, though. More like Armageddon."

"I can imagine."

Her eyes narrowed on him, doubting very much that he could imagine anything like

Samsara's implosion. "Who'd you say you were again?"

"Apologies! I'm Komodor McNally." He shook her hand again, gaze pausing on her bolo. "Oh, that's delightful! Meteorite, yes? Do you know which one?"

"Not a clue. But yeah, meteorite. My—Letnan First Class Nalawangsa gave it to me." She seized the excuse, still trying to extricate her hand from his. Sweat dampened her palm. "Have you seen her, actually?"

"Last I saw she was with the Nalawangsa boy."

Dar hasn't shown his face all night. "Gotcha, thanks! Better catch up, she wanted to show me the," she glanced back, searching for anything to fill the blank drawn in her mind, "forest. It looks amazing. Great to meet you!"

She wove through the crowd, annoyed enough to don a furrowed brow in hopes of preventing further conversation. She didn't trust slimy, middle-aged men at archaeology conferences—or any conference, really. Space conferences were no different, it seemed.

"Scuse," a low voice remarked. An arm reached across her to a bowl filled with vials of clear and faintly orange or blue fluid.

Nel glanced up into an open face under an elaborate swoop of pale blonde hair. "Hey, you're one of the tech people, right?"

"Yep! Teera." The smile was bright. "Want one?" She offered an alarmingly large tube.

"No port," Nel explained, showing her bare arms. Curiosity warmed her gut. "What are they?"

"Mingle-ease. Calms the nerves, lowers inhibitions, settles the stomach a bit."

"So, IV beer?" Nel snorted. "Guess my awkwardness is that obvious, eh?"

"No, but I remember my first gala. They don't get easier." She wrinkled her nose.

"Thanks for the thought. I'd kill for Black Pond's jalapeno saison though." As if in answer, the pastry she popped into her mouth smacked her tongue with smoky heat and a sweet bite. She hummed in approval and grabbed another. "Man, the food is almost good enough to keep my feet off the ground forever."

Teera laughed and cringed. "Doesn't make me feel any better about whatever I'll be eating once we're planetside."

"I heard something about beer."

Nel turned to see Arnav hum up. The rims on his wheelchair were decorated to match the elaborate caps to his sleeves. Angular structures rose from either side of the back of his chair, framing his head.

"Dude, you look badass," Nel remarked.

His mouth quirked. "Thanks. Just for your kind words..." He opened the draped front of his jacket and produced a heavy flask. It was battered, the metal covered in dings and the wrapping soft and warm.

"Shit, this what I hope it is?"

"If you're hoping for grade C recycler distilled starshine, then yes, yes, it is."

Nel knocked back a sip, then a second before returning it with a pleased shudder. It was burning ice in her gut, setting off the fire of whatever spice she ate a second before. "Fuck, that's good. You've made a best friend of me, that's all I need tonight."

"You're welcome to it, I've another in my pack, but I'm starving—what do they have out? Anything good?"

Nel shrugged. "Don't know what half of it is, but this spicy stuff is nice. I've my eye on that fruit thing that looks like caviar."

Arnav laughed. "I honestly wonder what the Nalawangsa girl is doing with you, upbringing that she had."

"Opposites and all that—maybe I'm good for her." Nel offered a wink, belatedly realizing she was already slipping up on the professionalism. She scrubbed a hand through her gelled hair. *Dammit, now I'm gonna look like a cockatoo.*

"Where is she?" Teera asked. "I'm always dying to see what the elite end up wearing."

Nel's gaze was pulled up to the upper levels. "Haven't found her yet. Sure she's busy though. I'll rescue her later from some boring intellectual nightmare."

"Oo, well it looks like the department heads are already at it," Arnav groaned. "I swear verbal sparring over ethics is the only joy Dr. Ndebele gets these days."

"Best be off before she realizes I've holed myself up over here." Teera flitted off, gossamer cape and fascinator bobbing above the crowd.

"This is all very space fairy," Nel decided. "Odd food, ephemeral costumes, highly educated."

Arnav laughed. "I don't know, this is just a piece of it. Everything looks pretty on *Odyssey*. How well do you know your Homer?"

"Enough, why?"

"Well, the *Odyssey*? It wasn't easy. Took a long time and a lot of blood." His gaze followed a cluster of people that seemed to move over the crowd instead of through it. "And more than a few monsters."

Nel followed his gaze, caution flitting up her spine. She was tired of distrusting, but nothing surprised her these days—warring space factions? Sure. Exploding mechanical planets? Just another Tuesday. "I hear that." She itched to ask him more, but surrounded by gleaming strangers made her feel more than a bit out of place. "Except I'm pretty sure the fae have to tell the truth."

"Only if you're asking the right question," a deep voice rumbled from behind her.

Read the rest of *Heretics* at Books2read.com/hereticsnel

Explore the events leading up to *Travelers* through Lin's eyes in:

Disciples

Cryosleep was a temporary death. The lights were dim, a twilight between waking and sleep. Lin blinked and rolled her shoulders, stretched her neck, curled her toes. Viscous stasis fluid drained silently, leaving goosebumps across her beige skin. Nausea shuddered through her. She ignored it. Instead she drifted in the peace of momentary amnesia. The hiss of heated air punctured the stillness. She flexed her fingers and tapped the smooth metal embedded in the flesh of her wrist. "Commence waking sequence in five...." She counted the seconds down silently.

"Good morning, Opsir Nalawangsa." The low voice was male, and just shy of truly human. The lights rose, gradual and faintly yellow.

"Good morning, Phil. Where are we?" She pushed out of her tank, rising in the zero G of her cryo tube. The lights were fully bright now.

"We're in orbit, 437 km from the surface of the planet Earth." There was a pause, and she almost thought the ship's voice held a smile. "Welcome home."

She snorted. "My genes may come from that ball of dirt, Phil, but I certainly don't." The air rolled over her skin, drying as it went. A click and pop echoed from beside the closed door of the cryo tube. She grabbed the vial from the ship's delivery system and held it up.

NALAWANGSA, LIN
IMMUNIZATION LEVEL 2
STABILIZERS
PROTEIN
CARBOHYDRATES
ELECTROLYTES
VITAMINS A, D, B, C
SALINE

She groaned. "What does a woman have to do to get proper grilled fish with her breakfast in bed?"

"When you cure cryo-sick I will personally deliver you a plate of fresh milkfish in bed upon waking."

She rolled her eyes and snapped the vial into the port in her arm. A moment passed then her nausea subsided. Aching in her head ebbed. "How was the trip?"

"Uneventful. You are wanted in Trajectory." Phil's tone often trod the line between a butler's deference and a captain's rebuke.

"Dar?"

"Yes. It appears Komodor Muda Nalawangsa has requested you personally. Shall I tell him you're on your way?" *Probably just to rub in his new rank of Komodor Muda and the fact he's now senior enough to just 'request' me.* "Thanks, Phil. I'll see you there." She unwrapped the plastic from her uniform and slid it on. After seven years of drifting naked in a vat of saline, the stiff electro-fiber felt cumbersome. She flexed her hand, aligning the contacts inside with the conduits tattooed on her skin. A hum. A rush of energy not-quite-her-own. *Paired.* The word wasn't spoken, not heard in the traditional sense, nor was it a thought. It least, not hers. *Increase temperature by 0.5 degrees C.*

Her goosebumps sank back into her skin. She slid the door open and slithered from her cryotube. The lights here were brighter, the snaking lines of green and blue illuminating the stark white of walls and the sharp silver of glass. Her finger brushed the pad in the wall, changing a panel from cycling photos to a mirror. She scraped her hair back and straightened her collar. It was always alarming how little her face changed during years of cryosleep.

"Opsir Nalawangsa—"

"Yeah, Phil, I know. On my way." She shoved through the next door into a corridor. The steep curve told her still-disoriented mind she was on the interior of the ship. A gentle press indicated they were just inside the gravitational field. *Planet-side is starboard.* She kicked off the floor and sailed along the corridor. Other than several bots and the usual techs, the hall was deserted. *Debriefing already started then.* It took days for the ship and crew to recover from a cryo-trip to open space. Longer when they arrived at a planet's orbit. She found the first drop-door to the exterior rings of the ship and pressed the symbol for Trajectory. The ground trembled with the rings' gentle turning. When the doors between the outer rings and a transport shaft were aligned the door slid open. Lin dropped, her grin broad. This was her favorite part. The slight artificial gravity brought by the rotation grew the farther from the core she got, so what started as a gentle drift accelerated into a true free fall.

WARNING: Falling from high places can result in damage or expiration. Engage mag-catch. She ignored the suit for another moment, enjoying the rushing air. Lights flickered past as she hurtled through dozens of levels. She clenched her teeth against biting her tongue. *Suit: Engage mag-catch.* Electromagnets in her suit kicked on with a hum and lurch. By the time she arrived at the door emblazoned with the symbol for Trajectory she was floating. A panel slid across the transport tube and she touched down. Gravity settled over her like a blanket. Even her organs felt heavy. Her palm on the door granted access to the waiting area. Another palm on the next door prompted a cheery robotic voice very unlike Phil's.

"Good morning! Please state your rank, full name, and purpose clearly into the speaker."

Lin leaned forward. "Opsir Muda Udara First Class Lin Nalawangsa, to see Komodor Muda Udara Dar Nalawangsa."

"Accepted, have a lovely day!"

Lin smiled, wondering if the security bot's voice grew irate when you weren't allowed through. The door slid open and she stepped through. Trajectory was as messy and chaotic as the rest of the ship was tidy. The bank of screens to the left showed their past trips, and those of other ships in the fleet. One blinked with a digital scan of Phil's face as he debriefed the crew and discussed issues with other ships' minds. The right was a whirlwind of orbit physics and gravitational maps. Her brother stood within the ring of navigation and communication computers that dominated the center of the room. He snarled something at the image of Phil's head on one of his screens. "I don't really care what the ISS has to say. Our orbit takes precedence. It's much harder for us to navigate then for them."

"Sir," Phil offered, "I think they feel differently. They're expecting a shipment and new crew. Their flightpath has been planned for months, and the weather won't hold forever—"

"I'll show them fucking weather…" His mutter almost drowned in a chorus of beeps that rose from Navigation. "Then put me on the comm with NASA."

"Paging NASA."

Lin saw her opening and stepped up to the raised floor of the Captain's Ring. "You wanted to see me, Dar?"

Dar frowned, but did not look up. He could have been her twin: black, smooth hair, warm beige skin, and deep oval eyes. Their features and parents, however, were the only things they shared.

"I need you to go planet-side."

Lin's stomach lurched. The tingle crawling up her arms had nothing to do with electromagnets or her suit maintaining temperature. "Excuse me?"

Read the rest for free at vsholmes.com/disciples

ACKNOWLEDGEMENTS

As always, there are more people to thank for this book's creation than there is space. *Strangers* is here in part to the incredible people at the Iceland Writer's Retreat, The amazing people there helped inspire me, and focus my energy on making this book happen against, at the time, what seemed like all odds.

Thank you to my fantastic editors, formatters, and designers, and to the wonderful, welcoming community of authors I've found online.

Thank you, of course, to my archaeologist community, including my incredible partner for putting up with my singular hyper-focus.

And thank you to my father, whose strength and grace through all of life's myriad bumps and potholes, has taught me how to live.

ABOUT THE AUTHOR

V. S. Holmes is an international bestselling author. They created the BLOOD OF TITANS series and the NEL BENTLY BOOKS. *Smoke and Rain*, the first book in their fantasy quartet, won New Apple Literary's Excellence in Independent Publishing Award in 2015 and a Literary Titan Gold in 2020. *Travelers* is also included in the Peregrine Moon Lander mission as part of the Writers on the Moon Time Capsule. In addition, they have published short fiction in several anthologies.

As a disabled and non-binary human, they work as an advocate and educator for representation in SFF worlds. When not writing, they work as a contract archaeologist throughout the northeastern U.S. They live in a Tiny House with their spouse, a fellow archaeologist, their not-so-tiny dog, and own too many books for such a small abode.

www.vsholmes.com

Made in the USA
Columbia, SC
15 September 2023

22924450R00170